Vicki was in the Jac[uzzi] [up to her] neck, holding the C[hihuahua above the] churning surface.

The lawn chair wh[ere Mimi had] been hanging was em[pty.]

Leo said, "Are you [crazy?"]

"Get in and find out [for yours]elf," Vicki said.

Mimi had been appealing to Leo with her eyes. Just her luck her mistress would be the one person in the world who thought this was a cute idea, a Chihuahua in the hot tub.

The sliding glass door was locked. Leo tapped the Jag's ignition key against the pane, a clinking that brought Beaumond's eyes, yellow and dilated, out from behind the curtain. The dining room table was cluttered with boxes of baking soda, a roll of sandwich-sized baggies, and a jar of unlabeled powder.

Beaumond and Fernandez had gotten hold of two triple-beam scales, strategically angled near their places at the table. Dumped on the Business section of the Sunday Herald, the kilo sparkled under the glow from a hanging lamp.

"How'd you make out?" Fernandez wanted to know. He was puffing the tobacco part of the Newport.

"Not too good," Leo said, grabbing his lighter and sparking a Marlboro. "I'm supposed to meet El Negrito in a little while."

"What're you gonna tell him?" Beaumond asked. He was using a yellow sandbox shovel to blend baking soda and cocaine. He dumped a heaping tablespoon of the jarred powder into the batch.

"I'm gonna deny everything."

Fernandez said, "You think that'll work?"

"What choice do I have?" Leo said. "I don't know about you guys, but I'm too young to die..."

**OTHER HARD CASE CRIME BOOKS
YOU WILL ENJOY:**

GRIFTER'S GAME *by Lawrence Block*
FADE TO BLONDE *by Max Phillips*
TOP OF THE HEAP *by Erle Stanley Gardner*
LITTLE GIRL LOST *by Richard Aleas*
TWO FOR THE MONEY *by Max Allan Collins*
THE CONFESSION *by Domenic Stansberry*
HOME IS THE SAILOR *by Day Keene*
KISS HER GOODBYE *by Allan Guthrie*
361 *by Donald E. Westlake*
PLUNDER OF THE SUN *by David Dodge*
DUTCH UNCLE *by Peter Pavia*
THE COLORADO KID *by Stephen King* °
THE GIRL WITH THE LONG GREEN HEART
by Lawrence Block °
THE GUTTER AND THE GRAVE *by Ed McBain* °
NIGHT WALKER *by Donald Hamilton* °

° coming soon

Dutch UNCLE

by **Peter Pavia**

A HARD CASE CRIME NOVEL

A HARD CASE CRIME BOOK
(HCC-012)
July 2005

Published by

Dorchester Publishing Co., Inc.
200 Madison Avenue
New York, NY 10016

in collaboration with Winterfall LLC

If you purchased this book without a cover, you should know that it is stolen property. It was reported as "unsold and destroyed" to the publisher, and neither the author nor the publisher has received any payment for this "stripped book."

Copyright © 2005 by Peter Pavia

Cover painting copyright © 2005 by R. B. Farrell

All rights reserved. No part of this book may be reproduced or transmitted in any form or by any electronic or mechanical means, including photocopying, recording or by any information storage and retrieval system, without the written permission of the publisher, except where permitted by law.

This book is a work of fiction. Names, characters, places, and incidents either are the products of the author's imagination or are used fictitiously, and any resemblance to actual events or persons, living or dead, is entirely coincidental.

ISBN 0-8439-5360-8

The name "Hard Case Crime" and the Hard Case Crime logo are trademarks of Winterfall LLC. Hard Case Crime Books are selected and edited by Charles Ardai.

Printed in the United States of America

Visit us on the web at www.HardCaseCrime.com

Miami Beach, 1996

Chapter One

Strolling Ocean Drive on his third day of parole, Harry Healy ran into Leo, whose last name he didn't learn the weekend they threw Leo into his cell, at a sidewalk café sipping espresso.

Harry started out just Drunk and Disorderly, but when he landed a left on the chin of arresting officer Kenneth Simms, a pack of O'Learys fell on him and dealt him the beating of his life. They knocked out two teeth and fractured the fourth rib on his left side, and one cop bent his arm so sharply behind his back it separated from his shoulder, still popping out from time to time so that Harry had to realign it himself. That didn't bother him too much, and neither did the rib after the first eight weeks or so, but he was still pissed about the teeth, holes where an incisor and a bicuspid used to be, making him look exactly like the ex-con he now was.

Leo was Drunk and Disorderly too, and he spent the weekend getting orderly while his father's attorneys tracked down the connections who got him undone.

Leo was twenty-five or thirty. He had a wiry build that was going soft, a superstar jock who got hurt and had his shot at baseball glory ruined. To hear him tell it, anyway. Leo knew a lot of baseball, good memory for stats, and kept Harry entertained talking about great stars Harry had never heard of. He was an okay guy to spend a weekend in jail with.

Harry squinted into the sun. He asked Leo for a Marlboro.

Leo said, "Why don't you sit down?"

"Because I don't have any money I wanna spend here, and I hate those faggy little cups of coffee, and I ain't all that fond of broiling on the concrete, either."

Leo looked at him from behind his sunglasses and his mouth got tight. He waved his Marlboro and shrugged one shoulder. He said, "Hang out, man."

A brunette sashayed past the table. She was carrying a portfolio and switching her hips, wearing patterned hose over a g-string. Or, possibly, no panties at all. Peering at life through lenses tinted brown.

In the sun-bleached afternoon, Harry missed his shades, the spanking new Ray Bans that were among his personal effects when he went inside, but weren't when they let him go.

Harry made his hand into a visor. He followed the brunette with his eyes. "She's probably a model," he said.

"You think so? What tipped you off?"

"Look at how tall she is and look at her clothes. And her face, well, you can't see it now, but she was beautiful."

"C'mon, Flash, of course she's a model. They're all models down here. It's the number one industry in this town. I'm thinking of taking a shot at it myself, soon as I get my book together."

Leo was over six feet tall. He had smooth skin and a pointy chin and a nose that had never been broken, and Harry supposed he was good looking, but no more so than a dozen other guys he'd seen that afternoon alone. Besides, the modeling racket meant getting up when the sun was right and wearing make-up and having somebody blow air at you so your hair went flopping in a certain direction. Not a job for a man, he thought, but he didn't say anything.

"Harry, what're you doing?"

"Right now? I'm trying to get back to New York."

"Is that right," Leo said. "How much money you got?"

"I don't know, I got a few bucks." He knew the amount to the penny, $12.97, but there was no reason Leo had to know it, too.

"You feel like making some?"

Harry didn't know if he liked the way that sounded. "What do I have to do?"

"When was the last time you saw your uncle?"

"My uncle," Harry said. "What uncle? How do you know my uncle?"

Leo looked at him like he knew a secret. "I'm talking about your uncle Manfred."

"Manfred?" Harry said. "You mean Manfred Pfiser?"

He wouldn't in a hundred years have paired Leo and Manfred. Manfred was New York by way of Rotterdam, a Euro-wiseguy who dealt with the Chinks, in town two, maybe three times a year, and Leo, Leo was strictly Miami. "How do you know Manfred?"

"I know a lot of people," Leo said. "Now listen to me. Your uncle's here."

"In Miami Beach? No shit."

"He likes the weather. And he heard about your predicament. As your Dutch Uncle, he feels obligated to lend a helping hand."

"Yeah, right," Harry said, "a helping hand. He's so fucking concerned about me, where was he when they had me locked up like a dog, just for trying to defend myself against a dozen steroid-crazed freaks? Dutch Uncle, my ass."

But Harry sat down anyway, and after he settled in with Leo's cigarettes and the ten dollar whiskey Leo was paying for, he figured he might as well hear Leo out. Three things became clear: It was easy, it was illegal, and

Leo was cutting him a break. Harry wondered why.

Leo was profiling a lilac-colored Guayabera shirt over a white guinea-t. He pulled a container from the left breast pocket, a canister with the Eastman Kodak logo on its lid.

"After you shoot a roll of film, you stash it like this. On the Beach, it's the most inconspicuous package you could possibly be carrying. 'A photographer friend took these for me, officer, but since he did the work as a favor, I have to pay to get them developed.' One of these bad boys holds a quarter ounce. You pack like a dozen rolls in a satchel. The live ones you bury at the bottom. You're betting he doesn't get to what he's looking for. That's if he stops you at all. See what I'm saying? Totally plausible. Specially if you look the way I do. Hi, darling."

Leo waved to a girl. He pressed the canister into Harry's palm.

"What's wrong with a paper sack?" That was the way Harry did it whenever he was holding something the law would rather not have him holding. In a plain brown wrapper, an ounce of blow or a sizzling .38 might just as well be a tuna salad on whole wheat.

"My way's more creative. That's the trouble with you, Harry. You've got no imagination."

"I got plenty of imagination, and what I'm imagining is getting my ass busted collecting Manfred's money and being thrown back inside, only no Dade County lock-up this time, but a big league jolt in a fucking State Penitentiary. That's what I'm imagining right now." He put the canister down.

"You don't wanna do it, don't do it," Leo said. "Suit yourself."

"I didn't say that," Harry said. "But I've gotta be wondering, what's in it for you? You know what I mean? What angle're you working here?"

"Let's just say I was hung up one time and somebody really helped me out. I believe in karma. I believe in giving back."

Harry doubted Leo believed in a single thing outside his five senses. But what were his options? Knock over some granny for her Social Security check? He'd never hurt anybody that didn't have it coming, and he wasn't about to start. He could hustle pool, but that'd only be good till the other sharks got wise. Besides that, he had no back-up here, he was way off his game, and what if he lost?

Leo took off his shades and posed, the tip of an earpiece to a corner of his mouth. His eyes were the same green as the ocean beyond the asphalt and sand on Harry's right. He looked at Harry and waited, the kind of guy who wanted to make you think he had all the answers.

Harry had to admit, he was curious about the Manfred-Leo connection. Maybe Manfred would shed more light on it.

He took two Marlboros from Leo's box, lit one, and slid the other behind his ear.

Never a hard-knuckles hood, Manfred Pfiser directed a thriving import-export business from several outlets in Holland.

After suffering forty-seven years of Flemish latency, two marriages and three children, Manfred charged out of the closet and threw his arms around a lifestyle he was twenty years too old for. He loved his cocaine, piles of it, though only when he was partying, compulsive behavior he reserved for New York and now, Harry guessed, Miami Beach, the ideal hideout for any late-flowering fag.

He reveled in his reputation, playing the role with relish during his sprees, benefactoring dozens of runaways and beefcake queens who always had something nice for their Dutch Uncle when Uncle had something nice for them.

Harry met him working security at one of Frankie Yin's events at the now shuttered Wonderland. It was easy work for a hundred bucks a night, and Harry was happy to get it. He wished Frankie Yin promoted more parties.

Manfred made Yin's scene three weeks running and cruised Harry a bunch of times before he screwed up the nerve to actually speak to him. His opening, "You look awfully lonely back here," was a line he had to repeat twice on account of the thudding blast of Super Sound, and the cartoony accent that made him hard to understand in even the quietest moments. Harry gunned him down politely, letting him know he wasn't gay, and on top of that Frankie Yin had a strict rule against yapping with the clientele when you were supposed to be working for him.

And that would've been it, if fate hadn't schemed to bring them together the next afternoon at a bagelry near Harry's apartment. Harry munched eggs and bacon and toast, and a savagely hungover Manfred, bloodshot and wheezing, sipped black coffee and smoked half a cigarette at a time. He concluded the only cure for his misery would be more coke and more booze, and when he asked Harry where he could score and Harry answered "What's in it for me?" they had the seedling of a working relationship.

Manfred appeared in the doorway dressed in a monogrammed robe that fell just to the tops of his thighs, his sunburnt skin a radish red rushed by Bain de Soleil.

He said, "Harry Harry Harry." A hefty shot of Ballantine rattled in his hand. "So sad to hear of your recent sorrows, but I only recently learned the news, and why, here you are, among us once again." He sounded like every bad actor who ever played a Nazi. "You really must control that temper."

Harry said, "How about we talk inside?"

"Please, please." He did a hop-step and closed the door. He wasn't wearing underwear, and as he flounced around the room rearranging chairs, his balls were swinging free outside the robe.

"Let me offer you a toot," he said, fishing for a vial. "And a drink, please have a drink. Have a drink with your Uncle Manfred."

He got nellier and nellier the deeper he got into a binge. Auntie Manfred. The graying bags under his eyes hinted at about a thirty-six hour jag.

"I just finished one drink," Harry said, "which is one more than I need at four o'clock in the afternoon." He paced to a spot where he thought he'd be comfortable, but he wasn't comfortable. The darkened room was smoky and frigid, the canned air chemical and stale.

Manfred put the spoon to his nose and sucked up some powder with a wince. "Is this what you call a reunion? Come on, Harry, you can do so much better than this." He acted like his feelings were hurt, but he always did when he didn't get his way.

"I'll tell you what I will take," Harry said, "is one of those mongrel Dutch cigarettes in the orange pack."

Manfred said, "Shore," his accent thick with scotch. He shook a cigarette out and Harry took it.

"So," Manfred said, "you found Leo? He's a good boy, Leo."

"Leo's a punk. And I'm pissed off with you."

Manfred clicked his tongue and collapsed on the bed. His robe fell open.

"What is this, some late-breaking bulletin? Leo got locked up with me weeks before my court date, and if somebody, you for instance, had coughed up a couple grand, I wouldn't have spent the last nine months inside. Do me a favor? Put on some shorts or get dressed or do something so I don't have to have that dick waving in my face. Don't tell me this is the first you're hearing of it."

"Five days ago when I got to Miami. I swear, Harry. Would I let you suffer like that?" He was pouting now, and Harry didn't know whether or not to believe him. He walked to the dresser and slipped on a pair of silk boxers. He said, "There. Feel better?"

"When I get off the Beach for good is when I'm gonna feel better. Leo said something about a package."

"Patience, Harry. Patience, patience."

Harry's head was splitting. Manfred was annoying him more than ever, and the roaring air conditioner put a pressure on his sinuses that made him dizzy. "Look," he said, "let's get this out of the way. I'm wasting time here."

Manfred took another slug of scotch. "Your appointment isn't till tonight. The only product I've got now is in this little jar. I'm waiting for delivery."

"When's that gonna be?"

"Early this evening. No worries, nephew. We'll have you on your way by nine o'clock."

Nine o'clock. Five hours to kill. Wonderful.

The Hotel Fiorella was situated south of 4th Street in a part of town the neon didn't reach, where the Harleys rumbled off the strip and where no heart-stopping brunettes strutted with portfolios under their arms. It cost thirty bucks a night and Harry was one of two or three current residents who wasn't getting the tab covered by welfare.

It wasn't the crazies or cripples, the winos or crackheads, that sickened him about life at the Fiorella, it was the idea of lives that had stopped. Of people who'd fallen over the edge and weren't coming back. They slumped in the lobby, paralyzed by the television's buzzing, unblinking eye, chain-smoking and dropping butts on the tiles, butts nobody bothered to sweep up, sixteen hours a day.

One evening, Harry'd seen a red-skinned infant, a week out of the hospital, tops. It hung at its mother's breast, wailing at the world from the bottom of its tiny lungs. Harry couldn't stop thinking about that kid. What were the odds it wasn't going to die in a place exactly like this one, or worse?

With the blinds shut and a chair wedged under the doorknob, Harry calmed in the cool grey of his room. He sank into the rut of the mattress, smoking a Dutch cigarette, the evening ahead unfolding like a movie in his mind. He floated back to Manfred's hotel through the neon-lit mob, and took directions from the Dutchman. Money in hand after the job, he saw himself sweating out the dawn in some Greyhound station.

He rolled out of the mattress and peeled off his shirt. He dropped to the floor, squeezed off fifty pushups. Harry struck some poses for the mirror, shoulder flex, biceps flex, side view. Jailhouse muscles. He shot a sneer at the mirror, then two jabs and a right, mumbling curses at his reflection. Starting another combination, his left went long and whacked the mirror flush. The mirror shattered.

He ran cold water over his knuckles and lay down again. He thought he was too wound up to sleep, but before long he lapsed into a dream. He was eating a sandwich in a glassed-in café, his eyes traveling over the gardening column of a newspaper. There was a photograph of a tulip, but the caption claimed it was a rhododendron. Harry had no idea what a rhododendron looked like, but the flower in the picture was a fucking tulip if he ever saw one. A guy he thought he knew started knocking on the window, pounding so hard Harry was scared the pane would come crashing in like the mirror had, and then he was awake and somebody outside was hammering on the door.

Harry said, "What time is it?"

"Time for you to either pay up or get the fuck out," a voice said, and Harry listened as feet shuffled away from the door and down the hall.

There wasn't much to pack, underwear and socks, some toilet things he threw into a bag, crunching shards on his way out. He took the back exit to an alley, then cut through to the street and into the first sluggish trickle of the throng on Ocean Drive.

If he'd been looped in the afternoon, by the time Harry got back to Manfred's room the Dutchman was in a full-on frenzy. One hand on his waist, one wrist flapping a faggot burlesque, the whites of his eyes laced with ruptured capillaries that shone pink in the half-light.

The air conditioner was still blasting, and the refrigerated air roiled with cigarette stink and a new offender, a musky cologne Manfred had slathered on. Somebody'd been dispatched to the liquor store. The Ballantine bottle sat drained on a nightstand, but there was a fresh one riding shotgun.

"Okay," Harry said, "where am I going?"

"You know, Harry, you must never fix those teeth. The gaps, I find them terribly hot." He brought out a two-gram vial. It brimmed. "Tootski?"

Harry glared.

"Do a little bump with your uncle. Harry, for old times."

Harry turned in his bottom lip. The last thing he needed was a toot. A hit, a bump, a blast. He wiped his palms on his jeans. "You know what, Manfred? I'll take a drink."

The bathroom door was open, and the shower was running. Steam humidified the room, and a whiff of the hotel's brand of shampoo churned in the gumbo of odors. Harry stifled a gag.

He swallowed Manfred's stingy measure, grabbed the fifth and poured a shot that'd loosen the knot in his gut. The vial was uncapped again, and Manfred held a heaping spoonful under Harry's left nostril. Harry passed. Manfred pumped the coke into his own head.

"What I need from you is the package and the address, and I need to get this over. I don't feel good about committing another felony three days out of the joint, and I'd just as soon put it behind me. You know what I'm saying?"

Harry was desperate to get out of the room before whoever it was, the juvie boy-toy, he guessed, climbed out of the shower, but it was already too late. The water quit splashing and he heard the clack of plastic, hooks sliding along the curtain rod. A second later, out stepped a blonde making a show of covering her body with a towel. Two things Harry noticed: her skin tone, basted to a succulent bronze, and her nipples, peaked, brown, peeping over the edge of the towel. How full of change-ups could one degenerate Dutchman be?

"Har-ry," he said, drawing out both syllables like he was calling him from another room, "This is Jennifer." The old queen pronounced the J like it was a Y, Yennifer. He knew the difference, but he was way past the point of caring.

She played it cute, this chick, making no attempt to pull the towel higher. She took a few things from a suitcase, then glancing at Harry, she went back into the bathroom and clicked the door shut.

"You yum yum," Manfred slurred. "Shore you can't spend a few more minutes with your uncle? And Yenny?" He cupped his hand over Harry's crotch and gave his balls a squeeze.

Harry gave him an easy shove and said, "Will you give it a rest? Are we gonna do this deal, or what?"

Jennifer warbled a Patsy Cline tune from behind the door, way off key. Manfred weaved a circular path toward the closet, really gone, and turned around clutching a double-bagged bundle the size of a bar of soap. He stopped to freshen his drink, and handed Harry the package. "One ounce," he said. He had one eye closed. The other pinwheeled Harry into focus. "One thousand dollars."

"What's the guy expecting to pay?"

"You be a do-right nephew. You don't fuck around."

"What'd you say I'm getting paid for this?"

"Come on, Harry. Leo told you the deal. Two hundred bucks."

Small potatoes all around. Manfred must've been doing somebody a favor. Somebody besides Harry. This was embarrassing.

"One more question, uncle. What's to stop me from beating town with your cash? Seriously?"

Manfred tried to give the impression that he had that

angle covered, but Harry saw the possibility was just dawning on him. He blinked twice and said through a squint, "Tragic. Positively tragic. You have no idea how deeply wounded is your uncle."

He considered. "Of course. There is nothing to prevent you from this terrible deed, nothing but your conscience." He admired Harry through a single, loving eye. "Dear, dear boy. You would never do such a thing in a thousand years. You don't have it in you."

It was a postcard Miami evening. Palm trees rippled with the breeze, the scent of salt water on the air.

At the wheel of Manfred's rented Mustang, Harry hadn't counted on this traffic: Tourists captained convertibles idling alongside hot rods cranking brass-brittle Latin tunes; family wagons stuffed with dusky chiquitas, lacquered and spritzed for a night of clubbing. Waiting through three light changes at Espanola, Harry saw the same valet jog past him twice, once coming, once going, and it took half an hour to drive ten blocks.

Traffic didn't start to flow till Harry hit the mid-20s, rolling past hotels that lodged legitimate Manfreds. He cruised into the 40s, where non-divorced Manfreds lingered whole seasons. From there it was another ten or fifteen minutes, prowling a hushed suburb, before Harry had to pay attention to the street signs. The address wound up being an efficiency motel designed in the classic South Florida style, an L-shaped two-level affair that boxed a drained pool and parking spaces.

Neon letters spelled out CANCY. The building was a charmless knock-off on the Fiorella theme. Harry headed for the north wing of the L and scaled a staircase to a catwalk, pink and pea-green paint chipped off in splotches. Where they weren't flickering or blown out, florescent tubes crackled outside each room. The door to 206 was thrown open. Harry flinched behind TV gunplay, glanced at a man in Bermudas, smoking and watching a cop show. He didn't look up as Harry walked by.

Room 202 occupied the northernmost tip of the L. Electronic disco thumped behind the door. Harry gave it three sharp raps. The noise cut out and the door flew open on a muscular man about Harry's age.

His arms and shoulders were swollen like a lot of guys in the joint who pumped massive iron. If there was ever any hair on his chest he'd had it shaved smooth. He knew what Harry was there for, but his eyes betrayed a nervous, scheming gleam. He was obviously expecting somebody else.

"You are not Leo," he said, in some kind of accent from Scandinavia. The guy could've been a Swede. Possibly a Dane. He had both nipples pierced with thick-gauged pewter rings.

"You got me there, pal. I'm not Leo. My name is Harry. Manfred sent me."

"We don't know you." He skipped a beat. "Did you bring the stuff?"

Harry had the package hidden under his jacket, rewrapped in a brown paper sack. He showed it to the guy. "Be better if we did business indoors, wouldn't it?"

The Swede stepped aside, wearing leather hotpants that laced up the crotch. He had a partner, a bald black man with a charcoal complexion who must've gone 6'6". He was built like an unraveled wire hanger and sported a baby-blue negligee over a matching bra and briefs. He gave Harry the up and down and said, "Bon soir."

Harry said, "How you doing."

The black guy told him his name was Javier, and introduced the Swede as Sven. Sven. Harry bit back a laugh.

Sven was tugging a nipple ring, antsy. "Let's have the stuff," he said.

"You have to forgive my husband," Javier said, "for being so impatient. You are quite late, but I understand South Beach traffic is positively murderous, especially on these high season evenings. Make yourself at home."

Harry scanned the room. He would've sat on one of the two chairs, but both were stacked high with laundry, some of it clean and, from the smell of it, some from an afternoon at the beach.

"You know, I'd stick around, but with that traffic, I should get back to Manfred. He's probably already wondering what happened to me."

"Manfred can wait," Sven said. "He can wait and so can you."

Okay, so he'd caught a pair of aces. Leo hadn't said a word about these two. Presumably he'd been able to handle them. Maybe Leo wasn't such a creampuff after all.

The Swede was the one to watch, jonesing heavy for his blow, getting edgier by the second. Harry figured he'd have his hands full with this guy, who outweighed him by twenty pounds and, judging by the muscles, had to be strong. He took a glance, to see what he could use as a weapon, then lit a cigarette, the last of Manfred's, which could always be ground into an eye or a pierced nipple. He looked over at Javier. Hard to imagine this skyscraper drag queen as an ally, but that was the way it was shaping up.

Harry handed Sven the package. Sven took it out of the sack, dropped the sack on the floor, and unraveled the baggie. He held up the coke to the naked light bulb, kneading it, but the bulk of the ounce was one rock, and it didn't break.

Sven said, "Hmmmm." He set it on the table. "You first."

Javier was on the bed, his back against the headboard, his ridiculous spider legs double-crossed. He dangled a backless slipper from the biggest foot Harry had ever seen. "Your drama is boring. This is our Dutch Uncle. All the boys are very dear to Uncle Manfred."

"This is not Manfred," Sven said. "This is not Leo. This is somebody we've never seen, and you want to hand him a thousand dollars for a product we haven't even tested. You stupid faggot."

Javier gave him a stricken look, then stared at his giant feet.

Harry was done being polite. "Listen, sport, you either want the shit or you don't. In fifteen seconds I'm walking out the door with this package or a thousand dollars. Your move. Make up your mind."

"My mother always said it," Javier said. "Rudeness begets rudeness."

"Shut up," Sven said. He took three steps to the dresser, and reached into the back of a drawer. Instead of the bundle of bills Harry was hoping to see, the Swede was holding a pistol, a Colt .45 automatic, and he was pointing it at Harry's chest.

Harry said, "Terrific," and Javier started a gasp that got stuck in his throat.

Sven wagged the Colt toward the chair that was cluttered with beach gear. "Move that shit and sit down. Javier," he said, "get up. My hands are full."

Javier teetered on his mules. He dumped the one big stone and whatever shake there was onto a mirror, working the smaller pieces with a razor blade, slicing and dicing, a rhythmic clicking. His pink tongue poked through his lips in concentration.

Harry eyed the gun, the hand that held the gun, the arm attached to the hand that held the gun. Here he was, kept at bay by a muscle queen in leather panties. Two comic book fags making him look bad. No getting around it.

Javier chopped three lines. An entire half of him bent over the table, he had a straw to his nostril, about to suck up the powder.

Sven stopped him. "He goes first."

Harry kept quiet about blow not being his thing, how it always got him in trouble. He already was in trouble. He huffed half the line into his right nostril, the other half into his left. A little sting, the coke was up his nose and into his head, trickling down his throat. He gagged. Too much. He gagged again. A-1 product. His heart was thumping and his palms remoistened.

"Outstanding product," he said, feeling brotherly toward the Swede threatening his life. "Excellent."

Sven looked unconvinced. He cocked one blonde eyebrow, flipping his gaze between Harry and Javier. He gestured to Javier, who deadpanned, "I know what to do. Trust me."

It was a long line, about five inches, and fat. Javier horked it all in one short sniff. He pinched his nostril closed and rolled his eyes heavenward.

"Ho, yes, child," he said. "Ho, yes." He pressed his fingertips together and smiled a jack o' lantern smile, except he had straight white teeth. Every single one.

Sven took his turn hunched over the powder. He snorted. Half the line went up. He straightened and smacked his lips, both eyes looking left, like he was trying to remember something. On the return trip, Harry slammed both forearms down on his neck, driving his face into the mirror. Cartilage crunched, and glass. The gun hit the carpet. Harry dove for it and tumbled, rolling crouched to his feet.

Javier froze flamingo-like, one knee pulled up, screeching. Two hands, enormous hands, waving. Six feet six and fucking useless in a beef. Unbelievable.

Harry faced off against the humbled Swede, palms overlapping his beak, blood running onto his hairless chest. Harry was stunned, realizing this was all the fight he was going to get, but once he figured it out he leaned in and cracked Sven over his left ear with the Colt. Sven dropped to his knees. Harry fed him another short sweet one. He sank to all fours, then crumpled, nighty-night, to his side.

Javier's eyes, locked on Harry's, darted down to the gun. Two yips from hysteria, the perma-howl of joy or fear an inch from his throat, Javier did not scream, and for this, Harry was grateful. A chuffing sound came from Javier's lips, forming words. "Did you?" he managed. "Is he?"

"His nose might sit a little to one side, and he'll have a headache with some genuine staying power, but he's far from dead. Listen." Harry wound up and kicked the Swede square in the gut. He coughed and sputtered, moaning low.

"See?" Harry said. "Told you. Now you, Javier, are who I'm interested in. A fully conscious, able-bodied individual, holding Uncle's money. You are going to find Uncle's money and you are going to give it to me now, right now, or I swear to Christ I'll blow your fucking head off. I don't see you moving."

"I cannot allow you to use that vile language in the same sentence with the name of my personal Lord and Savior."

A tremendous piece of work, this Javier.

"You're a decent guy, Javier. You're a freak but you're a decent guy, and as a decent guy, I know you're determined to do the right thing. Do me a favor, buddy. I need to get that money, and I need to get out of here."

Javier sifted through the pockets of a suede carcoat and pulled out a knot that was probably hundreds. With shaking hands, he tried to count out a thousand, or whatever it was Harry was supposed to get. It was almost like it didn't matter anymore.

Harry said, "Javier, get in the bathroom." He leveled the gun. "Now."

Javier obeyed, walking toward the toilet, the stack of bills in his fist.

"Javier. Stop. Leave the money on the table. Okay, now go on, get in there."

"What're you going to do?"

"Why don't you just let me worry about that?" Harry said. "When a man aiming an automatic weapon at you tells you to do something, you don't debate him. You fucking do it. Are you with me?"

Harry dragged a chair across the floor and wedged it under the doorknob. Once Javier was scared enough, he'd find all the strength he needed to break out of there, but Harry would be miles away before that happened, or before the Swede scraped himself off the carpet.

He stuffed the Colt into his jeans and leafed through the bills. Seventeen hundred and change. The change, two twenties, a ten and a five, he left on the table. The rest he put in his pocket. Thinking twice about ripping off their ounce, too, he carved a thick line and sucked it up with a twenty. Sven whimpered in Swedish. He rolled from his side to his belly, but that was as far as he got.

For a guy with fairly good intentions three days out of stir, Harry was having no trouble racking up the felonies. Let's see, you had possession, intent to distribute, and sale of narcotics, for a start. Robbery, assault with a deadly weapon, and the all-time classic number-one no-no for any ex-con, concealing a handgun, although not too well, in his waistband.

Steadying the wheel with his knee, Harry twisted out of his jacket and wiped down the Colt. He was about to cross a bridge on some back road that ran parallel to Collins Avenue. He pulled over. He could smell the ocean. No streetlights, not a single car or the dimmest headlamp in any direction, just a crescent moon waning against a star-splattered sky. He held the gun by its trigger guard and dropped it into the canal.

Harry ran through his story to Manfred. Basically, there was no story to Manfred. It all went smooth. Here's your cash, I got lost on the way back. Take care and thanks. I am so gone from this miserable town, the man you see before you is but a hallucination.

He drove on, fighting South Beach traffic all the way back to Manfred's hotel.

On the way up in the elevator, Harry thought about his trip to New York. Seven hundred dollars to the good, the bus was out. Harry would be flying. He was going to report to that parole officer, all ready to be good, and he was going to say, Hey, I'm right here.

Only something wasn't right. It wasn't adrenaline or nerves or cocaine jitters, though Harry was feeling all of those. But something wasn't right and he didn't know what. From behind Manfred's door, he could hear a Pasty Cline song blaring, a recording of the real thing this time. Nobody answered when he knocked, so Harry tried the knob and let himself in.

Manfred was sprawled in the center of the room, one leg pulled in, the other stiffening straight out from his torso. He'd been shot with a small caliber pistol, once real close from what Harry could bring himself to see. Powder burns rimmed a wound at the base of his skull. The satin bathrobe was thick with blood. His mouth and eyes were set in mischief, like Manfred had been poised to float one of his idiotic suggestions before the bullet went in.

Harry's forehead was wet at the hairline and his breath got short, fear choking off his air. He'd better figure out what to do quick, and get out. He tiptoed around the pool of blood and shut up Patsy Cline. The silence made it easier to think. He swallowed three thirsty pulls of Ballantine, and wiped down the bottle and both glasses with a towel. Bringing up one acidic belch, he switched off the lights. He walked out and shut the door.

A drunk couple nattering in French fumbled with their keys, oblivious as Harry went past.

Leaving the scene of a murder. Another felony. No question.

The upside was this: He had just made a considerable accidental score. The down: If they caught him they'd try him for murder, and he'd have a bitch of a time talking his way out of it. And they'd catch him. Nobody had seen him on the way in, but there was Leo, and Jennifer, and the Surfside fags, and the fact he was registered under his real name at the Fiorella. They'd find out about him, and then they'd come for him. He'd have let the whole roll ride on that. The question was when, and where.

He took the Mustang and immediately regretted it. He was on the Interstate headed north, putt-putting in the right hand lane, every car on the road whizzing past him. The Florida Highway Patrol car tailing him for the last ten minutes changed lanes, gaining speed. The trooper closed to an eighth of a mile. His lights flashed silently and Harry closed his eyes. You stupid motherfucker. What were you thinking?

He pulled onto the shoulder, scattering gravel under the tires.

He hurled a prayer into the indigo sky. Holy Mary, Mother of God. The trooper screamed past and hit the siren. A second unit was on his bumper. A third, in the southbound lane, hooked a U and joined them. And then a group of motorists cruised past, in exact replicas of Manfred's rental, in Sunbirds and Escorts, in mini-vans and pick-ups made in Japan. The road was still for a moment, then the next cluster of vehicles zipped by.

Harry got off the highway in a town called Hollywood, and drove around the back of an all-night mini-mart. He wiped down the keys and the steering wheel and the seats and pitched the keys into some thick weeds next to the lot. Breaking a hundred, he bought three packs of Marlboros and a bag of peanut M&Ms. The cashier snapped suspicious gum and wore huge pink-framed glasses connected to a chain. Three o'clock in the morning, she was telling him to have a nice day.

This street was like Hollywood's main drag, Florida route something or other, running north and south. Where he was going and what he was going to do when he got there, he didn't know, but he walked north. North was as good a direction as any. They'd catch up to him eventually, he had to admit that, but not tonight. No way. Not tonight.

Chapter Two

Detective Arnie Martinson was standing in the lobby of the Bird of Paradise hotel, talking to the patrolman who had responded. His name was Kenneth Simms. Simms was in his mid-twenties, and he had a rusty-brown mustache, and though Martinson had seen him around for the last couple years, he couldn't say he knew him. Simms let him know that the room where the homicide occurred had been taped off and that the Crime Scene Unit had been dispatched to the hotel. Martinson asked him to go back upstairs and wait.

The hotel manager was dressed in grey slacks and a grey cotton shirt. The hair he retained was cropped super-close to match the this-is-not-a-beard length whiskers fuzzying his cheeks and chin. A pair of reading glasses hung around his neck, and he put them on as Martinson approached the desk.

"I'm Detective Martinson," Martinson said. He shook the man's hand.

"I don't suppose there's any way not to turn my hotel into a three-ring circus."

"Well," Martinson said, "no. What's your name?"

"Howard Rutger."

"And you're the manager?" Martinson flipped open a notebook.

"I'm the General Manager."

"General Manager. You reported the crime?

"That's right."

"Found the victim?"

"No, that was Mrs. Lopez, one of our housekeepers."

"Where is she now?"

"She's in my office. Would you like to speak with her?"

"Is she alone?"

"One of our other housekeepers is with her."

"Where's your office?"

"Right through that door behind the desk," Rutger said.

"If you could ask the other maid to come out of there, I'd appreciate it. Explain that a detective is going to interview her, and the detective'll be along shortly. Could you do that?"

The CSU rolled up, represented by Carl Burns and Shug Petrie. Another detective from the Beach Bureau, Lili Acevedo, walked a few steps behind them.

"Second floor," Martinson said to Burns. He and Petrie proceeded straight through to the stairs, and Martinson said to Acevedo, "A maid found a body in a room up there. Go and see if she can remember what she saw."

Pink was the pastel theme of this operation. The lobby's walls were pink stucco. Pink neon alerted weary travelers of the hotel's existence, and the housekeepers wore pink uniforms. A woman dressed in the regulation smock walked out of Rutger's office with a balled-up tissue in her fist.

Rutger had taken a call. The top of his head reflected the lobby's pink interior.

Martinson said, "Can you get somebody to cover for you?"

He pushed a button that sent the caller to some Muzak'd limbo. The phone chirped again, then a third line started ringing. Rutger caught the attention of a passing bellman. "Arturo," he said, "get on these phones. We are not interested in speaking to any newspaper or television station at this time. Do you understand that?"

Arturo rushed behind the desk to put everybody on hold. He said hello to the first caller when a fourth line started chirping.

"I can do this," Rutger said. He extended his arms, making his hands into stop signs, then touched two fingers to his forehead. "I can do this."

He turned to Martinson. "Do you realize what's happening here? I'm fielding calls from fishwrappers that don't normally cover anything more serious than some bimbo jumping agencies. This is going to kill my season."

"What do you know about the victim?" Martinson asked.

"His name was Manfred Pfiser." Rutger blew out a sigh and squared his shoulders. "He was a businessman from the Netherlands."

"Remember when he checked in, off hand?"

"One day last weekend." Rutger's features pinched, his eyebrows closing in. His nose wrinkled like he was getting a whiff of sour milk. "I'd have to look it up."

"Was he traveling alone?"

"Yes," Rutger exhaled. "He always traveled alone."

"So you knew the guy."

"He's been a frequent guest," Rutger said. He pursed his lips.

"Can you think of any reason why anybody would want to hurt him?"

"None."

"What sort of company did he keep?"

Rutger said, "I think I'm drawing an inference here, and I think I'm resenting it."

"I wasn't implying anything, Mr. Rutger, I'm asking if you knew who his friends were. If you don't think I know fifty percent of the visitors to Miami Beach are gay, then you've got a poor understanding of my knowledge of my jurisdiction, and I resent that. Was he a homosexual?"

"The sexual orientation of my guests is the least of my concerns."

"That's a very progressive attitude. You think you could answer my question?"

Martinson saw a reporter homing in on him, Jason something or other. He worked for a weekly that concentrated mostly on restaurant critiques, but he was their police blotter guy. They'd spoken once or twice before.

"Hey, Arnie," Jason whatever his name was said. Arnie. As if they were cousins.

Jason was wearing faded dungarees and a white golf shirt, shoes that looked like moccasins without socks. Martinson remembered when these guys dressed like they wanted to be taken seriously.

"I've got nothing for you," Martinson said. "Call the Bureau this afternoon."

"C'mon Arnie," Jason persisted. "Give me a little piece of something."

"I said call in later today. I'm talking to this man." Martinson turned his back.

Rutger said, "Mr. Pfiser was often in the company of young men." He snapped off the glasses and let them hang from their chain. "Beautiful, young men. Feel free to draw your own conclusions." The two fingers were back at his forehead, massaging. "You know what else is going to get killed? My business. At the peak of our peak season."

The phone lines had not stopped bleeping. Arturo stonewalled them in the order they came in.

"Media frenzy," Rutger said, tilting his chin toward the desk. "Psycho Killer Strikes on South Beach."

"Would you know how involved the victim was in the scene?"

Rutger composed himself. He looked left and he looked right and he shot a tight-lipped smile at two guys walking through the door. Sand clung to their ankles.

"Manfred Pfiser was a raging queen so desperately out of control I'm surprised he lived as long as he did. How's that?"

"Fairly substantial. Now, who was on duty last night?"

As an up-to-the-minute example of the evolutionary process, Arnie Martinson might've been considered tall, had he lived five hundred years ago. Though he hadn't begun to think of himself as short until very recently, there was no denying it: He was shrinking. His last physical proved it, when the wizened Doctor Eusasky extended the measuring stick attached to his scale and gave him the news. Sixty-eight inches. Five feet, eight inches. When he joined the Miami Beach PD, he was five-nine. This was the ineluctable effect of gravity on the body. People got shorter as they got older. Arnie had watched this happen to his father.

And he was getting fat by anybody's standards. He was always stocky, but that extra weight used to make him feel strong. For most of his life, he carried it well through the chest and shoulders, maybe not so well around the gut, but the distribution seemed to shift right around the time he started to think of himself as short. He was not short enough, however, to duck under the tape denoting this new, expanded crime scene without some unintentional grunts escaping his throat, so the new, expanded Martinson lifted the tape up over his shoulder.

Simms had himself posted opposite the elevators, and another patrolman was standing outside the room. Arnie cleared another yellow obstacle and walked onto the scene as Burns was completing a chalk outline around the body.

The victim was lying in the center of the floor, a middle-aged white male with white hair taking a goofy, surprised expression into the next world. His lifeless hands were stained black with fingerprint ink.

Manfred Pfiser had taken a single bullet to the back of the head at very close range. The powder marks provided an impression of the barrel on his whitening skin. Entering at the base of the skull, the bullet struck the jawbone and sent shattered bone fragments tearing through the flesh, creating massive exit trauma. Burns focused his Nikon and snapped a nice, tight close-up of the fatal wound.

Shug Petrie reminded Martinson of the guys the Department was top-heavy with when he was just starting out, old boys from Kendall and Homestead whose daddies knew judges or somebody in the mayor's office who could get their son a job. Petrie was a throwback, a relic of a bygone day, holding out until he could swat mosquitoes and spit tobacco juice outside his trailer while drawing the pension on his twenty-five years of faithful service. He was a tremendous pain in the ass, a cop Martinson exchanged as few words with as he could, but he was a competent, patient technician.

A mediocre seascape, an original, depicted a deserted beach at sunset. Except if the artist was painting Miami Beach, it would have to be sunrise. The water was greenish-black, and the sun, making either its entrance or exit, was a band of orange on the horizon.

Acevedo cleared the tape like she was slipping a punch and popped inside the room. She was in her early thirties, and long-legged, an inch in height on Martinson. The name and the family were Cuban, but Lili's wan complexion was more Prague than Havana. She had green eyes and black hair Martinson originally thought she dyed to combat encroaching grey, but the hair stayed that shade always, and not a single root ever gave it away, not in the florescence of the squad room, not in the hot, bright Florida sunlight.

Giving the body a nonchalant once-over, Lili said, "The maid found him around ten after eleven, ran out of here screaming and tracked down her boss, who made the call. She insists she didn't touch a thing. I took her phone number and told her to go home. The woman's a wreck."

"Alright," Martinson said. "Start knocking on doors. Take this floor first."

Acevedo repeated that same tight move and popped up on the other side of the tape.

Petrie was brushing aluminum powder on the nightstand where two bottles of Ballantine scotch sat, one empty, the other about half-full. Two eight ounce tumblers crowded between them.

"Whoever it was did some housekeeping," Petrie said. "See the wipe marks?" He indicated the swirling trails made on the bottles, like the streaks a rag might've made on a window. "Same thing with the glasses."

On the opposite side of the bed, in a drawer of the nightstand, Martinson found Pfiser's wallet and passport. Multiple Visa cards representing many banks sat snug in their individual slots, but the wallet was empty of cash. His Dutch papers said he was born in Rotterdam in 1947, three years before Arnie Martinson. So that was how long the guy had been alive. Martinson wanted to find out how long he'd been dead.

Burns said, "I thought somebody notified the Medical Examiner."

Martinson said, "I did. Where is this guy?"

"On vacation," Petrie said. "You're getting Leviticus,

mon." He was mocking the doctor's Caribbean accent. Arnie felt sorry for Burns, having to work so closely with this asshole.

A gold Rolex sat on the dresser, keeping imperfect time. The drawers were stocked with boxer shorts and those see-through kind of socks that went up to the knee. Pfiser was not bashful about spending money on clothes. The man liked his silk.

Martinson opened the closet door. Every one of the hotel's theft-proof hangers was holding something, a suit, a shirt, a tailored jacket or a pair of trousers. Two suitcases sat on the floor, one housing a few days laundry, and an overpowering male scent puffed out of the bag as Arnie flipped it open, sweat mixed with a thick cologne long gone sour.

He pulled down a carry-on bag and undid the latches. It was empty except for some traces of white powder. Arnie touched the tip of his pinky to the powder for a taste. It was cocaine. A potent batch that numbed his tongue and deadened his teeth as he clicked them together. So let's say the deceased was doing more than sniffing little-bitty spoonfuls out of a twenty-dollar envelope. Let's say this dust leaked out of a big fat package.

Then let's say the shooter knew the deceased was holding heavy.

The Assistant Medical Examiner had arrived and was squatting over the body. Dr. Leviticus Williams was a dark-skinned black man with conked, orangish hair he greased straight back. His eyeglasses were so thick they magnified his eyes and made him look like he was in some hypnotic trance. He did some poking and he did some touching and he said, "Gunshot wound to the head."

It might have come off like a grim gag from somebody else, but Williams had almost no sense of humor. Your class clown rarely wound up in forensic medicine.

Two of Williams's men came in bearing a collapsible gurney, dressed in hospital green. Somebody took the trouble to close Manfred's Pfiser's eyes for him before he got zipped into a black vinyl bag for his trip to the morgue.

Lili Acevedo was in Room 224. At first, with the almond eyes that were the exact same shade of cobalt, Lili made this French couple for a father-daughter team. The woman answered the knock, dressed in a pair of pink nylon shorts and a halter top, typical South Beach for a girl her age, with the body to show off. Through an accent like quicksand, she wished Lili a good morning. They were the last two words she attempted in English.

She was a generation younger than her boyfriend, who was in front of the bathroom mirror training a blowdryer on the salt and pepper hair he wove over the bald spot on his crown. A bathrobe was sashed tight across his pot gut, and a chain, featuring both a crucifix and a diamond-studded Star of David nestled in a thatch of black-grey chest hair. He introduced himself as Allain Marcoux, the girl as Annick Mersault, and Lili scribbled both names into a notebook, way too much alike to be clear in her head.

Acevedo had to use simple words and short phrases, but Marcoux understood and answered her questions deliberately and with some thought. The only problem was, the guy hadn't seen a thing, was by his own admission shit-faced, a condition he illustrated by twisting a fist in front of his nose. He rolled his eyes and whistled, giving his head half a shake to unhinge the cobwebs.

Annick snuggled on the bed with her boyfriend. He had a hairy arm across her shoulders. After an unnerving round of chatter, Marcoux told Acevedo that Annick had seen a man in the hallway late last evening, leaving the hotel as they were coming in. Neither of them could recall the time, but it was after midnight. Marcoux recalled at one vague point looking up at the clock on Washington Ave., the one above the bank, and that it said 11:59. How much later it was when they got back, he couldn't say, and Annick, when the question was put to her, turned down the corners of her mouth and blew out a puff of breath.

Acevedo said, "What does she remember about this man?"

Marcoux translated and relayed Annick's answer. "She says he seemed like he was in a hurry to get out. She also says that yesterday afternoon, when she was returning from the beach, she saw the same man leaving the victim's room."

"How does she know it was the same man?"

Marcoux dealt the question.

Annick Mersault had expressive eyes and twitching, hyperactive lips. She was looking at Lili when she said, "Je m'souviens tout les beaux garcons."

"She remembers all the handsome boys."

Annick took her time giving Marcoux the details, and when she was finished talking, she gave him a kiss behind the ear. The little love bug. She just couldn't help herself. She studied Marcoux's face as he translated for Lili.

"He had dark eyes and dark hair cut short. Handsome features, about my height, and muscular." Marcoux improvised a seated, pumped-up pose. "He stuck out because he was so pale, white like a ghost."

Acevedo recorded the few facts Annick Mersault provided her with, skeptical about how much help she would actually be. She asked the girl through her translator-boyfriend if she would have a couple hours, perhaps later this afternoon or tomorrow, to look at some photographs and see if maybe she could identify the man she saw. If that failed, would she be willing to help a police sketch artist put together a drawing of this man?

Marcoux gave her the request and Annick lifted her head and nodded gravely. She was new enough in life to believe in a few too many things, a girl solid with the unshakeable convictions of youth. She spoke directly to Acevedo in French, knowing full well Lili couldn't understand a word she was saying.

Marcoux handled the interpretation. "She says it would be an honor. She has a sense of justice that is," the man groped for a word, "visceral."

Martinson had the image of an old television commercial in his head. There was an animated, cut-away model of a skull on the screen. The sinus areas of the skull were highlighted in blue. When sinus membranes are inflamed, a voice-over explained—here the blue parts turned to red and red lightning bolts shot off them—the sinus headache sufferer experiences pain. The commercial was for an over-the-counter medication that Arnie swore by until a few years ago, when it stopped working, and he developed headaches that were less like sinus and more like migraine.

Eusasky let him know his sinus status was unchanged, but he was concerned about the severity of these new headaches. He referred Arnie to a specialist named Boring—that was the physician's name, Dr. Boring—and Boring ran a raft of tests on the Martinson noggin, up to and including a CAT scan that to Arnie's immense relief revealed nothing. Dr. Boring scribbled a prescription for another kind of medicine that sometimes worked and sometimes didn't.

He sensed a real monster coming on, but that feeling could be deceiving. It might turn into a migraine, or it could just be a sinus thing. He didn't have enough experience with the migraines to differentiate between the two, at least not at their outsets.

But there was something starting behind his eyes as he stood in the first floor room directly under the room where Pfiser had been shot. He was talking to a woman named Marcy Lowenstein, and his sensitivity training was flunking him, maybe due to his fear of a headache.

He took one look at her and thought, full-on, man-hating bull-dagger. She was wearing no-nonsense wire-rimmed glasses and her mouse-brown hair was short and thick like the rest of her, pushed back in a no-nonsense cut. She kept thinking it could've been her.

"This happens right upstairs while you're sleeping, it shakes you."

Martinson understood that.

"My entire life in New York, nothing even close to this, ever."

She was wide-shouldered and widened some more at the waist. Her massive thighs touched from the knee up. She had both sandaled feet on the floor.

"When did you check in, Ms. Lowenstein?" This was sensitivity training in the field. That Ms. couldn't have been any clearer.

"Wednesday night, for a long weekend. I was going to stay until Monday, but now I don't know."

"You told Detective Acevedo that you heard loud music coming from the victim's room. What time was that?"

"All day. Patsy Cline. All day and all night. You know, they made the movie with Jessica Lange."

"Sure," Martinson said. He remembered when Patsy

Cline's records were hits, sometime before this woman was born, and she wasn't all that young.

"I called the desk and complained."

"Do you remember what time that was?"

"After eleven. I was watching the news, getting ready for bed."

"And the music was turned down?"

"The music got turned off, and I fell asleep before the weather. I wanted to see what the weather was going to be. But then it came back on again, even louder. I tried to sleep through it, because I didn't want to be a bitch and call the desk again."

Martinson zeroed in. His headache was a minor sinus flare-up. Nothing to worry about. "Can you remember the time?"

"When it went off for good? Ten to two. I was actually looking at the clock. I couldn't believe anyone would be so inconsiderate, and I couldn't believe I was the only one it was bothering."

"And after that?"

"Like in the song," Marcy Lowenstein said. "Sweet dreams."

"Is there anything else you can think of, Ms. Lowenstein"—there, he said it again—"that might assist us in our investigation?"

"I'll tell you this much. He's going to be missed. He was a really popular guy. People coming and going at all hours. He must've had a lot of friends here."

Martinson was waging a ferocious battle against his first impression, recalling the sensitivity trainer's words. Remember the old saying. You can't judge a book by its cover. Lowenstein was homely, with her glasses and her big schnozz and her fat thighs. But fat thighs did not a dyke make. Half the female population looked like

Marcy Lowenstein, and they weren't all lesbians. She liked to spend long weekends in South Beach. And she went to sleep after the news. Just another dull vacationer, spending a lonely time in an overpriced Ocean Drive hotel. So what if she had hairy shins? That didn't make her one thing or another. What business was it of his, anyway?

Arnie needed to review his sensitivity training.

Chapter Three

The house was way up Pine Tree Drive, behind a high row of hedges that hid it from the street. It featured a gravel driveway and a two-car carport, an aluminum overhang with shingles nailed to its roof and tacked to the side, a whim the owners thought would make their property more rentable. But what did the owners know? They hadn't lived in Miami in years. They were from Montana, or was it Missouri or Minnesota, some place with an M, and were now in either Saint Moritz or Saint Bart's, Saint Somebody's, Leo forgot what they told him.

Renting this pad was the first move he made after he got his inheritance. Leo turned thirty, and the money was his, just like it said in grandpa's will. Thinking of his grandfather, wearing a powder-blue cardigan and finishing the back nine in the pinkish pre-twilight, made Leo feel like puking. It was a good thing the old man was dead. First, because Leo didn't get the money until he died, but second, had he been able to see how his loving legacy was being squandered, it would've blown the toupee right off his head.

The house seemed like a good idea. The South Beach thing was getting hotter and hotter with each passing season, the narrow streets swarming with pussy, fine young pussy, pussy from all points of the compass. The world's next supermodel had to start somewhere, and she needed to have a good time before the appointment of that divine hour, a good time that Leo, with his six rented rooms and his Jaguar and his Jacuzzi, was more than willing to provide. Boozed-up, coked-up nineteen-year-old Icelandic blondes, two at a time for Christ's sake, that first month felt like a dream. But all that changed so fast. Where did it go?

Leo steered the Jaguar, British Racing Green and leased, through the opening in the hedges. He parked it next to the Eldorado that JP Beaumond had arrived with, and told Rex, the neighbor's Rottweiler, to go home. Rex woofed. Off he loped.

Leo picked his way through the piles of shit, the grenade-sized turds Rex laid down—he was going to have to speak to those people about their dog—and the thinner, neater work of Mimi, the long-haired teacup Chihuahua. Mimi was her own set of problems, and Leo didn't particularly care for her. Come to think of it, he never much liked dogs, and now he had one under the same roof with him. But Mimi was tiny, and quiet, for a twitching, trembling mutt. When she wasn't in Vicki's lap, she was sniffing out new hiding spots around the house. Mimi was a dog Leo could live with.

Vicki, on the other hand, he could not. She was in the Jacuzzi with Mimi, in the water up to her neck, holding the Chihuahua's head just above the churning surface. She was a friend of Lawrence the Model Dude, who Leo hadn't seen since his New Year's Eve party, the night he introduced Leo to Vicki. New Year's Day, Leo woke up next to her, and she'd been at the house ever since. It turned out to be a chore just getting Vicki to keep her clothes on, which was fun at first, but by now Leo was so over her that a mere glimpse of her nude, evenly browned body gave him a headache.

"Hey," Vicki said. "C'mon in, the water's fine." She splashed some his way.

The lawn chair where a towel or a bathrobe should've been hanging was empty.

Leo said, "Are you naked under there?"

"Get in and find out for yourself," Vicki said.

"Because this Lady Godiva routine is getting tired."

"That's the way mommy likes to dry off," she baby-talked to the Chihuahua. "It's good for her. Sun-dried, like a tomato."

"Over-ripe," Leo said. "Like a fucking hothouse cantaloupe. Okay, new rule. No walking around the yard without a bathing suit. Period."

"If somebody wants to look, let them look. I don't mind."

"The neighbors mind," Leo said. He jabbed a thumb at their exposed southern flank. "Their kids can just gander this way and set their little brains on fire. They mind that. And let that poor dog out of the water. Look at her."

Mimi had been appealing to Leo with her eyes. Just her luck her mistress would be the one person in the world who thought this was a cute idea, a Chihuahua in the hot tub. Mimi sighed.

Vicki set her on the ledge and the dog hopped down with a single yip of gratitude.

The sliding glass door was locked. Leo tapped the Jag's ignition key against the pane, a clinking that brought Beaumond's eyes, yellow and dilated, out from behind the curtain. The dining room table was cluttered with boxes of baking soda, a roll of sandwich-sized baggies, and a jar of unlabeled powder. A bunch of bananas was going brown in the fruit bowl.

Beaumond and Fernandez had gotten hold of two triple-beam scales, strategically angled near their places at the table. Dumped on the Business section of the Sunday *Herald*, the kilo sparkled under the glow from a hanging lamp.

Like the house, the plan to rob Manfred had seemed like a good idea the night it was born, over an eight-ball and a bottle of Jose Cuervo Gold. The gun was supposed to be for show. Nobody said anything about murder.

Fernandez was taking a break. He'd cleared out the end of a Newport and was loading a pebble of coke into it, crushing it up so the coke and tobacco mixed. He twisted it closed, lit a lighter that had a flamingo decal on it, and sucked. The paper went like a fuse. The stink of burning cocaine hung over the table. Fernandez held his hit, then exhaled a thin stream of grey.

Leo met Alex Fernandez on a high school all-star team. He had the livest arm Leo ever saw, but every schoolboy had a fastball, it was the amazing assortment of junk Fernandez worked around his heater that made him so special. He threw a sinker, a sharp-breaking curve no lefthander could touch, and a slider, all for strikes, plus a screwball his coach wouldn't let him use. Then he entered USC, where every guy was an all-star. He didn't earn a spot in the starting rotation, and just walked away from the game.

Leo'd never forgiven him for that. You didn't walk away when you had the stuff like Fernandez had it. Leo didn't have half the raw talent Fernandez had, but he'd been disciplined, had thrown a baseball every day except the day after a start, and he'd been undefeated in Dade County his senior year. Of course, after the injury, none of that mattered. Leo remembered the afternoon. His elbow felt like a cherry bomb had exploded under his skin, but every pitch was working, so he kept throwing. Never threw any harder in his life. The next day, he couldn't raise his arm to scratch his head, and after two surgeries and two rehabs, the scouts stopped calling.

"How'd you make out?" Fernandez wanted to know. He was puffing the tobacco part of the Newport.

"Not too good," Leo said, grabbing his lighter and sparking a Marlboro. "The Quiet Man is reported to be totally pissed off, and I'm supposed to meet El Negrito in a little while."

Though the central air was set at sixty-five degrees, the sight of all that coke and the scales and the baggies scorched Leo with a hot, dry feeling. He wondered if he was coming down with something besides a chicken heart.

"What're you gonna tell him?" Beaumond asked. He was using a yellow sandbox shovel to blend baking soda and cocaine. He dumped a heaping tablespoon of the jarred powder into the batch.

Leo said, "What is that shit?"

"Procaine," Beaumond said. He stuck a pinky into the glistening heap that wasn't yet cut and swiped the finger over his gums. "Gives 'em that sting they expect. The numbness. Masks the other cut."

He had a down-home panhandle twang. He was Alex Fernandez's buddy from Leo forgot where, and as Leo watched Beaumond's fat, bone-white arm working the shovel, he wondered how it was that Beaumond had been staying in his house so long.

"The bigger the count, the less we step on it," Fernandez said. "Fifty-fifty an ounce, sixty-forty a half, so on down the line, to grams. But that's the smallest we're doing. Grams."

Fernandez had unraveled into a full-on fashion victim, sporting white hip-hugger bellbottoms, and a belt that fastened with a circular buckle. His long-collared shirt was unbuttoned, a pattern of crimson and gold revealing a stripe of hair in the center of his chest. Rocking a blown-out afro, doing that 70s thing from a few years ago. There was an oily sheen on his forehead and nose. The last few drags of that Newport hung from his lips, and he was generating a rancid, chemical smell.

"Grams," Leo said. "You guys are doing grams. A kilo of top shelf rock, and you're gonna knock it down till you're dealing what, ten percent product?" Welcome to Amateur Hour, with your host, what was that guy's name? Not Arthur Godfrey. Some old-timer like that. "The whack you're selling, who's gonna come back?

"Don't need 'em coming back," Beaumond said. "Move it down to Big Black Mule and Statsonic, three, four in the morning. Snowbirds. Who's gonna see 'em again?"

Beaumond's face was shaped like an upside-down pyramid, the low, wide forehead giving way to a flattened cranium. He reminded Leo of the guy on the descent of man timeline, the one a generation or two away from the dude who first walked upright, not quite monkey, not quite man yet, either.

"Tell you the truth," Leo said, "I don't give a shit what you do with it. This—" He waved his cigarette at the table and cut himself off.

Beaumond said, "You never answered my question,

Leo. What're you gonna tell Nigger-ita?"

"Negrito," Leo corrected. "I think he knows I was in on it, but I'm gonna deny everything."

Fernandez said, "You think that'll work?"

"What choice do I have? I don't know about you guys, but I'm too fucking young to die."

Beaumond finished bagging an ounce. He sealed it with two strips of tape. "Never woulda happened a'tall, 'cept that German queer hadda go and get brave on us."

"Dutch," Leo said. "Manfred was Dutch."

Beaumond took a rat-tail comb out of his back pocket and dragged it across his hair. The comb made a ripping noise as it tore through his split ends.

Leo knew Beaumond was lying. He couldn't imagine Manfred doing anything but surrendering the second he saw the gun. He would've been scared, and no matter how fucked up he was, he wouldn't have done anything reckless. He liked his life too much to have it end over 2.2 pounds of totally replaceable white powder.

Vicki tapped on the sliding door, stark fucking naked. After Leo hurried over to let her in, she sprinted through the kitchen on her toes, through the dining room and up the stairs, trailing water, cradling Mimi, seized with a spasm of modesty.

Her footsteps faded. "We have got to do something about that girl," Leo said. "She's nothing but a liability."

Beaumond said, "A what?" He was looking at Fernandez.

"Vicki's cool," Fernandez said. "She can hang." He wiped some oily sweat on the back of his hand, and shook another Newport out of his pack.

"She sucks my dick good," Beaumond said. He had his sandbox shovel in the coke. He lifted some up and vacantly dropped it back in the pile.

"Look," Leo said, "the party's over here. We've got some serious fucking trouble on our hands. She's gotta find some other place to stay."

Beaumond's narrow eyes turned to yellow-brown slashes. "There's where you're wrong, dude. My Victoria ain't going nowhere."

His Victoria. So it was like that, was it? Okay.

"Anybody leaving this house, it's gonna be you. Want you to keep that right here." Beaumond stabbed an index finger into the center of his forehead. "Don't fuck with me."

He screamed the word fuck. Leo flinched. He said, "Take it easy, big guy."

Leo figured Beaumond probably thought he'd be easy to get over on, with his soft skin and his high-fashion cheekbones, but Leo wasn't about to get vic'd by this white trash piece of shit, not in a million years.

There was something about him Beaumond didn't understand. Leo was as tough as he needed to be. Let Beaumond think he was squishy. This was the way he lulled you to sleep when he was pitching. Blockheads muscled up to the plate to dive into pitches, all macho and shit, trying to pull everything, the way they saw major leaguers do it on TV. Leo stayed outside, outside, tossed one in the dirt, then—how ya doing?—buried his fastball in your ear. That was the danger of underestimating Leo.

Beaumond hadn't blinked since he handed up his warning, the muscles in his neck tense, his jugular blue and pulsing. Leo looked at him, at the place where he had touched his forehead, and pictured a smooth round bullet hole squirting blood, Beaumond tipping over backwards in his chair, his Wal-Mart sneakers and his graying socks dangling in the air. It was going to be his pleasure.

There was a way out of this, Leo told himself, definitely a way out, if he just kept his cool, if he didn't panic and let the situation get the best of him.

The situation. All baseball was situations. All of life was situations, too. He was on to something here. He'd have to think it through when he had some time. When he had some time and his head cleared and he wasn't worried about whether Negrito was going to take him for a ride to the Glades and feed him to the fucking alligators.

At the corner of 17th and Washington, Leo coughed and gagged and lowered his head between the bumpers of two cars. He heaved a few times, but nothing came up. When his eyes stopped watering, he peered out from behind his shades, hoping he wouldn't see anybody he knew. Because there were tons of people heading back from the ocean in the dying afternoon light, the streets buzzing with girls in bikinis and beach wraps.

The Barbarossa announced its existence in indigo neon, a ten-year-old update that did nothing to distinguish it from a half-dozen other restaurants within walking distance. The place was usually empty, though on occasion the overfed Cubans who ran the joint would be forced to set down their cigarettes and coffee, or beer, depending on the time of day, and actually maneuver their fat asses around the tables. A waitress wiping the counter moved toward the window that opened onto the sidewalk, where somebody was signaling for something to go.

The tables were fitted with lilac-shaded linen, and glass tops with cracks and chips that cost the owners zero credibility with their budget-minded clientele. Each one was adorned with a plastic vase that held a single paper flower, and every chair had a laminated placemat in front of it, fun facts over a map of Florida, Spanish on one side, English on the other.

Negrito's name was Ramon Santiago, and he wasn't Cuban or even Colombian as Leo first suspected, but was born in a banana republic down that way, Ecuador or Venezuela, something like that. Leo never asked and Negrito did not offer extra specifics about himself. He was a nephew of Miguel Santiago, better known as El Negro, which was how he got his nickname. Leo didn't know where they came up with this Big Black-Little Black business. Negrito and his uncle were both medium-toned Latin guys.

Negrito was hogging a booth that probably fit eight. The table was clear except for that paper posy, a small saucer, and an espresso cup he was drinking from. He was alone. Leo wasn't sure if this was a good sign or not, whether Negrito's uncle or one of his thugs weren't going to slip up behind him and strangle him with a piano wire, like in *The Godfather*.

Negrito was about thirty. He wasn't more than 5' 6", a rock-solid fat guy who never touched a weight but would bury the biggest Body Tech blockhead in the sand and cut off his head if he was in a bad mood, and Negrito was never in a good one. He looked like he'd gained a few pounds since the last time Leo saw him.

He had a head like Rex the Rottweiler, and his eyes were set way apart like Rex's, but the animal he most resembled was a hyena, no neck, the head sprung straight from shoulders knotted tight with muscle. His fat cheeks made his thin-lipped mouth look smaller. Handsome, no. But his strong chin saved him from being homely.

He sipped his coffee. He looked Leo up and down. He

set the cup on the saucer. After what seemed like a long time, Leo just standing there, he said, "I suppose you think you're pretty slick."

Leo could hear him breathing through his nostrils, snuffling like he had a cold. He said, "Why would I think that?"

"Shut up, Leo. Shut up and sit down. You arranged a delivery. That delivery was made. Then they guy who took the delivery got smoked in his hotel room." His English had no accent. "You gonna tell me you don't know anything about this?"

"Well, no. I saw the papers. And it was on TV. They said it was, I knew it was Manfred." He waited for Negrito to say something, but Negrito kept quiet, so he added, "The guy I arranged the delivery for."

"You thought this would be good for my business? My uncle's business? Using us as the set-up men in your pea-brained scam?" He smoothed the corners of his mustache.

"You know I, I mean I..."

"We've got friends, Leo, all kinds of friends, and you know what our friends told us? They told us none of our product was found in the man's room. Now that's odd. What happened to our delivery? That's what I don't understand. Maybe the guy was able to flip the whole kilo between the time our people left and the time the murderer arrived. Hey, maybe the cops stole it. Maybe the package grew wings and flew across the street into the ocean. What do you think?"

He wasn't waiting for answers, Negrito getting down-right rhetorical.

"Or maybe, just maybe, somebody who had inside information on this deal let his friends in on his secret, and they got themselves an idea. Let's steal it. C'mon, who's gonna know? Negrito's too stupid to figure it out, so let's tie his operation to the murder of a man who was no trouble to anybody. Bring a blast furnace of heat right down on Negrito. Let's make an asshole of Negrito. Fuck El Negrito."

"I swear to Christ and on my mother's grave I did not rob that guy and I had nothing to do with his murder."

Negrito raised his fist and swung it down in an arc, slamming the table top. The cup jumped off the saucer and tipped, spreading espresso out on the glass. That earlier nausea Leo was feeling crept further down his intestinal tract. He was struck with the overwhelming urge to shit.

Negrito took a breath and collected himself, letting the red go out of his face. "This is a complicated situation, Leo, but all life is situations. Some you can get around, and some," he paused, and Leo wasn't liking the sound of this silence, "you can't."

"Man, that is so weird," Leo interrupted. "I was just thinking that exact same thing—" He was about to say "on the way over" but Negrito cut him off with a ringing slap that made his eyes water up again.

"I'm responsible for this particular situation. That's lucky for you." He was totally calm, not a note of emotion in his voice. "Because if it was up to my uncle"—he shrugged to show Leo there'd be nothing he could do—"or the Quiet Man, forget about it." He shook his head. Slowly. "You hear me?"

"I think I do," Leo said.

"You might never be completely forgiven," Negrito said, "but I'm gonna give you the chance to right this wrong. And if I were you, I'd be hoping Negrito was pleased with my solution. Understand what I'm saying?"

Leo understood. He was getting a reprieve, but it

wouldn't last long. He wondered if the solution Negrito was referring to meant he was supposed to kill Fernandez, too, but his voice got smothered with fear, and he didn't want to seem so stupid he had to ask. This was the difference between Negrito, a genuine tough guy that people were afraid of if people were smart, and that shit bucket JP Beaumond, always fronting how tough he was. Negrito didn't need to act crazy or dangerous because he *was* crazy and dangerous.

It wasn't that long ago, two, three days, Leo's luck was running hot. He thought about it, walking back to where his car was parked. He was calling the shots, sketching the plan for Beaumond and Fernandez, finding out when Harry would be getting out, sending him to Manfred. Admittedly, meeting Harry in the first place had been pure, unconscious providence, but figuring out how to take advantage of it—that had all been Leo, and he'd been on fire. So when had it all gone to shit?

Then he thought of something else. What if Negrito was using him to take care of Beaumond, or Beaumond and Fernandez, he hadn't decided yet, and then planned to kill Leo anyway? He started feeling sick again.

This was a situation that had taken a dark, dark turn. It was like getting shelled in the ninth when you'd been cruising through the line-up all day. There was definitely something to this, his baseball-situations theory. Once this whole mess was finished and his mind wasn't cluttered with so many other things, Leo was going to start carrying a pen and a pad. He got a lot of ideas. He'd write them down. Work them out.

Chapter Four

When operating under an alias, Harry felt it was best to hang on to your own first name. For example, if you switched to George or Bill, that's what people would call you, all the people who had no idea your name was Harry, and after thirty-five years of answering to Harry, you might ignore a George or a Bill aimed your way. That'd make people suspicious, or it could lead them to believe you were a moron who didn't even know his own name. Either way, potentially embarrassing. So Harry lopped off the Healy and substituted his middle name for his surname, becoming Harry James, like the bandleader his old man named him for.

First order of business was finding a place to stay. Fort Lauderdale worked hard to shake its image as a municipal frat party, but the Fiorella-type fleabags that warehoused whatever college kids still showed up in spring were legion. Harry had lots of choices.

The Wind N' Sand, set close to the street at the top of a shallow horseshoe driveway, was eighteen rooms laid out in a row, wedged between a Muffler Man and a Pancake Palace. Breakfast All Day. It lacked the least hint of anything resembling glory, past or present. A sign promised prospective lodgers TV and air-conditioning. In red and blue block letters it said SPRING BREAKERS WELCOME. The torn screen curling from one of its windows looked very encouraging.

The office was a Formica counter and an empty mail grid, an ice machine, a soda machine, and a glass box that vended pretzels and orange crackers stuffed with imitation peanut butter paste.

A woman in her late twenties was working a word search puzzle in the same newspaper that brought Harry to Fort Lauderdale, pinching the last drag out of a Kool 100. She was a dishwater blonde with ears that winged her skull at 45 degree angles, and she told Harry she didn't have any vacancies.

"That's not what it says on your sign."

"It says Spring Breakers Welcome. My guess is the last time you were inside a classroom, Gerald Ford was president."

"Jimmy Carter," Harry said, "but I don't see what that's got to do with anything. My money's as good as any college kid's." He was holding a twenty dollar bill on the counter between his thumbs.

"I'll tell you right now, that's not gonna get it," the woman said. She had a diamond of acne on her right cheek, pimples she'd been picking at, a furious fuchsia bomber on her chin.

"Okay," Harry said. "What're we talking about here?" He went into his pocket for a fifty and laid it over the twenty.

The woman looked at the bill and she looked at Harry. "How long did you plan on staying?"

"I'd like to pay for the week."

"And what name did you plan on using?"

"I'm Harry James," Harry said, getting used to it.

The woman stood and slid Harry's seventy bucks into a pair of brown corduroys washed and worn so many times that the nap had gone flat at the knees and the ass, a plum of an ass, wide and thick and high. Her navel was exposed under a white halter and she was wearing a silver chain around her belly. Too bad about her skin.

"You know, Mr. James, it isn't about money."

"It never is."

"That's not what I mean. I can tell you got trouble. You look like trouble from across the street, and if there's one thing I don't need, it's somebody else's trouble. My name's Darlene," the woman said finally. "Please don't ask me for anything."

South Florida's News Leader kicked off a telecast with Manfred's murder, and the story made the papers a few days running, in paragraphs of shrinking size. The reports said police had no suspects at that time. Which may or may not have been the case. Law enforcement only leveled with the media when it served their purpose, and Harry wasn't setting his clock by those guys.

There seemed to be an inordinate amount of cops in this town, but that could've been his imagination. Harry spotted them cruising the wide streets and held his breath, not looking at them, forcing himself not to look away, either. Then the Manfred story lost steam, and nothing happened.

Harry tracked the Lauderdale strip, two boulevards that right-angled the ocean, and skipped the places that looked too small or too hard-core local to hire out-of-towners. He thought he'd give Myrtle's a shot. Its antiseptic scent threw him, its cool dim interior. The place was supposed to be a supper club, but there was no stage and no dance floor Harry could make out, and with its tight-assed fuss of tables and chairs, the joint looked like a cafeteria.

Harry poked around until he found the manager processing words in her office. Glazed in the green glow of her computer, she had auburn hair. She was wearing a beige suit and glasses. She said most of their security people were off-duty police officers, but Harry could fill out an application if he was interested. She sent him into the cafeteria with a pen. As she turned her head to face the screen, Harry saw her right eye flutter with a nervous tic.

Okay, for a residence he could provide a fleabag motel. He couldn't think of a single reference outside of Frankie Yin, and he couldn't remember Frankie's phone number, never knew his address. He didn't recall graduating junior high school. He passed the sixth grade with flying colors, but that seemed to fall into the grammar school category, an academic milestone the application ignored. And hadn't she mentioned they employed off-duty cops? Harry folded the form and stuck it in his pocket. He left the pen on the table, and held the door as it was closing, so he wouldn't make any noise on his way out.

He stopped at a club called Sailor Randy's, an indoor-outdoor multiplex that featured two outside bars flanking a crabgrass garden. Some Mexican was hosing down the patio, and Harry got mad because he didn't understand English. The kid twisted the nozzle on the hose, cutting off the water, like he was about to launch some back and forth finger alphabet, but Harry got spared by a guy drinking out of a plastic tumbler.

Harry liked the looks of him, rumpled and bony, but with a potbelly that bulged over his jeans. His hair was going extra thin on top, but he wasn't trying to hide it, just brushed it straight back from a savage widow's peak and left it long on the back and sides. He looked like somebody who rode a Harley and hung out in titty bars. Not exactly the type Harry was friends with, but he liked his chances with him a lot better anyway than with some linen-suited redhead suffering facial spasms.

The man stuck out his hand. "I'm Bryce Peyton," he

said. "What sort of work were you looking for?"

Odd name, Bryce. It reminded Harry of a hustle he used to run out of the joints on Ludlow Street, with a dope fiend chick named Sam. The marks were straight off the train from New Haven, these suckers, fine arts majors acting hip on the Lower East Side, khaki pantsers who would've been burned by anybody anywhere, then slapped around a bit for their trouble. They usually had names like Bryce.

Harry bluffed his way through all the experience he had in the security field. Peyton called it.

"I bet you got plenty of experience cracking heads," Peyton said, "but that's not what I'm after. Tell you the truth, you're a little small to be a bouncer."

Harry didn't argue. The other guy inevitably compared himself to you. Peyton had him by an inch or two, and Peyton wasn't really somebody you'd think of as a big guy.

"If I stick a walkie-talkie in the mitt of somebody six foot eight, I got sheer intimidation on my side. Maybe the guy hasn't fought with anything more than a lobster special in fifteen years, but then again, he hasn't had to. You hear me knocking?"

Harry wondered whether it was too soon to weigh in with the name, but after this first trip down the strip, he figured Bryce Peyton was the employer most likely to hire a guy like Harry Healy. Or Harry James. James. Harry told him he was down from New York, which impressed Peyton, that he'd been working for a guy named Frankie Yin. Maybe Peyton had heard of him.

"Sure. Who hasn't heard of Frankie Yin? From the Wonderland on Second Avenue. That's a mighty rugged crowd he caters to." He started laughing and loosened something that was sticking to one of his lungs. "Nothing scares me quite as much as a stockbroker wearing a dress."

Harry was about to tell him to take his job and stick it up his ass, but his thinking would run this way whenever his pride was taking a beating.

Peyton emptied his tumbler with two swallows, and when he exhaled, Harry caught a blast of the vodka inside. What was it, noon? This guy'd give Manfred a run for his money.

Shit. Manfred. Harry was trying to forget about Manfred and the hole in the back of Manfred's head, Manfred bloody on the floor in his bloody bathrobe.

Peyton said, "I can tell if I'm gonna like somebody within the first five minutes of meeting him, and I like you. You strike me as somebody who could use a break."

He was going to keep talking, but a hacking fit turned his face scarlet and kicked up the louie crackling in his chest. He hawked and spat but missed the crabgrass, and a quivering blob of brown landed on the Mexican's pressure-cleaned flagstones. When the coughing subsided, Peyton patted his pockets for the pack of cigarettes he must have forgotten inside.

He caught his breath. "And in this business, that fucking Chink is a legend. If you're good enough for Frankie Yin, you're good enough for me. We'll start you tonight around ten."

Bryce Peyton turned out to be a decent enough guy, and he paid cash out of the drawer at the end of a shift, but Sailor Randy's was the cheesiest joint Harry had ever set foot in. He had to be at work by six on Monday, for the drive-time promotion put on by a classic rock radio outlet. Broadcasting live from the club, an on-air personality exhorted listeners to get themselves over to Sailor

Randy's to collect scads of useless shit, visors and bumper stickers emblazoned with the station's nickname. The Storm. They arrived in herds the minute their bosses let them go, guzzling Peyton's rotgut cheapies, caterwauling over lyrics they knew by heart. Harry endured his ten-thousandth listening of "Carry on My Wayward Son" and "Won't Get Fooled Again," two overwhelming favorites of the Broward County workforce. Tuesday was Dress to Kill night, which encouraged all manner of local hag to climb up on stage and flash her tits, while no-assed fat guys, Peyton's cronies, hooted from the floor.

The only bouncer Harry had any respect for was Palmero, who everybody called Big, or when he wasn't around, The Gila Monster. He held down a day job at a hospital, a 6'5" ex-lineman from the U of Miami who was currently looking down both barrels at four hundred pounds.

Palmero handed out assignments at the beginning of a shift, and Harry usually got stuck at the small bar by the bathrooms. He was supposed to keep an eye out for rowdies hassling the bartender, and the unisex toilets, which were one hole each, to make sure people went in alone. If somebody stayed inside too long, Harry'd have to go after them with his key. He'd find some tenderfoot passed out with vomit on his shirt, and then the kid would have to be bounced. Puking was not allowed at Sailor Randy's.

By the start of his second week, the Spring Breakers landed and Harry was earning every pink penny of his one hundred nightly dollars. He had never seen so many kids in the same place at the same time, blown out on booze and hormones and the stupidity of feeling immortal. Tuesday's Dress to Kill contest attracted the usual assortment of cycle sluts, but the less weathered collegiate competition hot-wired the room with a different kind of tension. The two finalists were last week's winner, a biker broad who stripped off her tank top to reveal thunderous, surgically untainted breasts, and a sorority sister emboldened by baybreezes and the whistling crowd. The college girl was prettier, and, for the record, had nicer tits, full and round, but firm, with a slight upward curve and quarter-sized nipples that looked rouged from where Harry was standing. The reigning queen's subjects left her high and dry. Not only was she dethroned by this show of non-support, actual boos peppered the lukewarm applause.

She sent a few bitchy words the college girl's way. The college girl, flushed with victory and all that vodka, made a couple of remarks, too. Some hair got yanked and a slap landed, but the winner was no match for this grizzled veteran of dressing to kill, and before she realized what she'd gotten into, she was catching a beating. A frat boy trying to break it up absorbed three quick rights from a guy twice his size and twice his age. He spit one tooth out of his orthodontically corrected thirty-two.

Harry grabbed a big drunk kid around the biceps and muscled him toward the door, but the entire security crew was inside, and there was nobody to hand him off to. A biker pulled a buck knife. Harry let go of his man and cracked the biker on the jaw, blindsiding him just below the ear. The guy belly-flopped to the concrete and bounced, out cold. His knife skittered across the floor. One of Bryce's whacko bartenders clobbered a frat boy with an unopened fifth of gin, a shot worthy of any cowboy movie. The kid went down. The bottle didn't break. The bartender ran off, one eye bloody, fifth of gin held high.

Head-up on a brass-knuckled biker who threw a

hissing right, Harry blocked it with his left. He kicked the guy twice in the same shin, and once in the balls. He caught a left that backed him up, and the knucks came in again, a roundhouse. He ducked, digging his right into a jelly gut. His shoulder stayed in place, but a hard left connected, and Harry's ass touched down. He sprang back up.

He didn't come out of nowhere, because Big Palmero never came out of nowhere. It took him too long to get where he was going. But he was moving quick for him, quick like a landslide, and snatching that brass-knuckled fist at the wrist, Palmero pushed his palm straight through the guy's elbow, snapping the arm clean at the joint. The biker hit the floor and cradled his crippled limb, screaming.

No shots were fired.

The cops blew in behind helmets and masks and billy clubs that went whap whap whap. Harry vaulted the bar he was supposed to be watching and stayed right there until they cleared the club and Peyton came over to vouch for him, which Harry needed, in spite of his black t-shirt with the periwinkle lettering of Sailor Randy's logo.

Harry ducked everybody with a camera.

The melee was front paged in the *Sun-Sentinel*, and it led the morning newscasts, file footage of the outdoor bar on calmer nights, clean-cut college kids whooping it up, shots of the dance floor and stage, "…where the riot"—they weren't calling it a fight—"is said to have erupted." The Chief of Police and the Mayor got quoted and so did some EMS guys. The paper ran a photo of Peyton, with a big black eye. "Dozens" of arrests were made, nobody said how many, and fifteen people had to be hospitalized.

Harry would almost have been all right with all of it. Almost. But the next night he had to listen to Peyton's juiced-up blockheads, whose conversations were usually restricted to how many big plates they could squat, crowing about their heroics. Like they'd achieved something. It made Harry sick to think he'd been on their side, right there with them, C-note-a-night muscle in a classic mug's job.

The chicks Bryce Peyton employed as bartenders weren't at Sailor Randy's because they were especially skilled at mixing cocktails, or because they could handle a bunch of customers all at once or had the kinds of personalities people were willing to shell out money to be around. They were there to preserve the myth of the beach bunny as ideal woman, modern version: bottle blonde where nature fucked up, sun-tanned, cap-toothed, tattooed and pierced.

Agatha stuck out because she was none of these things. Big Palmero handled the introduction. It was early. Bryce had just turned down the lights, and Agatha was toweling lime juice off her fingers, getting ready to go. Harry asked her if people called her Aggie.

"With a name like Agatha," she said, "they better."

Harry told her it was a nice name, though what he meant was it was an old-fashioned name, and if he had a daughter, he sure as shit wouldn't be naming her Agatha.

"Double double, toil and trouble," Agatha said. "It sounds like the name of one of the weird sisters."

With the possible exception of Bryce Peyton, who could surprise you with the things he knew, Harry would've laid ten to one that he and Aggie were the only two souls in the place who knew the line was from *Macbeth*, and he said so.

Her hair was light brown, and her dark eyes were bright with intelligence. She had a nice, compact body, and the shape of her legs looked great, even in her jeans. She stepped down the bar to pour two drinks, and Harry pictured her walking away from his bed at the Wind N' Sand, panties riding high, baring one cheek of her ass.

"You don't seem like Bryce's type," he said.

"I'll take that as a compliment."

"Why'd he hire you?"

"Because he trusts me," Aggie said.

"You know him a long time?"

"Eight years. We worked together at a place called Mead's. There's a Dunkin' Donuts there now."

"So you're local."

"Fort Lauderdale, Florida," she said. "But you're not."

"I'm from New York."

"The city so nice, they named it twice. Why on earth are you here?"

"I needed a change of scenery."

"Uh-huh," she said. "What's your story?"

"Let me take you out for breakfast, and I'll give you the condensed version."

The bar accumulated a handful of customers, waiting with bills in their hands. Standing money, Peyton called it. He was glaring across the dance floor, his eyes locked on Harry's, his arms spread wide and his palms turned up. Harry made a gun out of his hand, and fired it by pushing down his thumb. Right you are, boss.

"I thought you had to close," Aggie said, reaching for a bottle of Midori.

"Not tonight," Harry lied. "Listen, I gotta make it look like I'm working. I'll catch up with you later."

As a matter of fact, the toilet cop always had to close. So if he was going to see Aggie after work, he needed somebody to cover for him. This was going to be tough. He had no friends on this crew, and everybody hated closing.

The first guy he hit up was Tommy, no last name learned or cared about. He was looking a tad tender from Tuesday night's festivities, though his left eye had started to open a bit. Tommy was a good bet. This was his only job, and the most important thing he had going the next day was polishing up his tan.

"Dude," Tommy said, "you serious?"

"Like a capsized cruise ship."

"I can't," Tommy said. "It's Thursday night." Like if it had been a Monday or a Friday, Tommy'd be happy to oblige, the muscle-bound closet-case.

That led Harry to William-Not-Bill, a puppet-legged blockhead with Cuban blood and a prizefighter hairdo, spiky on top with rat-tails curling out the back. When Harry asked him for the favor, Not-Bill wanted to know if Harry'd been smoking crack.

This left only the Big man himself, and Harry stalled asking the whole night, till he noticed Aggie counting out her money and getting ready to split.

"I give you the twinkiest gig in the whole house, and y'all wanna run outta here," Palmero said. "Why you gotta do me like that?"

"I got a date with Aggie," Harry said. "I mean, I do if you cut me loose."

"That right?" Palmero said. He nodded his enormous head, impressed. "Ain't she the sweetest?"

"That's what I'm trying to find out, Big."

"Well, shit," Palmero considered, "I gotta be at the clinic by nine, otherwise I would. Don't suppose none of these tough guys is gonna help you out."

Harry shrugged.

"Course not." He thought a minute. "Alright, look. I'll

do it tonight and tonight only. Not on your account, you understand, but because I like Agatha."

"Thanks, Big," Harry said. "I owe you one."

Palmero said, "You don't owe me shit. Just do me a solid. In the future, make time on your time, not on my time."

Agatha St. Denis pronounced her name like the French martyr, San-duh-nee, and unlike the rest of her family, who Americanized it so that it rhymed with tennis. They were sitting in a Stuckey's in Dania, being waited on by a begoggled biddy who moved like she had arthritis in her ankles.

Aggie didn't pour syrup over her pancakes, she made a puddle in a saucer and dipped bite-sized chunks into it. And she didn't use butter. Bad enough she was eating at this hour, a snack like this could wipe out an entire week's worth of sensible dieting.

"What're you worried about?" Harry said. "So long as you're eating, I figure you're okay."

"If you live in a Third World Country," she said, "which we don't. A few more late-night pig-outs, and you're asking one of Bryce's sand bimbos to have coffee with you."

They talked about exercise and nutrition. She tried to cook at home as much as she could.

Harry said he was in the best shape of his life. No sense filling her in on his recently completed training regimen as Florida's guest, but since he'd been in Lauderdale he'd kept it up, swimming in the ocean and running and doing his push-ups on the beach. He rarely thought about what he was eating.

"I'm just the opposite," Aggie said. "I can't get with this whole sweat-culture thing."

Harry fired questions at her so he wouldn't have to field any about himself. He found out she was married and divorced from some guy named Bob.

"I thought I was supposed to be getting your story," she said.

"The one buying breakfast gets to ask the questions."

She studied his face and she made a gesture with her hand like she was going to speak a few seconds before she did. "You the trouble man?" A glimmer of a smile brightened her eyes. "You come up hard?"

"Tremendous song," Harry said. "Great song. That's my favorite song." He attempted a creaky, Marvin Gaye falsetto.

"We know one thing for sure," Aggie said. "You were never a singer in this or any life. You're also really good at weaseling, like any trouble man."

She had him pegged for a roughneck and he wasn't a roughneck. He knew some Shakespeare, didn't he? "What is it," he asked, "the teeth? Soon as I get some money, I'm gonna get them fixed."

She wrinkled her nose, dismissing. She slid a Marlboro out of Harry's pack, and he put a match to it. Aggie covered his hand with hers.

"I thought you didn't smoke."

"I quit," she said.

"Why do you think I'm so tough?"

"You're hiding something with a tough front. It's your whole vibe," she said. "But I don't think I buy it."

"I know," Harry said, not listening, "it's the accent. The accent makes me sound like a tough guy."

"New Yorkers have very definite accents, but you haven't got one. Take Henry Miller, for example."

"Henry Miller, huh? When did you ever hear Henry Miller speak?"

"In that movie *Reds*. Remember how they kept cutting in with those talking heads? It was like a documentary that interrupted the narrative?"

The narrative. Why couldn't she have said story?

"Henry Miller was one of the people they interviewed."

It was time to get the check. Harry looked around for that waitress. "Warren Beatty played John Reed, the commie writer," he said, "and Diane Keaton was his girlfriend, I forget her name."

"Right," Aggie said. "Remember?"

"I never saw it."

The waitress was resting her bones at the counter, studying the local section of the *Sun-Sentinel*.

"Excuse me," Harry said with a bit more edge than he intended, "can we have the check?"

"There was a guy with a real New York accent," Aggie said.

Who? Warren Beatty? John Reed?

"Henry Miller."

Henry Miller grew up in Brooklyn and acquired the accent that made even the smartest people sound like retards. If you had money, you sent your kids to schools where they made sure that didn't happen. Now, Harry was born and raised in Manhattan. People from Manhattan sounded different than people from Brooklyn, but it didn't mean they didn't have accents, and people from Brooklyn sounded different than people from Queens. Harry was too tired to explain all this to Aggie. He was tired, period.

Aggie drove him home in her Miata. When he told her to pull into the Wind N' Sand, she was startled to learn he lived there, but she didn't say anything.

Harry was startled to learn he lived there, too. He

said, "Be it ever so humble." He climbed out of the car. "Thanks for having breakfast with me," he said, not looking at her. "I'll see you over at the job." Turning and heading for his room, he heard Aggie kill the ignition.

"Hey," she said. "Get over here."

He walked back to the car and was about to give her a peck on the cheek when she grabbed his face and gave him a big wet kiss right on his mouth. No tongues or anything, but still.

"Tough guys don't get their feelings hurt."

"I'm like James Cagney in *Public Enemy*. I ain't so tough."

She said she didn't know the film. A minute later, Harry was back in the car and they were smoking his Marlboros and he was telling her about Tom Powers and his brother, and Putty Nose, and if she saw *Miller's Crossing* and remembered that scene with the guy begging for his life, that was ripped right off from *Public Enemy*.

Aggie thought maybe the next night they were off she could make dinner and they could rent the movie, and watch it at her house. Harry said that'd be great, he'd look forward to that, and as he got out of the Miata for good, bad as he wanted to drag her into the Wind N' Sand, he knew that part could wait.

Chapter Five

Lieutenant John Kramer was a rock-jawed, crew-cut Dick Tracy of a cop who'd had his cold eye trained on his current job since before he made detective. He enjoyed giving orders, and he didn't enjoy leaving his office unless his squad was about to make a headline-grabbing collar, and then it was a shoo-in he'd be on the scene to provide the media with a statement. With many statements.

It was essential that Kramer keep himself looking sharp for those appearances on the six o'clock news, and today he was sporting a double-breasted suit, the jacket to which hung from a wooden hanger on a coat rack. The clasps on his navy blue suspenders were aligned, and he was standing, which meant he was going to keep it short, with Martinson at least, short and sweet and to the point.

"When are you going to bring me someone for this Pfiser thing?"

"We've got a witness going through mug books, says she saw somebody leaving the scene. Acevedo's with her now."

"That's all you've got?"

"So far. Robotaille's still canvassing."

Kramer looked like he was adding things up in his head.

"You figure what, bad drug deal?"

"What it looks like," Martinson said.

Kramer came around his desk. "Arnie, I need you to make something happen here."

"You catching shit from upstairs?"

"Let's just say this is coming at a real bad time for me."

Martinson almost admired how the man could boil down any situation into what it meant for him personally. Lieutenant Kramer wasn't bad at what he did, but Arnie had come to the conclusion that the man was completely consumed by his ambition to become Chief of Police John Kramer. If things worked out that way, maybe Mayor John Kramer. Ultimately, who could say? Governor John Kramer.

"You mean it's making you look bad." With your pals in

the State House, Arnie could've said, but didn't.

Kramer touched the knot of his tie.

"I'm on my way to the ME's office," Arnie said. "The autopsy should be done. I'll get back to you with the details soon as I can, probably this afternoon. Relax, John. The investigation's proceeding."

"Alright, Arnie. Just bring me back something good."

Taking advantage of her union's dental plan, Lili Acevedo got braces put on her teeth to correct an overbite her family'd been too poor to fix when Lili was growing up. She'd taken advantage, too, of the fact that her parents' generation was the one that Americanized, attending public school all the way through her Master's degree in Criminal Justice. She spoke peppery Spanish and network TV English and sometimes used words Arnie had to look up in the dictionary after Lili wasn't around.

And she took advantage of always knowing what she wanted to do, which was to be a cop. Here she was, bang, a female on the Detective Squad at age thirty-two, hammering out fifty words a minute on the old Selectric, finishing a page without having made a single mistake. Arnie's four-fingered method frustrated her, though Arnie thought he did well, and he did, for a cop, compared to the old-timers he used to work with. Fifteen, twenty years on the job, fully half their time spent doing paperwork, you'd think a guy would learn to type in self-defense.

Lili could be sexy, very sexy if Arnie let himself think of her that way. He was more attracted to the all-American blue-eyed blonde type, but there was no denying Lili had a lot of what a lot of guys went for. He asked her once, and he hoped he wasn't out of bounds, why she wasn't dating some nice young fellow. She blushed and that made Arnie blush, but her answer was a hundred percent honest: If I met some guy I liked and that guy asked me out, don't you think I'd go out with him?

He knew for a fact that Lili and Robotaille saw each other a few times during Robotaille's divorce proceedings, but it hadn't worked out between them. Nobody's fault and no hard feelings, just one of those things. Martinson had been pulling for Robotaille. He was a good cop and a good man, handsome enough for Lili, but it was supposed to be this big secret, so Arnie never opened his mouth about it to Lili or Robotaille or anybody else.

Feeling his eyes on her, Lili looked up from her typing. "What?" she said. "What is it?"

"I thought you were with the French girl."

"I handed her off to Robotaille. What're you doing?"

"Going over to the morgue," Arnie said. "Cranston's still on vacation, I think."

Lili typed a few more words. He was distracting her.

"I hate dealing with that assistant of his," Arnie said.

"Which one?" Lili said, still typing. "Williams? Not exactly the life of the party, is he?"

"He gives me the creeps, that guy."

"Whereas Cranston leaves you with a fuzzy glow."

"Cranston I'm used to. Williams is in a different league of creepy. What is it, the accent?"

"I'm trying not to draw any racial inferences here, I want you to know that."

Lili had attended the same sensitivity training session as Martinson. It was one of their running jokes. "Race, gender, and socio-economic background," the sensitivity trainer summed up, "these are the three categories most likely to arouse prejudice in any of us. Break the pattern of stereotypical thinking. This," he allowed, "will be more difficult for some of us than for others."

The last comment seemed to be directed at Martinson. Afterwards, Arnie and Acevedo got a good laugh out of the bias suffered by overweight Miami Beach natives from Jewish families whom nobody thought of as Jewish.

Martinson did not much identify with being a Jew. He couldn't remember the last bar mitzvah he'd been to, and in the last wedding he was at, his niece got married by a Unitarian minister. Anybody who would've said a peep about it on the Martinson side had been dead for a decade, and when he'd been married briefly himself, it was to a Catholic girl of German-Irish ancestry.

This, Martinson remembered his mother saying, was how a Jew lost his Jewishness. She had a Yiddish word for it, though the truth of it was, she had never been what you'd think of as religious, and his old man believed in nothing, ever, and had encouraged the same in his children. In his opinion, it would only hold them back in life. That sensitivity trainer would've had a field day with Arnie's father, but he'd been gone twenty years before afternoons like that were ever dreamt of.

"It's all that hoogus-boogus island shit," Arnie said of Williams. "Where's he from, Haiti?"

"I believe his country of origin is Trinidad. He is now, however, an American."

"Tell me the truth, Lil," he said, leaning in toward her, his palms on her desk. "Couldn't you just see the guy as a witch doctor?"

"Stop it," Lili said.

"Grass skirt, headdress, whiteface?"

"I am not hearing this."

"Dancing with a torch, maybe casting a spell?" He had his fist balled and he opened it twice quick, throwing the fingers at Lili, casting a spell of his own.

As much time as Martinson spent around the morgue, he'd have thought by now it wouldn't faze him, but the combination of florescence and formaldehyde left him cold with a sense of futility that fell just short of panic. The sheet spread over the body, the repeating squares along its fold lines screaming for order, mocking the scientific discipline that could give you what and when, and where and how, but wasn't going to tell you why. But if you got yourself all twisted up in why, you'd eventually take your service revolver and hold it to your temple and send your brains steaming out one side of your head, just like Frank Matzalanis.

Matzalanis was the best homicide investigator the Beach Detective Bureau ever had, and as far as Martinson was concerned, ever would have. Because Matzalanis was possessed. No wife, no family, no life outside of work, and no interest in one. He drank too much whiskey and soaked up the booze with fried chicken and donuts and solved every homicide that had the balls to cross his desk, except two.

The first was at the very beginning of his career. It involved a little girl who was thought to have drowned in Indian Creek, but an autopsy revealed ligature marks on her throat. She'd been strangled and dumped, and she'd been raped. The kid was nine. Her killer was never found. Twenty-some years after the fact, Matzalanis would periodically re-open her file, putting in whatever hours of his own that he could spare. That was Matzalanis. Haunted.

Then in 1987 there was a series of murders that scared the living shit out of every grandmother living in South Florida. The actor had done three. All women, none under sixty, all rape-strangulations. Martinson worked the case with Frank. They had it narrowed down to one very strong suspect, an ex-Florida Power and Light employee by the name of Karl Bogosian. Bogosian had read all the meters of the victims during his tenure with FPL and would have been able to ascertain that each of them lived alone. During a break-in of Bogosian's apartment, they found a uniform he neglected to return after he'd been terminated, and a trove of porno magazines and videos that featured old broads.

They couldn't match a single shred of evidence at any scene to Bogosian. That hurt their investigation. No judge would allow a blood test with such flimsy circumstantial facts. Maybe due to the strain of the investigation, or maybe just because his time had come, Bogosian died of a heart attack. The wave of murders stopped. Matzalanis was more convinced than ever that Bogosian was their man, and Martinson thought he was right.

But why hadn't he left anything behind? Not a fingerprint or a cigarette butt or a thread from the FPL uniform, nothing. Matzalanis theorized that Bogosian had gone in with a hand vacuum, which they did *not* find in his apartment, and was deliberate and meticulous and compulsive about cleaning up his various messes. He would have had all the time in the world.

Near the end, Matzalanis re-opened the case of the nine-year-old, and was attempting to establish a connection between her murder and the '87 series, defying the wild dissimilarities in their ages, the fact that the little girl had been dumped and the women left in their homes, and his own inability to tie any successive rape-strangulation to the original, the one that had eluded him, had escaped his instinct and his investigative genius. Matzalanis must have concluded the little girl's murder and the old women had to be linked, if only because he couldn't solve them.

A couple of interesting coincidences: the four of them, the three senior citizens and the little girl, had been strangled with a rope or a cord or a wire. In each case, a different instrument was used, but it was some kind of ligature device, not the hands. And every victim had suffered severe vaginal trauma, indicating violent sexual assault, but no semen was found. Not in the nine-year-old, not in the old ladies.

These bookends of failure would be Frank Matzalanis's legacy. That's what he thought. When Matzalanis was facing mandatory retirement with nothing to look forward to except directing security at some godforsaken shopping mall, Martinson encouraged him to take a teaching position. Or to write a book. His memoirs, at least. He had an obligation to share his knowledge. But when Matzalanis didn't show up for work one bright morning and didn't call in, Arnie knew it meant the worst.

He drove to Frank's house in Miramar, and let himself in through the front door Matzalanis had so thoughtfully left open. He'd known Martinson would come. He was in the kitchen. Happy, kitcheny yellows rang false as fire drills. Eyes squeezed tight in anticipation, finger still on the trigger, a single unuttered syllable dead on his lips.

Leviticus Williams didn't strike Arnie as a guy who was too hung up on why. Steeled against the whims of a vicious world behind the glasses that made him look like an African dictator, Williams radiated faith in science, in his own training, in weights and measures.

Martinson said, "Good afternoon, Doc." He called

everybody in a lab coat Doc, from the dentist to the ophthalmologist to the psychiatrist they made him go see after he found Frank Matzalanis in his kitchen.

Williams was crossing the T's on Manfred Pfiser's autopsy report. "It's ironic, detective, but without concerted medical attention, this man would have been coming to the close of a rather short life. He had the lungs of a coal miner, and he was in the nascent stages of heart disease. Also, his liver was enlarged to about one-and-a-half times the size of a normal organ, indicating the onset of cirrhosis, a far more painful death than the one he suffered, and a direct result of his chronic alcoholism."

Okay, he was an alcoholic. No big deal there. Arnie knew a lot of those.

"My assumption is, he ingested a liter or more of hard liquor per day for at least the last five years, though there's no way to be certain." Williams's swaying Caribbean accent made him easy to listen to, even when he got all esoteric and started babbling about things Arnie had neither the time nor the desire to hear.

"The level of alcohol in his blood at the time of death was point two-five percent, which again, just an opinion, could only be achieved over a prolonged period of consumption without producing acute alcohol poisoning."

"So he was really loaded when he got shot."

"He would have been extremely intoxicated," Williams said, "yes."

"I'm betting he liked his cocaine, too." This cold feeling started in Arnie's fingertips, which began to tingle. He rubbed his palms together, then on the legs of his trousers. He wasn't cold. Just his fingers.

"It would be safe to conclude he was a drug addict, as well. In addition to a medication he took for high blood pressure, we discovered trace amounts of marijuana, and a variety of amphetamines and barbiturates. I've noted them individually on the report.

"An extremely high level of cocaine, which indicates habitual use. The man was a toxic time bomb. He had, in fact, ingested cocaine shortly before he died. Nasal passages clogged with undissolved powder. He also had a deviated septum that had been surgically repaired.

"Death was caused by severe trauma to the brain, a metal object entering the base of the skull, ripping through the cerebellum and shattering the jawbone, which, not incidentally, resulted in the gross exit wound you noted. There is absolutely no possibility that the wound was self-inflicted."

Williams's bottle-bottom lenses magnified his eyes, giving them an eerie, bulging effect. He looked up at Martinson. "Unfortunately, lividity was difficult to determine because of the temperature of the room. The air-conditioning was set for sixty-eight degrees, making the body much colder than if it had lost heat in natural climatic conditions. We were forced to rely on the degree of rigor mortis, and the rate of coagulation of the blood to approximate his time of death."

"Which in your opinion was when?"

"Not before ten p.m. and not after ten a.m. Detective, are you certain the victim was standing when he was assaulted?"

"No," Martinson said, "I'd have to check CSU's final report. But I was operating on that assumption."

"If your assumption is correct, he was murdered by someone shorter than himself. From the angle and trajectory of the object, a person no taller than five feet, eight inches, and possibly shorter."

Martinson watched Williams's eyes move over his

report one more time before he signed it. The chill in Martinson's fingers inched past his wrists and up his arms, but he fought it, asking himself what his problem was with Williams. The man was a bit lacking in personality, without a whole lot about him to like, but that wasn't something that should make Martinson feel like he was going to freeze solid in the man's presence. Williams was just one of those guys with no interest and no ability to speak outside of his immediate field of expertise, kind of like Frank Matzalanis, a cop who got drunk with cops and rehashed homicides.

Leviticus Williams dedicated his life to a lonely, grisly function somebody had to perform. Without it, Martinson's job would have been impossible, and for gratitude and a couple of cheap yuks, Arnie had compared him to a witch doctor.

Williams stood up to say goodbye. Martinson hoped he wouldn't notice he was grasping a hand as warm as Manfred Pfiser's.

Lili had gone back to check on Annick Mersault, and she was doing all she could to stay in her chair while Annick described the man she had seen leaving the hotel. The boyfriend, Allain Marcoux, was having a tough time, too, translating Annick's subjective concepts into English for the Department sketch artist, an illustrator named Charlie Roth. Before Roth suggested they move to an interview room, Annick was using Ron Robotaille as her model, saying the man was handsome like Robotaille, except with a squarer chin and a thinner face.

"Thinner?" Roth was asking. "Or narrower?"

"That's good," Marcoux said after clearing things up with Annick, "she means narrow."

The kissy-kissy thing Marcoux had going with this little twit was making Lili sick. She was over the gap in their ages—young or not, Annick was an adult old enough to make her own decisions. But she'd have thought a man of Marcoux's years—he had to be as old as Martinson, and Arnie was what, forty-five?—would have the decency to be embarrassed by a gushing twenty year-old, but the sleazeball just fastened his necklace, slapped on more cologne and lapped the fawning up.

And it hurt to admit it, but Lili was jealous of Annick's beet-faced mooning over Robotaille. It was Robotaille's eyes she was stuck on now. The man at the hotel had eyes like his, Annick said, but the detective's were further apart.

"Do us a favor," Roth said, staying patient, "forget about Robotaille. Try to concentrate on the face you saw. Can you remember what the eyes were shaped like?"

Lili headed out into the squad room. Martinson was walking in, carrying an envelope. He nodded at Lili, stopped to pour himself a cup of coffee, and added two Sweet N' Lows.

"I can't stand to be around that French girl another minute," Lili said.

"She's seen too many Brigitte Bardot movies, that kid. How's it going?"

"Slow. She's hung up Robotaille's eyes."

"Uh-huh. And who's that with Robotaille?"

"Douglas Waters. He was the manager on duty at the hotel that night."

"Oh, yeah?" Martinson said. "When did he get here?"

"About five minutes ago."

"Here's the autopsy report, Lil. Why don't you go over it with our fearless leader? I wanna talk to this guy." She was about to head for Kramer's office when Martinson grabbed her elbow. "Hey, by the way, I'm sorry what I said about Williams."

"What're you talking about?"

He let go of her. "That shot about him being a witch doctor. I didn't mean anything by it. He's not so bad, you know."

Acevedo shrugged him off, but it made Arnie feel better, having said what he said. He moved toward the desk where Robotaille was babysitting his witness. Ron noticed him coming over and got up to meet him.

"Good timing. The guy's gotta be at work soon. Says he would've been in earlier, except he fishes the Keys on his days off. I don't know," Robotaille said, "he looks more like the country club type to me."

"Wherever he's been, it was in the sun. Check out that white stripe across his eyes."

Robotaille went and picked up a telephone and Martinson introduced himself to Douglas Waters. He took the chair Robotaille had been sitting in and said, "I'm sure you heard all about last Wednesday. On that night, did Manfred Pfiser receive any visitors?"

"Not to my knowledge," Waters said. He was a baby-faced guy with cool blue eyes and a close shave.

"Not to your knowledge?"

"We have a policy about announcing visitors, but the restrooms of the café are on the mezzanine level of the lobby, and you can't always tell who's who."

"The hotel isn't exactly a model of security."

"We have a team that works weekends," Waters said.

"Nobody during the week?"

Waters tightened his lips and shook his head no. His tie was tied perfectly, coming up flush against his collar, the knot in the dead middle between the collar points.

"Did you see or hear anything suspicious, anything that would've alerted you things weren't quite right Wednesday night?"

"I saw two men leaving the hotel, two men who weren't registered guests and didn't look like patrons of the restaurant. Something about them was just wrong."

"Such as."

"They were an odd pair," Waters remembered. "One was short—"

Martinson cut him off. With Waters seated, Arnie couldn't tell his exact height, but the man was probably close to six-three. Nearly everybody was short compared to him, and Martinson pointed this out.

Waters said, "Less than average height. With no kind of haircut, you know what I mean? Not combed or shaped or anything."

"Must've been pretty obvious, you noticing that in the two seconds it took him to walk past you."

"No, it took longer than that. I was on them when they got off the elevator, and I remember them walking through the lobby and out into the street. I was watching because I wanted to make sure they were gone. The guy's hair was horrid, looked like it had been cut with a lawnmower."

Waters's own hair was gel-tight. His sideburns, which reached the precise middle of his ear, didn't have a single whisker out of place. A bad haircut is something a guy like this would notice about someone. Maybe the first thing.

Martinson ran a hand though his own hair. "What about the other one, his partner?"

"Taller by a head, and thin. Cuban. I would've said light-skinned black but his features were Latin."

"What does that mean?"

Waters backpedaled. "Forget that. He could've been white, with an olive complexion, Italian or Jewish. I can't say. I didn't get a good look at him, but I do remember this. He had an afro."

Again with the hair, Martinson said, "An afro?"

"An afro. This might sound stupid, but you would've noticed these two by their hair alone. They rushed out of the lobby without wanting it to appear like they were in a hurry. Weird, it was like the taller one was trying to keep up."

"What's weird about that?"

"It should've been the other way around. Wouldn't the taller man cover more ground with a stride?"

"I suppose he would," Martinson said.

"In any event, there's no question they were together."

"Can you recall the time, Mr. Waters?"

"It was after midnight, that's for sure."

"Why're you so sure?"

"The waiters were stacking chairs in the café. That's the image I have of these two. Out the lobby and onto the sidewalk, past the piled-up chairs. The café closes at midnight on Wednesday."

"One of your guests told us that on that night she had to phone the desk to get Pfiser to turn his music down. You took the call, right?"

"I remember it clearly. Ms. Lowenstein in room 1207. I think guests like Ms. Lowenstein would be more comfortable at the Eden Roc, but her wishes do need to be respected. I went up to Mr. Pfiser's room personally, and asked him to lower the volume."

"Was he alone at that time?"

"As far as I know, yes."

"Was this before or after the haircut duo made their exit?"

"Before. I told you they left after midnight."

Martinson took a sip of his coffee and rubbed the back of his neck. He didn't have any more questions for Douglas Waters but he hoped that Waters could come back on another day when he had more time, to take a look at the mug books. Waters said he would.

Martinson got Robotaille to escort Waters downstairs, and he caught Lili coming out of Kramer's office. "What'd Big John have to say?"

"What's he gonna say? It's an autopsy report. The victim died of a gunshot wound. We knew that. What happened with the hotel manager?"

"He described the haircuts of two guys he saw getting out of an elevator."

Lili said, "You like this guy the French chick's describing?"

"I don't like anybody."

"Then who was the man leaving the room?"

"Couldn't tell you," Martinson said. "But we're gonna need to find out."

Kramer had his hair on fire over an editorial in some sporadically published model scene rag that accused the Miami Beach Police Department, and the Detective Bureau in particular, of negligence and sloth, not to mention indifference, toward solving the murder of Manfred Pfiser. Pfiser was a well-known figure among the gay set, and the editorial implied that the Dutchman's homosexuality was the cause of foot-dragging by the Bureau, an idiotic allegation the paper did nothing to substantiate. The piece was headlined EQUAL JUSTICE UNDER LAW?

Kramer was white. He tossed the paper on his desk for Martinson to read. In the third paragraph, somebody left the second 'p' out of inappropriate. Arnie said, "Why're you getting so worked up over a publication that doesn't even know how to spell? Nobody reads these things."

Kramer was pushing the idea of making the Annick Mersault composite public. They'd been back and forth over the relative merits of this strategy in the past, and for what it was worth, this was Arnie's theory:

Nobody, no matter how stupid, who had committed a murder, wouldn't think the cops weren't after *somebody*. Especially with a body left at the scene. But there was a huge gap between an anonymous, faceless suspect, and the specific mug that appeared in a police composite. By keeping the picture in house, so to speak, the killer might be lulled into thinking nobody had seen him. It would naturally follow that he'd think he'd gotten away with it.

Then, on some booze-addled morning, the actor's lips got loose, and he started bragging. Remember the Dutch guy who got it on the Beach? That was me. Next, somebody would rat the guy off. Which always happened. Too hot of a tip to sit on. Not to mention, there's no way the actor arrives at the point where he's pulling the trigger on a defenseless man in some hotel room without making a lot of people along the way hate his guts. This was your revenge factor.

They'd go pick the guy up. Using evidence detectives developed, the District Attorney's office built a case against him. If they had the right man, and everybody did his job, a jury convicted him. Nine times out of ten, anyway. After that, the guy had the pleasure of putting his life on hold for twenty-five years in one of Florida's garden spots. If he got lucky. If he got lucky and the prosecutor didn't decide he should do a little crackling instead. Because Old Sparky was always ready to receive.

Unfortunately, Arnie's scenario was encountering

furious resistance in the face of one quality John Kramer had in very light supply: patience.

"These miserable rags are more influential that you think," Kramer said. "The *Herald*'s bound to pick up this baton, then the TV stations, and then we're the do-nothing Miami Beach Detective Bureau that doesn't give a shit when somebody gets murdered in our jurisdiction. I can't have this, Arnie. I cannot have it."

"Relax, John. Who knows how hard we're working? We do."

Though it was lying perfectly flat against his perfectly flat stomach, Kramer smoothed his hand over his tie. The point of it touched his belt buckle. No suspenders today.

"If we take the composite public," Kramer said, "it could actually help us come up with a suspect, and that's more than we've got right now."

On the other hand, it could send all the hard work your detectives have done so far straight to hell, but Martinson didn't say that. And there was an outside chance Kramer might be right. There was a first time for everything.

Chapter Six

There used to be a lot more of these dives on the Beach, where a shot of no-name whiskey went for two bucks and you could buy a glass of beer for seventy-five cents, but those dirty saloons were t-shirt shops now, and the city Leo grew up with was gone. South Miami Beach had always been there—it had looked the same on a map—

but South Beach hadn't existed. Not by that name. The transformation was so complete that travel agents referred to the area by its cutesy nickname, SoBe. And although this revival played right into the hands of Leo's idealized self, there was something sad about the gouge that had been hacked out of his personal past.

Leo started drinking here, in Loby's Ron-Da-Voo, when he was going to Beach High. Everybody knew Leo's crew was underage, but since the youngsters made up about a third of the crowd, there were never any ID hassles. Florida lifers hung out in Loby's, guys who owned leaky tubs they chartered for tours of the Keys, and so did a claque of Cubans, Marielitas mostly, giddily drinking cheap and singing along with the jukebox.

If Loby ever existed, he was dead before Leo's time. Loby's Ron-Da-Voo was owned by Simon the Bartender. He poured drinks straight through all twenty-one hours of legal operation, and if you went to Loby's and you didn't see Simon, he had either just left or he was on his way in.

Leo didn't have time to kill with any of Simon's saggy-titted surrogates tonight, and he wasn't in the mood to fend off propositions from an end-of-the-line hooker or to make conversation with a stewed regular who smelled worse than the Ron-Da-Voo's men's room.

Fortunately Simon the Bartender was at his post, deadpanning and shaking the ice cubes in the pint glass of tap water he was always sipping from. He had to be over sixty, still beefy in the forearms, still handsome in a busted-up, old-guy kind of way. His wavy hair was mostly grey, but a touch of the brown it used to be was hanging on at the temples.

Instead of saying hello, he nodded at people as they walked in, to set the tone in case they were thinking he was the sort they could tell their troubles to. And if they were drunk or stupid or just plain bad at catching nonverbal drifts and they started in on him, he'd come right out and ask them why they thought he gave a shit.

The clientele was pretty much the same as Leo remembered, though the Cuban quotient had been watered down by tourists out for a slab of what was left of local color and slumming queers who got a thrill out of drinking in a real dive, not a chic, in-crowd place pretending to be a dive.

Leo told Simon he wanted a word and Simon signaled to his man Bruce, who got behind the bar and stood there, a bleary grin on his face.

A six-burner stove dominated the kitchen, its exposed, cobwebbed pipes connected to nothing. A double-doored refrigerator hummed against one wall and Bruce's cot was set up along another. What Leo needed, he told Simon the Bartender, was a piece.

Simon worked keys into a pair of padlocks securing a closet and opened the door. Leo spotted a mop, a bucket, and two brooms with their bristles worn to nubs. A pallet of cleanser was encased in shrinkwrap, and there was a stainless steel sink Simon hadn't gotten around to installing. He reached into a bowling bag and pulled out a black pistol that had a dull, oily sheen.

He said, "Know how to work an automatic?"

Leo said he did, though he didn't. How complicated could it be?

Simon the Bartender pulled back the slide. "Careful. It's loaded."

Leo closed one eye and brought the pistol level with his shoulder. "How much?"

"That's a SIG Sauer," Simon said. "P226, nine millimeter."

"Right," Leo said. He was thinking this baby would do a lot more than just leave a telegenic hole in JP Beaumond's forehead.

"The FBI's using these now, you know."

Leo held the gun at his hip and made a *High Noon* quick draw. Probably take a big piece of that Beaumond bean right off. "How much?" he said again.

"Six hundred."

"Six hundred," Leo said. "That's a lotta loochie." He had about five hundred on him. He gave the SIG Sauer back to Simon.

"That is not the way you hand a man a loaded weapon," Simon the Bartender said. "Barrel down, the way I gave it to you. I don't need any fucking accidents tonight. Six hundred and I throw in an extra clip."

"Can't do it," Leo said. "What else you got."

"I got this," Simon said, reaching into the bag. "Twenty-five caliber. A little short on stopping power, but you're not hunting buffalo, right?"

A chunk of the handle's knurled plastic grip was chipped off. "This's no good," Leo said. "It's fucked up."

"Don't worry. It fires."

"Who makes this one?"

"Phoenix Arms," Simon said. "That's your Model Raven."

"I don't know," Leo said. The SIG Sauer looked so much more menacing.

"And I got rounds," Simon the Bartender said. "About fifty rounds. I won't need 'em."

"Alright," Leo told him. "What's the price?"

"Everything? Tax included?"

Listen to him. Tax included.

"A hundred and fifty bucks."

"Seventy-five," Leo said.

"A hundred and fifty and I throw in all the ammo I got."

"You were gonna do that anyway."

"But I got two hundred into it."

"Bullshit," Leo said. "I'll give you seventy-five."

They settled on a hundred bucks. Leo was on his way out with the pistol tucked into his waistband when Simon the Bartender called him back. He made him come close. He lowered his chin and he lowered his voice.

"If you gotta use it, drop it and walk. Don't run. You call attention to yourself. Walk. Better if you can throw it down a sewer grate, toss it in some weeds or whatever, but remember, drop it and walk."

This bit of advice must have been included in the purchase price. Leo wondered what had gotten into Simon the Bartender. Turned into a regular chatty Cathy right before his eyes.

Every light in the house was burning, but there was nobody inside. A drained 64-ounce Diet Dr. Pepper and a flattened pack of More 120s cluttered the coffee table, but Vicki wasn't in her usual spot in front of the TV. The plate she'd been snorting from was licked clean, and it looked like she'd gotten a nosebleed at some point: a blood-spotted paper towel was wadded up next to the plate. None of her clothes were in the living room. Something wasn't right.

Leo thought Vicki might've gone out with Beaumond and Fernandez, but Vicki didn't go anywhere without Mimi, and the Chihuahua got car sick, so Beaumond wouldn't let it in the Eldorado. That killed that explanation.

The bathroom had been cleared of her shampoos and her eyes shadows and her laxatives. The panties always drying on the towel rack were missing. The closet in the bedroom she shared with Fernandez was emptied of her sundresses and her shoes. Vicki was gone.

Leo dismissed the minor possibility that she went to the cops. Considering it was Vicki who helped them get next to Manfred in the first place, she was as guilty as any of them. He hoped she realized that. Plus, she was ga-ga over Alex Fernandez. No way she'd give up Alex. Not a chance.

But motherfucker. Now he had a whole other bundle of worries to deal with, just as he was on the verge of getting everything sorted out. He wasn't going to let this setback throw him off. Oh no. He had work to do. He added Vicki to the list of potential problems that had to be dealt with, and he'd deal with her, too, in his own sweet time.

Using a wooden spoon to crush some rocks, Leo took a paring knife and diced the powder. He shaped the line into the curve of an S and sniffed it through the casing of a ballpoint pen, chilling to Gloria Estefan. She was singing in Spanish. Leo hardly understood a word. He wasn't crazy about the music, but he loved this sexy Cuban babe. He bet he'd do all right with Miss Gloria Estefan, if he ever got the chance to meet her. He bet she'd be right on his tip.

He stuffed some blow into the end of a cigarette and smoked it like that, took a bump for each nostril, a freeze for his gums. This coke was the bomb, the best he'd had in months, from his own secret stash. Now what did those morons do with his pipe? Here was a nice rock that'd cook up juicy, give him a real buzz.

Leo originally saw himself standing behind the door and whacking Beaumond the second he came in, but the problem was, he didn't know which door. So he sat on the couch with the automatic in his lap. Let Beaumond come to him.

The Eldorado's headlamps flashed though the living room window, and after what seemed like a long time, Beaumond's drunken voice came drifting in, warbling a current hit he didn't know the lyrics to. He let go of a belch that sounded like it came from his heels.

They picked the sliding door. Came in through the kitchen. Fernandez first, mutely blasted, the opposite of Beaumond, who got stupider and louder the more booze you put into him. Fernandez didn't say anything, blinking Leo into focus from the other room. He opened the refrigerator.

Beaumond was calling the dog, his voice getting closer, inside the house now. "Here, Mimi." He whistled three times. "C'mere girl."

Leo's lip was wet with sweat. This was worse than trying to play it cool with Negrito. Way worse. The gun was trembling in his hand, and he couldn't make it keep still.

He got off the couch and walked into the kitchen, the gun at his hip. He leveled it from about five feet away. He fired and missed.

The shitfaced Beaumond pulsed into stone cold sobriety, his eyes huge, reflecting pure fear. Leo liked that. Beaumond lunged for the gun and Leo fired again, grazing his head, the force of the shot spinning him to the linoleum.

Fernandez dropped a bottle of orange juice. It shattered on the floor.

Beaumond pressed his hand over his wound screaming, He shot me, He fucking shot me, and Leo squeezed off another round that went in above his ear and shut him up for good.

Fernandez was frozen in the refrigerator light, his mouth open, his hand on the door.

Leo said, "Are you gonna help me with this or what?"

Beaumond would've been enough of an idiot to hang on to the gun he used to shoot Manfred, and Leo found it wedged between the mattress and the boxspring of the bed JP'd been sleeping in. Also two hundred bucks in tens and twenties, and the latest issue of *Ass N' Bush*. Give the boy credit for selecting a unique spot where nobody would ever think of looking. Leo put the money in his pocket and collected the few clothes Beaumond owned and stuffed them into a Hefty bag. That made it one handgun, one garbage bag half-full of uncool clothing, and one body that Leo needed to get rid of.

Leo was spoiled by the tight-turning Jag. In the driver's seat of the Cadillac, Leo felt like he was piloting a tugboat, the Eldo squeaking and bouncing, badly in need of a front-end alignment. She kept wanting to drift right.

They were headed west on 19th Street toward the Causeway, Alex Fernandez riding shotgun, silent and jumpy, sucking the life out of a Newport. Beaumond's body was in the trunk.

He guided the car into the right lane, pulling the wheel left to keep it from hitting the restraining wall. He slid down the passenger's window. "Okay, kid," Leo said, peeking into the rear-view, "Good a time as any."

Fernandez got his torso outside, sitting on the door. Displaying the form that turned on so many scouts all those years ago, he brought back his left arm and heaved the gun over the wall and into the Bay.

"Nice delivery," Leo said. "Good mechanics."

He was watching his speed, but he thought they'd better get out to the Glades while it was still dark. He hadn't ditched the automatic he bought from Simon the Bartender, because he wasn't sure whether he was going to shoot Fernandez or not.

Alex was definitely catching that vibe. He lit one Newport off another and Leo thought, Wow, chain-smoking for real. He didn't think he'd ever seen anybody do that. Fernandez was about as sober as he got, but he was jonesing for the coke Leo refused to let him bring along. He could sniff himself right into a cardiac when he got back. If he got back.

"This is bad," Fernandez said. They were the first words out of his mouth since they loaded Beaumond into the trunk. "This is so bad."

"It isn't real good," Leo said. Shit, he was out of Marlboros. "Gimme one of those Newports," he said. He pushed in the lighter, and surprise, it worked.

Fernandez was fucking with the radio, trying to find something to listen to, all of it shit, until Leo lost patience with his button pushing and snapped the thing off.

The inside of the car went dead silent. Leo listened to the hum of the engine and the whirr of rubber on asphalt.

"He was my friend," Fernandez said eventually. "I know you didn't like him, but he was my friend."

Leo said, "Hey, Alex? What about Manfred, Manfred was my friend."

He was sweating again. Alex Fernandez was one oily, sweaty Cuban. That chemical smell came off him hard, and between that and the cigarettes, it stunk in the car. Leo peeled down the back windows, got some air in there.

A sliver of moon hung behind them, and the palest strip of violet lightened the eastern horizon, but it was pitch black everywhere, except directly in front of the headlights. Leo pulled onto an access road, but it was fenced off by a gate. Backing up across the highway, he got a running start, and plowed the Eldo through, the car dipping and diving on the rutted gravel. He left the motor running and the lights on and he motioned for Fernandez to get out.

He imagined it'd be quiet this time of day, but Leo was wrong. He heard all sorts of creatures rustling in the reeds and splashing around in the water. The trees shimmered with a thousand bird voices. It added up to a ton of noise.

Beaumond was wearing a Hefty bag, tied at the waist with some twine they'd found in the carport. This was Alex's idea. He didn't want to have to look him in the face, not even with the eyes shut. He was spooked, and Leo didn't blame him.

Getting Beaumond out of the trunk was a bitch. No way Leo could've done it alone. He grabbed the top half of the body, digging his fingers through the slippery green plastic. Fernandez took the legs. With nothing to support it in the middle, the body sagged into a V. Pulling it over the lip of the trunk, Leo lost his grip, and Beaumond's head smacked the bumper. It would've hurt like hell, if he'd been alive to feel it.

They rested for a minute, but Leo got rattled with the screeching birds and the dark all around them, and field-trip memories of gators chilling on logs. No guarantee a hungry one wouldn't come running right up and snatch him. Those fuckers moved quick on their stubby legs.

They dragged Beaumond through the weeds, right to the edge of where the water met the road. Fernandez went in with the feet, him pulling and Leo pushing, until the garbage bag ballooned and the body started to float. Fernandez tore open the bag, dug up a big rock, and fed it through the hole. Leo loosened two more and Fernandez put them inside. He climbed out of the water.

He had his hands on his hips, breathing heavy and watching the garbage bag send bubbles to the surface as it sunk into the muck. Leo stood in his blind spot, his palm on the grip of the gun. If he was going to shoot him, this would be the time.

He thought back to an All-Star game they both pitched in, the stands bulging with pro scouts. Alex Fernandez was the star among stars, a skinny lefthander who overpowered everybody, on his way to a full ride at USC. His mother and his sister—she was the same age as Leo's sister—cheering from the stands. Fernandez out there, holding the ball, looking in, and at that last instant, when it could've gone one way or another, Leo couldn't do it. He just couldn't do it.

Fernandez mumbled something about Jesus Christ Almighty and Leo said, "Let's get the fuck out of here."

The sun was up by the time they hit West Miami. Fernandez wasn't talking. Leo didn't have much to say either, and they were all out of cigarettes, including Alex's menthols.

Leo said, "We've gotta get rid of this car."

"Drop me off," Fernandez said, "before you do any other stupid thing."

Get a load of this guy, smart-mouthing him. Did he realize how close he came to dying back there?

"I can't believe this is my life," Fernandez said. "This is so bad." He was chewing his fingernails. "All I ever wanted to do was have a good time."

"It's done," Leo said. "Stop being such a pussy about it."

"Turn here for Hialeah."

"I'm not going to Hialeah. Hialeah's out of the way,"

Leo said. "I'll drop you off between here and the Beach."

Leo negotiated the thickening traffic. They were driving into a part of town where the streets seemed familiar, but Leo wasn't sure where any of them went. The Eldorado was stuck between a tractor-trailer turning left and a milk truck. Some idiot in a mini-van was nosing into Leo's lane, trying to squeeze between the Eldo and the semi.

"No, fuck you," Leo said to the driver of the van. He inched the Eldo forward, boxing him out.

The light turned green. Fernandez popped his door open and scrambled onto the pavement.

Leo tracked his orange soccer jersey like a visual SOS, his skinny arms flailing as he dashed across three lanes, scary close to getting clipped by a BMW that didn't look up until it was almost too late. *Let the cocksucker live, he wants to go and get himself killed.*

Two motorcycle cops flagged traffic around a wreck. Getting the hint, Leo turned north on SW 12th Avenue, cruising past an archipelago of used car lots, purple pennant streamers flapping above the acreage. Forlorn, buffed-out lemons lay in wait, Spanish words scrawled on their windshields. *Creampuff!* Leo imagined they said. *Original miles!*

He kept going north, rolling through the skanky neighborhoods that, if he wasn't wrong, should take him right into Liberty City. The turf had been poached by the wettest of wetbacks, Salvadorans and Panamanians and Ecuadorians, their pathetic hand-painted letters crammed onto signs outside their restaurants and shops. They ought to be getting a taste, right about now, of what this great country was all about, liquor stores and lottery tickets.

He veered down a street that dead-ended under an

overpass. The sun glinted off the silvery key chain that dangled from the ignition. Leo got out of the car.

He noticed a bus stop on the street he turned off of, and he walked back to it, slow, cool, nothing to worry about. It was in front of a building that at one point in its life was the Buenos Aires nightclub. Half its roof was collapsed and the other half had a huge hole burnt into it. The fire that knocked out the club must've been an inferno, the kind people died in, but Leo couldn't remember hearing anything about it. Imagine. Making it all the way from Nicaragua, then getting charred to a crisp, when the only thing you had in mind was blowing your dishwasher money on drinks and the possibility of pussy. It could almost make you sad, if you let it.

A bottle gang was passing the morning pint. They had watched Leo pull down the dead-end street. Now, they were eyeing him up hard. Looking black, talking Spanish, one could've had Chinese blood, slashes for eyes that were red and mean, a sinister, odd-looking hombre. Leo lifted his shirt and let the grip of his .25 stick out of his pants, in case anybody was getting any ideas.

The bus drifted to the curb. Leo stood in the stairwell, fumbling with his money. Boarding, he watched the gang fall out in the dead-end's direction. Buena suerta, he thought. Good luck, amigos.

As a demonstration of his good faith, Leo put out the word that he wanted to return the kilo that was more like two now after Beaumond and Fernandez got done stepping on it. Leo didn't want to be connected to a batch of blow that was attached to two murders. Way bad karma.

Maybe Negrito felt the same. He didn't seem too keen on getting it back. But any attempt to think along with Negrito was a lose-lose proposition.

Nestor Alameda contacted Leo and told him El Negrito would meet him in a bar off the Calle Ocho in Little Havana. Leo balked. Two things he wasn't going to do: Hook up with Negrito anywhere that afforded the slightest bit of privacy, or get into any car Negrito was driving. He countered with a parking lot off Collins. Nestor called him back and said it was a go.

He wasn't sure why this meeting would be any different than the one they had in the coffee shop, Leo arriving ten minutes early, Negrito already waiting, but he felt weird, a threat in the yellow of the parking lot paint. He got that same throw-uppy feeling he had when he dry-heaved between the cars, and he kept clearing his throat and swallowing, to keep whatever it was down there where it belonged. He really hated to lose the satchel he stashed his film canisters in, but he stayed quiet when Negrito snatched it out of his hand and tossed it in the front seat of his Monte Carlo. The one with the blacked-out back window and the stencil that told you Monte Carlo, in case there was any confusion.

Leo didn't know what to say that wasn't going to piss him off, and Negrito didn't appear to have anything prepared for the occasion. He glared at Leo, wearing no expression at all.

Leo tried this: "I hope you realize I've taken care of everything." He didn't want to come right out and say what it was he'd taken care of, and anyway, he was pretty confident Negrito knew about it, or Leo wouldn't be standing here talking to him or anybody else.

"The only reason there was anything to take care of was because you fucked up so bad in the first place." Negrito's mouth barely opened enough to let the words out. "That's what I realize."

Okay, something had changed since the last time they talked.

"I just want you to accept my apology, that's all." A rush of bile shot up Leo's esophagus. He swallowed hard twice, beating it back.

"I don't give a shit about your apology."

Not only did his mouth stay closed, his lips hardly moved. How come Leo never noticed this? The guy had an amazing untapped talent for ventriloquism.

"You did what needed to be done. That's all that matters."

Good. Well, then, if that was going to be all, Leo'd be on his way.

"And if I have an ounce of trouble with you again, ever, *ever*, you can kiss your ass goodbye. You got that?"

Leo was about to give him a one-word answer like "Understood" when he heard a crack and saw some things that weren't there. He glimpsed Negrito through tearing eyes. The guy just had a thing for slapping people.

Then Leo caught a punch. The second dug into his kidney. The third connected with his jaw and sent him to the pavement, three punches before he figured out he was being hit. He went down thinking, Man's pretty fast for a fat guy.

The ringing in his ears had just about quit when Negrito stomped on his neck. Leo heard a voice from somewhere far away say he wasn't fucking around, but Leo didn't think he was.

Chapter Seven

By the end of the month, Sailor Randy's slowed down. Bryce Peyton cut back security, and Harry only worked the money nights. He still had the money he'd gotten from Sven and Javier, though, and with only half his pay going to the Wind N' Sand, he was, in fact, accumulating cash.

The big news was, he had a genuine thing going with Aggie. She lived in an apartment complex in Sunrise, and they shopped for groceries and rented videos of black-and-white gangster movies. Harry slept at her place a couple of nights a week.

Aggie liked to cook, and Harry couldn't get over how cheap you ate when you made your own food. For eight or nine bucks, the two of them were stuffed and had things left over besides, to eat another night.

Aggie's dream was to be a writer. Harry could identify with wanting to be something other than what you were, but a writer? There was no money in the writing racket unless you hit big with something they turned into a movie. Otherwise, you were wasting your time. And writing took up a lot of time.

She was the theater critic for a weekly arts rag. The gig paid next to nothing, but she did get to see a lot of mediocre theater for free. Harry went with her once, but he was snoring before intermission, and Aggie didn't invite him again.

The paper had a predictable "anti-establishment" point of view, a way of looking at the world that Aggie didn't share, but since she was only critiquing bad plays, nobody cared about her politics. As a matter of fact, Aggie was quite the little capitalist, investment newsletters in the mailbox, on the phone with her broker in the morning.

Besides her newspaper duties, Aggie was hard at some secret project stashed in her computer files. Harry bugged her to show it to him. She said it wouldn't make sense to anybody but her, and when he pressed it, she changed the subject. He guessed this made them about even. She was in the dark about a big chunk of his life, too.

Harry was lounging around one morning, leafing through Aggie's hundreds of CDs, and she was trying to get rid of him so she could get some writing done, but since Harry didn't have anywhere to go or anything to do, he was stalling. The TV was tuned to some cable business show and something came up about one of Aggie's many stock picks. She clicked off the music and un-muted the TV.

"These fucking guys," Harry said. "Cheerleaders."

The screen flashed to a dark-haired good-looking guy extolling the virtues of some company Aggie was long in. Buy, the guy said. That made Aggie feel good.

"Harry," she said, "this guy looks just like you. It's uncanny."

His name flashed under his image. Arthur Healy.

"You think you two could be related?"

Harry said, "Uh, yes, I think we could be. He's my brother."

"Your brother."

"I think you heard me right."

"You never said a word about him."

"It never came up before. What's the big deal? He's on TV all the time. They gotta put somebody on these shows, right?"

"How come you two have different last names?"

Harry was about to say, What are you talking about? But he pulled himself up and said, "That's a longer story."

She said, "I've got time."

"I don't want to talk about him," Harry said, and when she didn't say anything, he said, "I just don't, okay?"

Aggie looked at him like she wanted to say no, but what she said was, "Okay."

It was a Wednesday night. Aggie had roasted a chicken with garlic and carrots and potatoes, and they were sitting around the remains of the meal, discussing that night's rental, *Dog Day Afternoon*.

Aggie was a huge Al Pacino fan, but it was the plain-looking guy who played the sidekick, John Cazale, who made the movie worth sitting through another time. Aggie couldn't picture him, but Harry told her she'd know him for sure once she saw him, he was the one who didn't go to Vietnam in *The Deer Hunter*.

Aggie was clanking dishes around in the sink and Harry said, "I'll get that," because that's what he always said, but she went on washing and he didn't argue. Back in the living room, he found the remote control between two couch cushions and pinched the TV to life.

The news was on. A DEA spokesman was announcing the largest cocaine seizure anywhere, ever. If it wasn't the biggest and the best with these guys, it was nothing. The anchorwoman blah-blah-blahed over footage of the haul, half a ton was the claim, DEA agents proudly wearing DEA caps and DEA vests. The picture cut to a head-and-shoulders of the anchoress in a hideous yellow blazer and door-knocker earrings, puffed-up hair frozen in place.

It reminded Harry of the gangster movies where the

bad guys always hear the law is after them on the radio. They just happen to be tuned to that station.

And Harry just happened to be tuned to this one.

The anchoress said, "Miami Beach Police today released a composite drawing of a suspect in the March Ocean Drive slaying of a Dutch businessman."

Cut to Composite Harry sporting the crew cut he'd let grow out, and the four or five days worth of beard he'd had at the time.

"Persons who may have seen this man are strongly urged to contact Miami Beach Detectives at 970-TIPS. Any information will be kept strictly confidential."

Cut to a promo of the weather. A graphic under the lady's madly grinning grill teased, Naughty or Nice?

Composite Harry's features were close enough to real Harry's, but the eyes, the eyes were scary close, and if you were a cop and you set your lights on Harry, you'd want to talk to him about what happened that night on Ocean Drive. Or if you were a ditzy chick who recognized Harry from Sailor Randy's, and you were clicking your way around the parallel TV universe, you might be tempted to call that number. Likewise if you were the clerk who wore holey t-shirts to your job, where Harry rented movies.

Chain-smoking through *Dog Day Afternoon*, Harry thought he remembered the movie being funny, but he didn't get a single laugh out of it. Aggie knew John Cazale, like he said she would, but when she went, "Hey, there's that guy," Harry just deadpanned his name. She mentioned he was in *The Conversation*, too. Harry said, "Hackman."

He was over the shock of running into his composite self on the cable waves. Right now, he was in desperate need of a plan. Before he executed it, whatever it turned out to be, he was going to tell Aggie everything. Most of it. Maybe. At the high cost of lying to himself, he'd enjoyed this four-week breather, but it was worse than dishonest not to think these cozy domestic moments had definite expiration dates. They were about to come due.

She misread his state of mind. When the movie ended she said, "I'll drive you back to the hotel if you want," but he didn't want that. He wasn't sure it'd be safe.

Aggie went to bed and Harry told her he'd be right in, he wanted to smoke some more and think some more, and after about an hour, when he walked into the bedroom, she was asleep. He slid in next to her and stared into the dark.

He tried to remember the first job he'd pulled. How old was he when they used to duck into supermarkets and drop steaks into the pockets they'd sewn inside the winter coats they wore till May, Harry and Ken Lupo and Gary Paris? Snatching purses from nightclubs they snuck into through side doors? The years ticked by and it all blurred together, Harry getting older and committing different crimes, but nothing really changed. Here he was, thirty-five years old, and he had never, not ever, done one worthwhile thing in his whole life.

Around three in the morning, he finally fell asleep. He dreamed he was in a lineup with Bryce Peyton and Big Palmero. Then Frankie Yin joined them, and so did Cavalero, a detective who rousted Harry for pickpocketing when he was sixteen. It was strange. He knew it was a dream while he was dreaming it. Besides random motherfuckers just shambling in, what tipped him off was he could see through the two-way mirror. Leo stood on the other side of the glass. And Harry could hear him.

"Arrest that man," Leo said in his cocky voice. "That's Harry Healy. He's the one who did Manfred. Murderer,"

Leo was saying, pointing a finger straight at Harry. "Murderer."

Harry said, "I never killed anybody."

It woke up Aggie. She had her arm across his chest, her face right up next to his. She said, "You're having a bad dream."

"I never killed anybody," he said. He was awake, too. He found Aggie's eyes in the dark, and he said it a third time, to her and not to the night, "I never killed anybody."

Harry climbed out of bed while it was still dark and made a pot of coffee. Aggie followed him into the kitchen. Pulling out a chair, she fixed her eyes on Harry's with a sleepy look of accusation, like he'd done something wrong.

Which he had. He'd done lots of things wrong.

He told her exactly the way it happened, told her about Leo and Manfred and the Surfside fags, how when he got back to Manfred's hotel with Manfred's money, there was the old Dutch Uncle on the floor with a bullet in his head.

He'd have liked to leave Julia out of this, but the reason he was in Florida at all was directly related to Julia, and the whole truth of it was, yes, it started with a woman.

This was about two years ago. Harry got a beep from somebody who needed half an ounce dropped off at a party on Spring Street. The party was stocked with chicks wearing black dresses that clung to their hips and made their legs look longer. They did the Bump with guys who were losing their hair, dressed in khaki pants, sporting wire-rimmed glasses with smudged lenses.

Pulling a Rolling Rock from a garbage pail full of ice,

Harry helped himself to sandwiches and pizza and cookies. He was digging around in a bowl for a potato chip wide enough and thick enough to hold the glob of dip he wanted to smear on it when Julia approached the table. She wasn't wearing black. Her dress was white with a pattern of roses, flimsy, loose, held up by two thin straps. She was picking over a plate of melon and sliced apple for a strawberry the right shade of ripe for her red, red mouth.

Somebody was yelling in her ear. She ignored him, eyeing Harry as she slid the strawberry between her lips. She set the stem on the tablecloth, then said to the yapping pest in a loud, clear voice Harry was supposed to hear, "Fuck off."

The guy's ears darkened, and he slunk back to the dance floor.

Julia asked Harry point-blank if he was the drug dealer.

"I am many things," he told her, selecting a strawberry of his own, "to many people. Who would you like me to be?"

"Sir Lancelot," she said. "And I'll be your Guinevere."

Harry was a pushover for literary references.

Aggie cut in. "Just like that, huh? Sees a cute guy, delivers a corny line. I suppose she fucked you that first night, too."

"Hey," Harry said, loosening up, "who's telling the story, me or you?"

He brought Julia to a place on Grand Street, where his friend Irish Mike was tending bar. Julia pissed Mike off by forcing him to make her margarita twice because the first one wasn't sweet enough.

"The drink's supposed to be tart," Mike explained. "That's fresh lime juice."

Julia said "What?" but Mike told her to forget it.

They sat and drank till last call. Mike was marrying bottles when Julia got up to go to the ladies' room. He leaned in toward Harry. "Watch that one, kiddo. She's nothing but trouble."

"Why, cause she doesn't like your margaritas?"

"She's in here all the time with guys who got money," Mike said. "What the fuck's she want with somebody like you?"

Julia owned a co-op north of Union Square. The building had a swimming pool on the roof, and the plan was to go skinny dipping, but when they got up there, Julia changed her mind because she said it was too cold. They spent the next eight hours draining her champagne stash and fucking. At one point, they were doing lines off each other's chests, but that was a detail Aggie didn't need to know.

Julia grew up on Long Island, under the diamond eye of a stage mother. Child-acting in commercials when she got her break, she was in a sitcom that ran until the actors got too pimply for their parts. It was still in syndication, and every time one of those miserable shows flickered across a screen, Julia got paid. She had four bank accounts, a stock portfolio, and a financial manager.

She had lost interest in acting, but she wouldn't have dreamed of having a job. Harry wouldn't have gone hard on her for that, except her time was completely empty, and he didn't care how loaded you were, you had to work at something. Look at those society broads. They oversaw pet charities or rounded up money for kids with cancer. Their energy went somewhere.

This was what he said to Aggie. He never mentioned it to Julia.

An ordinary day started between one and two.

Harry'd go make some low-key moves, flag down some cash, iron out the wrinkles in whatever the next thing was, while Julia ate lunch with her girlfriends and shopped. Around five, they'd hook up for cocktails in the most up-to-the-minute trend-o-mat. Eat dinner in some other restaurant. They got written up in a gossip column where Harry's name was misspelled. They were on the circuit.

Harry was raking a healthy profit off of Julia's friends, plus some jobs he did on the side, helping Jimmy De Steffano move hot TVs and VCRs from the warehouse where he worked. But all his money was going on these cocktail hours and dinners and nightclubs where he hated the music. That was another thing: For all the money the selfish bitch had, Julia never went into her pocket for a dime. Not for a cup of coffee, or a drink, or a cab ride, nothing. Her money was her money. She expected Harry to spend his money on her. And he did, all for the privilege of fucking her, which, as the situation deteriorated, he was doing less and less.

Julia decided she needed a break. Though it was July, she had her mind made up on Miami Beach. Harry went along with it, figuring the town would be dead. He pictured himself on an empty beach, Julia rubbing oil into his shoulders, but they landed in a neon-charged netherworld combusting with flashy hipsters untroubled by a single thought and a Eurotrash factor that made Soho feel like a mall in Topeka. There were a bunch of them in on it, this goofy road trip. Julia's whole circle was there.

It started in a Mexican restaurant. Harry was picking at a plate of quesadillas, and Julia was drinking margaritas and doing blow with a friend of hers named Yves. It would be just like Julia to trot out her boarding school French for this frog, and he corrected her when she needed it. Frequently. They giggled and played knees-y on the banquette.

Harry wasn't drinking, but when they got to Lefty's, a velvet rope dive, he ordered a double Dewar's and a beer, and lost Julia and Yves in the crowd. An hour and two doubles later, he found them. Yves with his hand up her skirt. Julia's tongue in the Frenchman's mouth.

He shoved his way across the dance floor and said, not to one or the other, "What am I, some kind of fucking asshole?"

Yves made Julia step away, like he had an idea he was going to get tough. He started to say something in his fractured English, and Harry popped him with a left and a right and followed with a hook that missed because Yves was on his ass, looking up.

The big difference between the South Beach fight and the brawl at Sailor Randy's was this: Harry got beaten like a borrowed mule.

He held his own against the bouncers, who were big and slow and didn't know how to fight, but they pinballed him out the door, which is where he laid nine months of time on the jaw of Officer Kenneth Simms, then half the Miami Beach police force used him as a punching bag. This was the way he lost his teeth, if Aggie was wondering.

The weeks before his trial felt like one long day. He kept hoping Julia would appear, serious and sorry, a cashier's check in her purse, but Julia and that moment never arrived, and before long he was pulling nine months of a year bid, including time served, twenty-three days.

The judge would've let Harry slide on the bullshit possession rap if he hadn't punched Simms into the X-ray room, but his public defender, whose angry African-American-ness didn't help Harry at all, refused to plea him out. This pissed off the judge like a charm, and when he handed down the sentence, he wasn't even looking at Harry. He burned slow, shaking his head at the black PD.

"This is the problem," he told Aggie. "My entire life has been getting fucked up and stealing and fighting, but it's starting to feel less and less like me. You know what I'm saying? That fight at Sailor Randy's? Last thing I wanted to have anything to do with."

"That's what Bryce pays you for," Aggie said. "You were doing your job."

"That's what I mean. When I was moving blow, I was doing my job. When I was stealing TVs, I was doing my job. I don't want to do jobs like that."

Which presented a dilemma. He didn't know anything else.

One thing he made sure Aggie understood, he never walked in anywhere behind a gun, and he never threatened to hurt anybody if they didn't give up their wallet or their watch. That didn't mean he wouldn't lift a wallet on a rush-hour bus, but that was a different kind of crime. Any job that involved a gun, it wasn't for him.

Using the gun, that is. He sold lots of guns. There was a good buck in that.

Sometimes he thought he might actually do something to change his life, but what? Unlike a lot of hoods, Harry never dreamed of the Big Score. His thinking didn't run like that. The hustle was just to get him through one day and into the next. Harry Healy was textbook small time, and he knew it.

"What about your family?" Aggie said. "Your brother, the one on TV?"

Harry was a mistake, born when his mother was forty-three. He had two brothers, ten and fifteen years older. Ernie lived in North Carolina, and Arthur, the big Wall

Street man, owned a house on Long Island that Harry used to visit on Christmas.

His mother worked forty years at the phone company, right up till the time she got sick. Diagnosed with liver cancer, she was gone, goodbye, six months. Harry was sixteen.

The old man was a trumpet player. Never had any kind of job besides playing trumpet. He still worked, or anyway was working off and on the last time Harry talked to him. Harry James was the old man's idol. Harry didn't get that one. Harry James was a suck-ass trumpet player if you asked Harry.

He hadn't talked to his father, or his brothers, since, well, he didn't remember, but it was a good long time.

What Harry had been doing all this time was waiting for something to save him. He didn't know what. An event, a person, something, some vague thing, was going to pull him up and turn his life around. He usually caved in for the rich-chick-as-savior scenario, which is where he supposed Julia fit, but just look at how that one turned out.

Like after he read that Brooke Astor was dissolving her Foundation, giving away the last of her money before she went down for the long count, Harry thought, If she only kicked a million or so my way, I'd be set. He pictured himself above the fold of the *Times*, beaming, flanking an Ed McMahon-sized check with the ancient Mrs. Astor. Harry had it spec'd out to the shoes he was going to wear.

Maybe he'd waited long enough.

"My family," Harry said. He let out a breath.

Every time Harry saw her, Darlene was looking better and better. The dermatologist gave her some pills that knocked out that skin condition, and she was coming off trashy and sexy in her cut-offs and halter, her baby-fine hair pulled back like a schoolgirl's. He waved to her from his end of the driveway as he was letting himself into his room.

Harry had chipped a hole in the wall behind the hot water pipe, covered the hole with masking tape, then slapped some paint that almost matched over the tape. His money was in a Marlboro box in the hole. Winding some small bills around the fifties and hundreds, he stuffed the knot into his jacket and buttoned the pocket flap.

He packed his duffel bag and folded the promotional t-shirts he'd accumulated at Sailor Randy's. He left the shirts in a stack on the bed. Darlene could help herself to them, cut them in half, some brand new halter tops for the siren of the Wind N' Sand.

He stuck his head through the window that opened on an alley. All clear. He dropped his bag and climbed out feet first. Cutting through the alley, he walked into some weeds still wet with a rain he didn't remember, and came out in a parking lot, where Aggie was waiting at the wheel of her Miata.

She wasn't talking, so Harry went over his story one more time. Leo, Manfred, the Surfside two. What happened, he had no idea, but he didn't shoot Manfred. Were they clear on that? Because there was a great chance the police were going to want to talk to her before too long.

"And you think you got set up," she said.

"No," Harry said. "No extra information. Don't do their job for them. Let them do it. You don't know anything. Nothing. You got it?"

She stared at the road, the wind sculpting her short

hair into a quiff. Harry had her drive him to Boynton Beach, and when they found the bus station, Aggie went in and bought him a ticket to Philadelphia.

Without the highway to distract them, and with a half-hour wait yawning, the tension was like a bug-zapper crackling over the wheezing of the buses. It attacked Harry's neck, that tension, but he didn't want to be the one who spoke first. He didn't know what to say.

Aggie said, "All I want to know is, where do I fit in?"

Harry flipped his cigarette to the asphalt and said, "What do you want me to tell you? You don't."

He turned his face flush into a slap and he blinked twice, reeling Aggie back into focus. Then he thought of something. What stopped her from rolling right over on him? If she got that in her head, they'd grab him before he got to Orlando.

"Look, I know this isn't nearly as romantic as you boarding a plane with some hero of the Resistance, and me walking away to run my gin joint."

She got the reference. She wasn't digging it.

"The last four weeks, Aggie... I've been happier than I've ever been. I guess I just wasn't meant to live like that. I guess God is saying, Harry, you can't have this kind of life."

"How moving," she said. She squeezed back the tears. They came out in spite of her. "Get out."

"Sweetheart?"

"I said get out," she said, gunning the idle. "Get the fuck out."

He lit another cigarette and walked over to where a dozen or so riders waited with their luggage, Aggie leaving rubber in second gear.

Chapter Eight

Manfred Pfiser had never been arrested in the United States, in his native Netherlands, or anywhere else. He chipped out a nice living for himself with his imports and exports, he was even-steven with the Dutch taxman, and he was all caught up on his alimony and child support. Another Euroman on an extended vacation, soaking up sunshine and neon. The difference between him and a few thousand other guys, besides his cocaine sideline, was that Pfiser left the party early, and against his will.

The traces in his suitcase tested out almost eighty percent pure. That much was rare in quantities under a kilo. Your strongest kick-ass street gram came in around twenty-five, and if you were copping in some after-hours dive, ten percent would be about the best you could get your hands on. Martinson theorized Pfiser went down holding large, a package that'd be worth killing for.

Being the savvy businessman he was, Pfiser no doubt had profits of his own to maximize, but to the heavyweights, to the real gangsters, he would've been a customer, and these people had grown far too shrewd to cut into their own market share. And the murder weapon, which Martinson didn't have, was a piece of evidence that mitigated against a professional hit.

Crime Scene recovered one bullet fragment from a chair and dug another out of the plaster. A third piece was removed from the wound during the autopsy. A small bit remained missing and it probably always would, but there was enough of the slug for Dade Ballistics to determine it had been fired from a Lorcin 380, a classic Saturday Night Special that could be bought brand new in the box for about a hundred bucks.

Cheap automatics had a reputation for jamming, and this particular model, manufactured after 1990, had had something shoved into it, scratching the inside of the barrel. That made it more inaccurate than it would ordinarily be. Actual discharge of this firearm was indulging in unintentional Russian roulette. The shooter would be lucky if the thing didn't blow up in his hand.

No self-respecting hood went anywhere near a gun like this.

The bad boys were goofy for sophisticated hardware. Berettas and Glocks, Walthers. It was a point of pride and street cred for these knuckleheads, who at least knew the difference between the real McCoy and a piece of shit like the Lorcin. So Arnie took a guess: The shooter was a punk who stumbled across a payday, a small-timer with the luckiest chance of a short, wasted life.

They found loads of fingerprints it took nearly a month to account for. Shug's team lifted a full set of ten from a windowsill, and there was a partial on the portable stereo that they couldn't match up with anybody, maid, electrician, or cable TV guy, who might reasonably been in the room. After exhausting his Florida resources, Martinson had the unidentified prints forwarded to the FBI's Science Crime Lab in Washington. It had already been a week, and it could easily take another, to find matches in their infinite computer files. That's if they had them at all.

The current crime of the century occurred in Colorado, and it might not have been a crime at all. A packed-to-the-vents 747 went down over the Rocky Mountains, shortly after take-off from the Denver airport. That was the plane-crash phrase. Shortly after take-off. The disaster cast suspicion on foreign terrorists and the usual knot of pissed-off white guys who blew up Federal Buildings and shot it out with over-armed G-men, but the FBI, backed up by the FAA, refused to issue any definitive statement until all the evidence was in, and since it was spread out over five or six square miles, it'd be a while before all the evidence was in.

The Colorado crash ended Pfiser's brief run in the headlines, the same way the Pfiser murder displaced the attack on Josephine Simmons, which had left people sufficiently appalled for several slow news days.

At approximately two o'clock on a February afternoon, Ms. Simmons, a seventy-nine-year-old woman, was trundling toward the efficiency she'd lived in since 1963, carrying a can of chunk light tuna, a frozen box of spinach, and two grapefruits. Her handbag dangled from her right arm. When an assailant ran up behind her to snatch it, Josephine Simmons, out of pride or fear or stubbornness, decided she wasn't going to give it up. Or maybe there hadn't been any decision-making process. Maybe she merely reacted the wrong way. Whatever it was, she fought for the purse. This left the perp no course of action but to pound the woman into submission, and in his rush to escape, he left the handbag on the sidewalk. It contained the grand total of eight dollars and fifty-four cents.

The media seized on the sum as if to say, See? See how cheap the life of an eighty-nine-pound old lady really is? Like if there'd been a few thousand in the bag, they would've understood.

Nobody witnessed the crime, or nobody came forward and admitted they witnessed the crime, and that was odd, considering it occurred in a residential neighborhood at two o'clock in the afternoon. Robotaille and Acevedo canvassed the area, but no one could furnish even a partial description of the attacker, and after two weeks, their investigation was pretty much dead in the water.

Until one concerned citizen responded to a call of conscience and a televised Crime Stoppers program, and phoned Beach detectives. Acting anonymously, the tipster fingered one Anton Canter, an area crackhead and two-bit dealer who'd taken a few raps for possession and sales, and was between jolts in the Florida penal system.

With some assault beefs on his record, Canter fit the profile flush, and Arnie, Acevedo, Robotaille and even Kramer at one point gave him the latter-day hot light and rubber hose. They held him for twenty-three hours without charging him. They kept him awake and they kept him hungry.

Through it all, Canter stuck to the alibi that he'd been in his outpatient drug-rehab program. The counselor vouched for him, and so did some of the other druggies in his group. His name was in the clinic's daybook. Anton Canter was a largely worthless human being, more than capable of this crime. However, the facts he based his alibi on suggested he didn't do it.

Martinson was driving north on Washington Avenue when he pulled over and made a quick dash across the street into Burger King. He ordered two Whoppers with Cheese. Hoping nobody would catch him committing this crime against his cholesterol levels, he skulked back to the car and wolfed down the burgers with a side order of guilt, one after the other. He polished off the last few bites of the second and wiped his fingers on the bag, before heading into the florist's. After selecting three yellow tulips and three sprigs of honeysuckle, he drove to Mt. Sinai hospital.

Josephine Simmons had lain in this bed, comatose, since the day of her attack. She looked like a child dying of starvation, minus the bloated belly. She was wired to one machine that displayed her heartbeat on a screen and a second that monitored her breathing. IVs pierced either arm and a hose pumped oxygen into her nostrils.

With a little bad luck, and who didn't have that, life could come to this. Three quarters of a century of loneliness and struggle, and here you were in a hospital, stranded between living and dying. It was scary. The chances were pretty good Martinson could wind up the same way, after a heart attack or a stroke or a bout with cancer. Retired and out of the loop, a couple people who remembered him from his cop days, Lili and Robotaille, say, would visit him and bring him flowers he couldn't see, until he became a nuisance people would rather forget about, wondering why he didn't just hurry up and die. Life was seldom fair. Martinson had gotten his mind around this a long time ago, but the cruel tricks it managed to come up with sometimes knocked the breath right out of him.

The water in the vase he filled last week had evaporated to an inch from the bottom, murky with dust and shriveled petals. He threw the old flowers in the garbage, rinsed the vase in the bathroom sink, and filled it about halfway. He put the fresh flowers inside. The scent of honeysuckle filled the room and chased away the modern, antiseptic smell.

Martinson chattered, arranging the flowers on a nightstand. "Here's a card," he said, spotting a religious greeting from an order of nuns. "It's signed by a Sister

Bridget in Des Moines. A picture of some saint." The icon had its arms spread, palms out and ready to embrace. "It says they're praying for you to get well."

The doctor told Martinson his visits might not be helping, but they couldn't possibly be doing any harm. He encouraged him to keep it up. This was an honest doctor, a short guy with tight curls, who gave Arnie the truth early on when Arnie was wondering who else came to see her. And when he asked about her condition, whether it was like being asleep or being knocked out or what, the doctor admitted coma was something they didn't know that much about. The young doctor hadn't honed his bluffing instinct. He was the first doctor Martinson heard say, I don't know.

Arnie took the chair at Josephine's bedside and let three meaty fingers rest in her palm. Josephine wrapped her hand around them, the way she always did. The first time, he jumped up to find that honest doctor and tell him what happened, thinking he'd been present for some major breakthrough. The man informed him it happened all the time. A reflex. Again, it wasn't bad, but it didn't necessarily mean all that much either.

But it convinced him Josephine Simmons was in there somewhere. Shallow chest moving up and down, eyes shut, bony fingers squeezing with a surprising strength, the way a baby could startle you with how much power they had in their tiny fists. Under the wires and tubes and plastic attachments, a human being whose life had basic fundamental value was fighting to get out.

He said, "You rest up and try to get better, Josephine. I gotta get back to work, but I'll be by to see you next week. The flowers are beautiful. Yellow tulips. And you can't miss that honeysuckle, right?"

Martinson made a move to get out of the chair, and as he stood, he thought he felt Josephine's fingers tighten their grip, but it was possible he only imagined it.

The prevailing sentiment around the job was that John Kramer's ascension to lieutenant had as much to do with his skill at navigating Department politics as it did with any leadership qualities he may have possessed. Kramer was in place before Acevedo got here, but Robotaille and other veterans related the disappointment they felt when Arnie Martinson didn't get the promotion.

Arnie would've claimed he wasn't interested in the job. He would have said Kramer made a fine lieutenant, and he would've denied there was any rivalry between them, but they often disagreed on policy. Like whether or not to make the composite of their suspect in the Pfiser murder public. Kramer was for, Martinson dead set against.

The following events proved the Martinson instincts sharp:

1) Patrolman Kenneth Simms, recovering from a gunshot wound and probably considering another line of work, dropped by the station to visit his buddies. Taking note of the composite on a bulletin board, he said it bore a glancing resemblance to a guy who broke his jaw at Lefty's, a bar on Washington that was now a coffee shop. The guy's name, Simms recalled, sounded Irish and started with an H. He asked somebody to look it up. Harold James Healy.

2) Later that day, a Fort Lauderdale sergeant called Beach detectives and told them they might want to take a look at a bouncer in a joint called Sailor Randy's.

And 3): Yesterday, an FBI fingerprint search spit out a match for a partial that had been lifted from the stereo in

Manfred Pfiser's room. It was identified as belonging to one Harold James Healy, last known address, New York City. With no help from the general populace, Harold James Healy was glowing super-nova hot.

Score one for Martinson.

The one thing they gained by releasing the composite was the likelihood of alerting the suspect to his status. And they created a task that would tie up Ron Robotaille for days. He was watching a tips hotline right now, unwrapping a piece of candy and sticking it into his mouth.

The FBI faxed a nice, neat package. Healy was born on 12/16/61 in Manhattan, and took his first fall on 5/23/78, for being a passenger in a stolen car. He earned an Adjournment Contemplating Dismissal.

On 11/12/90, he was arrested for possession of a controlled substance, codeine, and issued a summons. The judge slapped his wrist and Healy managed to outmaneuver the law until 8/15/94, when he was charged with assault in New York. His attorney plea-bargained it down to being a patron of a disorderly premises.

He did his very first bit a year later right here in the Dade County Jail. Tumbling on a slew of charges, including assaulting an officer, he got off easy. Nine months inside. Acevedo studied the mugs from Healy's most recent bust. The French chick had a point. He did kind of look like Robotaille. It was a stretch, but Lili could see it.

She slanted her eyes at Robotaille, who was wearing a bored expression, taking an obligatory note from somebody on the phone. She looked from the mug shot to the composite to Robotaille. Healy wasn't what you'd think of as ugly, but he was no Ron Robotaille.

Ron was great looking, and he was a nice guy, too, but

he was so dull he made you want to scream. It took Lili two dates to figure it out. They had a decent, unexciting time at a restaurant in Aventura, and another night they went to see a boring movie, Robotaille's choice, then for drinks in the Grove. Somehow or other, they wound up in Lili's apartment.

Wait a minute. This was dishonest thinking. They wound up in Lili's apartment because she was entertaining the idea of having sex with him, but when they got there, he wouldn't shut up about his soon-to-be-ex-wife, which turned off Lili like a light switch. Robotaille managed to put two and two together. He wasn't sure how, but he knew he'd blown it, and he didn't ask Lili out again. Only now, even their most mundane exchanges were strained with a clumsiness that wouldn't have been there if not for those two dates. Lili was sorry she'd bothered. If he wasn't so handsome, and Lili hadn't been so flattered, she wouldn't have.

Robotaille looked over, and Lili quickly averted her glance to Healy's mug shot. The look in Healey's eyes was one of half-drunk exasperation, not that dead-lensed, clench-toothed, tough-guy stare that jumped out of so many of these pictures. Healy was trying out the you've-got-the-wrong-man stare. You saw a lot of those, too. Annick Mersault, that syrupy little pain in the ass, hadn't done much with the shape of Healy's face, or his nose, or his chin. But the eyes, she had gotten the eyes exactly right.

Wispy clouds splashed white like brushstrokes against the sky. It was a bright afternoon, a day for the Department of Tourism. Martinson was driving with the windows down. It was hot enough for the AC, but Arnie held out for the muggiest weather to run it, afraid that the shock of the cold air blowing on him could trigger a migraine.

Traffic was one fact of South Florida life the tourism people never got around to mentioning. This ride between Miami and Ft. Lauderdale got more aggravating every time he made the drive, and he did it only when it couldn't be helped. The state started a highway improvement program a decade ago, and Martinson couldn't remember the last time all the lanes on the interstate were open. He drove past coned-off quarter mile sections. Long stretches of road he swore were finished the last time he came this way had somebody in florescent orange flagging traffic to a virtual standstill. What used to be a forty-minute trip could sometimes take an hour and a half if you weren't lucky. Highway improvement. He got off on Sunrise Boulevard.

Sailor Randy's was in a strip of yahoo-joints that catered to a young crowd, go-go bars and indoor-outdoor booze shrines roping them in with goofball promotions. A sandwich board at the entrance to the parking lot said TUE: DRESS TO KILL WED: LADIES DRINK 2-4-1 ETC. Arnie wondered what you got for that ETC.

The club featured two outside bars and a cinderblock building that looked like a warehouse standing behind them. Inside, the concrete and cement trapped the stink of stale beer. Two Latin teenagers were dealing with a delivery, restacking cases of Heineken on a handtruck that was as tall as either of them. They wheeled it into a storage room, one kid pushing, the other bracing the load so it didn't wind up on the floor. The deserted space had a weird feel.

Martinson knocked on a half-opened door and pushed it in. A man was sitting at a desk. He looked to be in his late thirties, with a rock star haircut and a beard flecked with grey. He looked up, saw Martinson, and said, "Hi."

Martinson badged him.

The man introduced himself as Bryce Peyton, and stood up to shake hands. He was about 6'2" and he had huge hands, his right covering Arnie's like a catcher's mitt. He said he owned Sailor Randy's.

"I'm investigating a homicide that occurred on March fifth," Martinson said. "We got a tip from the Sheriff's Office that this guy might be working in your place." Arnie showed him Healy's mugs.

Peyton pulled a variety of faces, squinting, bringing his eyebrows together, pursing his lips and pushing them out. No question in Martinson's mind he knew the suspect, but he might've been debating whether to give him up.

Peyton said, "Healy, huh? He told me his name was Harry James." He handed back the photos. "Am I gonna need a lawyer? Because if I'm gonna need a lawyer, you're supposed to tell me. That is, if I'm not mistaken and I don't think I am."

Where was this guy coming from? Martinson said, "What would you need a lawyer for?"

"In case I was under arrest." Peyton lit a Chesterfield. Now there was a brand you didn't see every day. He took a sip from a glass on his desk.

"I'm just trying to run a business here," he said. "Make a living and pay my taxes. Trouble with the law? I don't need it."

Martinson thought, pretty shaky. Maybe he was worried about the illegals he had stocking his beer.

The first two fingers on his smoking hand were stained to the second knuckle, from sucking those lung-busting Chesterfields right down to the nub, probably a good forty or fifty a day. Martinson wanted to tell him, There's a reason people quit smoking.

"Listen," Martinson said, "whatever you got going here, I don't give a shit about it. I'm asking you what you know about Harry Healy."

"He was this drifter type looking for work." Peyton picked up his glass and drained it. It wasn't water, it was vodka. "I felt sorry for him, but to tell the truth, I needed the help. By the time March rolls around, I get a thousand heads a night in here. Somebody's gotta control 'em. Harry seemed like a nice guy, and he did a good job."

Martinson said, "Where is he now?"

"I haven't seen him in a week. He took Tuesday off, and he was supposed to work Wednesday, but he never showed up. He said he had experience and he worked like he had experience. He's from New York, you know. He dropped the right name, so I hired him."

"What name?" Martinson said. He had his notebook out.

"Frankie Yin." Peyton inhaled a chestful of smoke and blew it toward the ceiling. "You ever hear of Frankie Yin?"

"Why would I have heard of Frankie Yin?"

Peyton's irises shined with a reverential gleam. His hands gestured loosely, as if words wouldn't do justice to the admiration he had to express. "Why would you have heard of Toots Shor? Or Josephine Baker? They're legends of this industry."

Martinson didn't know who the other two were, either. He said, "Is that right?"

"Legends of the time-honored profession of showing people a good time. Frankie Yin is a legend."

"And Healy worked for him, is that it?"

"Detective Martinson," Peyton said, switching gears, "May I offer you a cocktail?"

"Can't do it," Martinson said.

"Beer or something?"

"Thank you, no." This Peyton was a prize.

"Then if you'll excuse me, I'm going to help myself. You don't mind, do you?" Not really expecting an answer.

"This'll only take a minute," Martinson said, "if you'll bear with me."

"No problem," Peyton said. "I'll be right back."

His boots clopped across the concrete, and then Arnie heard the sound of bottles clinking. He checked out the photographs Peyton had mounted on a wall, pictures of himself with members of the Dolphins, the Marlins, the Miami Heat. He couldn't get over how tall the basketball players were, like they had to duck down to fit in the frame. The seven-footers dwarfed Peyton, a paw here or there on his shoulder, like he was a little kid.

"Would you believe," Peyton said, re-entering his office, "that Frankie Yin started out as a busboy?"

"I'm here to find out about Harry Healy, who I'm investigating on suspicion of murder. Frankie Yin does not concern me. What more can you tell me?"

"Not much," Peyton said, less enthusiastic now. "He seemed decent enough." He swallowed some vodka and looked through it to the bottom of the glass. "Likeable. He was a likeable guy."

"So he must've made some friends here."

"I don't know. He was polite, but he pulled up a bit short of being friendly."

"Nobody he was particularly close with?"

"He might've had something going with one of my bartenders," Peyton said. "Aggie St. Denis."

Martinson wrote down her name. "What was she, his girlfriend?"

"One night, he swapped shifts with another guy so he could leave with her. Occasionally, I'd notice them

Everyone is Raving About
HARD CASE CRIME
Winner of the Edgar® Award!

USA Today exclaimed:
"All right! Pulp fiction lives!"

The New York Times wrote:
"A stunning tour de force."

The Chicago Sun-Times said:
"Hard Case Crime is doing a wonderful job... beautiful [and] worth every dime."

New York Magazine called us:
"Sleek...stylized...[and] suitable for framing."

Playboy called our books:
"Masterpieces."

Mickey Spillane wrote:
"One hell of a concept. These covers brought me right back to the good old days."

And Neal Pollack said:
"Hard Case may be the best new American publisher to appear in the last decade."

Find Out Why–and Get Each Book for
43% Off the Cover Price!

(See other side for details.)

Get Hard Case Crime by Mail...
And Save 43%!

☐ **YES! Sign me up for the Hard Case Crime Book Club!**

As long as I choose to stay in the club, I will receive every Hard Case Crime book as it is published (generally one each month). I'll get to preview each title for 10 days. If I decide to keep it, I will pay only $3.99* — a savings of 43% off the cover price! There is no minimum number of books I must buy and I may cancel my membership at any time.

Name:

Address:

City / State / ZIP:

Telephone:

E-Mail:

☐ **I want to pay by credit card:** ☐ VISA ☐ MasterCard ☐ Discover

Card #:   Exp. date:

Signature:

Mail this card to:

HARD CASE CRIME BOOK CLUB
20 Academy Street, Norwalk, CT 06850-4032

Or fax it to 610-995-9274.
You can also sign up online at www.dorchesterpub.com.

* Plus $2.00 for shipping. Offer open to residents of the U.S. and Canada only. Canadian residents please call 1-800-481-9191 for pricing information.

If you are under 18, a parent or guardian must sign. Terms, prices, and conditions subject to change. Subscription subject to acceptance. Dorchester Publishing reserves the right to reject any order or cancel any subscription.

coming into work together. Does that make her his girlfriend?"

"Did you ask her, this bartender girl, what happened to her pal Harry?"

"As a matter of fact," Peyton said, "I did. She told me she hadn't seen him, and I took her at her word. She's not responsible for his behavior."

"I didn't say she was. But I'd like to get an address and a phone number for her."

Peyton said, "Sure." He opened a desk drawer and rummaged through a mishmash of catalogues and brochures and order forms. "I gotta have it around here somewhere." He unjammed another drawer overflowing with the same kind of mess.

A green metal filing cabinet sat between the desk and a wall. On the side that was facing out, somebody had taped a list of names and corresponding phone numbers. In black marker across the top it said STAFF PHONE LIST. Healy's name wasn't on it.

Peyton was rooting in a third drawer.

Martinson said, "What about that?"

Peyton straightened, red-faced and winded, and told him he could use the phone on the desk.

Unless Aggie St. Denis turned out to be a rabid, cop-hating brat, Martinson made up his mind going in, the right way to play her was soft.

She buzzed him into the building and waited in the doorway of her apartment. She was expecting him, after that phone call from Peyton's office, but Martinson showed her his badge anyway. She glanced at it, left the door open, and walked back inside.

She was pretty. Not a knockout model type, but fine-featured, attractive, with boyish hair she parted on the side. She was dressed in stiff new Levis, a man's cut that gapped at the waistband where her figure tapered in, and fit snugly over her hips. She wore a v-neck t-shirt without a bra. Her feet were bare.

They were standing in her living room, near a couch and a TV with a 19-inch screen. She didn't ask him to sit.

Martinson told her why he was there, and he asked her if she knew a man named Harold James Healy. He might have been going by Harry James.

She jumped on him. "Let me tell you something right now, detective. You're making a mistake. Harry didn't kill anybody."

Which told him Peyton was right. She did have something going with Healy or she wouldn't have come out of the box so defensive.

"We have a witness who saw him leave the scene shortly after the murder," Martinson said. "And we have corroborating evidence that proves he was there." He let this sink in. "If you were me, you'd be looking for him, too. When was the last time you saw him?"

"Earlier this week," she said.

"What does that mean?"

"Tuesday or Wednesday."

"It was one or the other, wasn't it?"

She kept the apartment neat, but she owned too many books for the bookcase that stood to the right of the entrance. There were stacks of books on the floor. Martinson unshelved an oversized, leather-bound edition of Shakespeare's tragedies. It was an old volume, the leather dry and cracked, and there were two more like it that made a set. He thumbed through the first few pages.

Aggie St. Denis closed the cover and put the book back. "I'd rather not have you sorting through my things," she said, "if it's all the same to you."

"I'm sorry, I was just trying to find out when it was published."

"1897," she said.

"Wow, that's a hundred years ago. That set must be worth some money."

"Ten dollars each," she said. "I tried selling them when I was broke, and that's the offer I got." She refolded her arms, remaining near the bookcase, but her shoulders had dropped down a bit.

"That's funny," Martinson said. "The same thing happened with this watch my grandfather gave me when I was a kid. I kept it in a cloth bag that closed with a string, and put it in a jewelry box and forgot about it. Long story short, I recently came across the watch. I thought, hey this is probably a really valuable piece. I took it to a jeweler and he appraised it for a hundred bucks."

"But is has sentimental value," she said. "That's different."

Martinson pretended to think about what she was saying. He said, "I guess so."

"You weren't close with this grandfather?"

"Nobody was. He was an ornery son of a bitch. Lived in the same apartment on the Lower East Side of Manhattan most of his life. In '57 or '58, he was supposed to come and live with us. My father hired a contractor and was all set to build an addition to our house, but then grandpa died."

"That's sad," Aggie St. Denis said. "But what you've got is a family heirloom, and I've got a set of books I bought at a garage sale."

Martinson said, "Family heirlooms are usually worth something besides sentiment, aren't they? Although when you think about it, nothing has any value, except for the value we assign it. I'll give you an example. A painting sells for twenty-five million dollars. Twenty-five million. What makes a piece of canvas with some colors splashed on it worth even one dollar? Basically, just somebody's say-so. Then a second guy comes along and says, Hell, twenty-five million? That's a bargain. I'll take it. There you go. That's what your picture's worth.

"Same thing with the watch," Martinson went on. "I take it to three jewelers, they all say the same thing. It's worth a hundred bucks. But let's say I had a totally different relationship with my grandfather. Let's say I loved him more than anybody I ever knew. I'd starve to death before I sold that watch. That watch would be priceless."

Aggie St. Denis was getting lost following the Martinson logic. She shook her head, and Arnie knew his argument, if he was trying to make one, was falling apart.

"But isn't that what I said in the beginning?" She sounded like she genuinely didn't remember. "We're talking about two distinct quantities. On the one hand, money. On the other, what, emotional attachment? Anyway, that's a weak example. Your watch's got nothing to do with my books."

"Maybe not," he said, though he'd forgotten where they were, and he wasn't thinking about whether he agreed with her or not. Arnie felt the first twinge of a headache boring in under his eyes. He took two deep breaths and hoped whatever was coming would go away. Just for a while.

"I guess I was taking the long way around to the point that all of us cling to various things, convinced they're so valuable, and then something happens, or somebody comes along, and proves us wrong.

"Now let me ask you a question," he said. "You're an intelligent woman. What's more important, living up to some false sense of honor by protecting a potentially dangerous criminal, or helping society make this individual answer for his behavior?"

"We're back on Harry."

"That's what I'm here for."

"He didn't do it," she insisted. "Harry wouldn't hurt anybody."

"That's odd," Martinson said. "Because he's been arrested for assault, and he certainly hurt one of our police officers. Put him in the hospital. I would say that not only is he capable of hurting people, he already has."

"He wouldn't do what you said he's done. He couldn't have. I know his side of the story."

"Then why don't you let me in on it?"

"Would it change your opinion?"

"It might."

"Harry went to do a job for the man who was murdered. When he returned to the man's room, he found him dead."

Martinson said, "A job, huh? What kind of job?"

She double-clutched and broke eye contact. She said, "I don't know." She was lying.

"Let me guess. He made a delivery for the victim."

"I don't know," she said again.

"And wonder of wonders, the victim was already gone by the time your boyfriend got back with his money? Is that what he told you?"

This time, she didn't answer.

"And you believe him? Look, at one point there had been a fairly large amount of cocaine in the victim's room, and by the time his body was discovered, those drugs were gone." Martinson went right at her. "Your boyfriend stole those drugs and killed that man. This guy you're trying to protect."

"Then why bother with the story?" she argued. "Why

wouldn't he just steal my money and steal my car and disappear in the middle of the night? If he's the kind of man you say he is?"

"What was he selling you? A frame? Prisons are full of guys who didn't do it. You know that, right? If he's so innocent why didn't he give himself up?"

No answer for that, either.

Martinson said, "So where is he now?"

"I have no idea," she said. Another lie.

"I don't believe you. And I wonder if you know that aiding and abetting a fugitive is a felony you could be prosecuted for?" Put some heat under her ass.

"And I'd like to meet the prosecutor who'd try me on those charges. You're not scaring me, detective."

"I'm going to find your boyfriend, Ms. St. Denis, and I'm going to bring him back here to stand trial for this crime, with or without your help."

"We hung out for like a month. We ate some meals, we watched some movies, we worked together. But I want to separate you from the notion that I have some special knowledge pertaining to this case. I don't. And I don't have anything more to say to you."

She walked to the door and held it open. She was lying about not knowing his whereabouts, but Healy did have her convinced he didn't do it. When she said she didn't know anything thing beyond Healy's version, she had told the truth. About that, anyway. Which was more than he could say for himself, and that yarn about his grandfather, who had been dead for years before Martinson's parents even met.

Chapter Nine

With a reminder beamed at him just about every time he turned on the TV, Leo was feeling guilty about Manfred's murder. But then a rapist got loose in Gainesville, forcing these college chicks to do it at knifepoint, and after that, some Homestead trailer-court mom buried her twin daughters alive. She claimed she had visions the kids were agents of Satan, who was behind like every other shrub in rural Florida, and this was way bigger news than some drunk getting offed in his hotel room, fabulous South Beach or not. In about a week or so, the Pfiser story died down. Leo's feelings about him died down along with it.

Though he felt zero remorse over smoking JP Beaumond, Beaumond did come to visit him in a nightmare. Beaumond showed up in his army fatigues, settling once and for all the question of whether you dreamed in color. Leo distinctly saw the brown and khaki, the olive drab that made up Beaumond's foul camouflage pants. Shirtless into the next world, his pink potbelly hung over his belt. The scary thing was, he had a huge bite out of his chest, a big chunk shaped like an alligator jaw. It wasn't bleeding. Just a hunk of flesh that wasn't there. Leo could see light coming through the back of him.

"Yew sum bitch," Beaumond said in the dream, "Ah'm gwan git yew fer this." It came out slow, like Beaumond had to think about it.

"Hey," Leo said, startled by the wound and the fact he could hear Beaumond's drawl so clearly, "you're dead. Fuck you."

Beaumond looked disappointed with the news, but he didn't bother Leo at all after that, and Leo didn't devote him any waking thoughts.

Alex Fernandez called and said he was sorry about jumping out of the car that day, but he was really freaked and he hoped Leo would forget it. He told Leo he was thinking about going to Cuba until things cooled off, some story about a sick relative he was going to peddle to Immigration, if it wouldn't fuck with his green card. Leo thought it was a good idea. He also thought it was a good idea if Alex didn't call the house any more.

Before he hung up, he asked Fernandez if he'd seen Vicki.

"Vicki?" Fernandez said. "Not at all. Do me a favor, Leo. If you see her, don't tell her where I am."

Since Leo didn't know where he was, and didn't want to know, he didn't think that was going to be a problem.

But now he had to worry about Vicki. Leo hated worrying. It got in the way of his fun.

He would've started worrying before, had he run into Vicki anywhere, but he hadn't. Which was weird. South Beach was an incestuous scene that got smaller by half if you lived here year round. You saw the same faces, whether you wanted to or not. It was inevitable. But now that he was looking for Vicki, she seemed to have disappeared. She wasn't wandering Washington Ave. in the afternoon, or haunting the clubs at night, the stuff she did every day when she was on bivouac at the house.

Leo made up his mind to find her. He was sitting on a café terrace overlooking Ocean Drive, hung over bad from chugging cheap champagne at an agency party. Drinking espresso and profiling with a Marlboro, he peeped the parade of Euros and crude modelitas from behind his Revo wraparounds. Not a hide or a hair of airhead Vicki, her Chihuahua either, whose snout would be poking out of a basket bag that matched the hat Vicki was sure to be sporting. He ordered another espresso to stay alert. If he did get Vicki in his crosshairs, he wanted to be sharp, in case he had to reach some kind of decision.

After two hours, he still hadn't seen Vicki. But the time hadn't been wasted, since this bouncing blonde bundle two tables over was staring right at him. Leo played it off with a dramatic drag on his Marlboro, pushing his hair off his forehead, and sipping from an empty espresso cup, as if he were deep in thought, which he was not. He snuck a peek back. No question. She had the Kid locked right in the old pin-spots.

She had a rocking tan under her white bikini and the white shirt she had tied around her neck. Leo scanned the table for signs of neurotica. There were dozens, if you knew how to read them, but on the positive side, every blonde signal was go. She was drinking a glass of wine. Excellent. Sometimes they didn't drink because they were uptight about their weight, and that could mean they'd be in the bathroom after a pricey meal, barfing up their supper.

Another positive vibration: no miserable mutt anywhere near her. And if Leo was not mistaken, that binder sitting on the empty chair was a portfolio. The genius of it all. Now he could walk up and ask what agency she was with.

He got the waitress's attention and told her he'd be drinking a Cuervo margarita, straight-up with salt, at that table where the blonde was sitting, and to bring the blonde another glass of whatever she was having.

He picked up his cigarettes, walked over, and introduced himself. Did she mind if he joined her? Of course she didn't. Leo lifted her book off the chair and asked who represented her.

"I'm not with any agency right now," she said, implying she'd been with some agency in the past, though Leo knew that was impossible, unless she worked when she was a kid.

Was that a nervous giggle he heard? He believed it was.

Her name was Whitney and she was nineteen, a real corn-fed, hand-spanked, all-American type with either blue eyes or green eyes, a tough call from behind the shades.

Pretty was not Whitney's problem. Height was. She wasn't tall enough to model any kind of clothes, and she had the wrong shape for it besides, her plump titties touching the tabletop. Leo imagined she was thick through the waist and the hips, too, stealing a glance downstairs without being too obvious. The girls who got work were all starvation skinny, five-nine at least (a six-footer was not unusual), all legs and necks and big flat feet that held them up.

Leo took a look through her book. A natural disaster, it was, in a way, better than he could have hoped. The pictures were poorly lit and the styles were so whack the clothes must've come from her closet. A photo of Whitney wearing a floor-length gown chopped a much-needed three inches off her height. Somebody sausaged her into a one-piece bathing suit with a horizontal pattern; she looked like a zebra-striped fire hydrant. There wasn't a single tear-sheet, not one shot from a magazine or a catalogue or any actual job she had done.

But toward the back of the book things got interesting. Whitney had a banging body she wasn't bashful about showing off, and there was no denying those boobies, flowering fully in one photo, no annoying bathing suit blocking his view. The last few shots—the whole cheese-bucket, woolly little pubic patch and everything. If her sights were set on the pages of *Ass N' Bush*, this was a fine example of her work, but she'd get laughed out of every office on the Beach.

"This is a terrific book," Leo said. "You've got a lot of talent."

"I'm glad you think so," Whitney said. "Now all I've gotta do is convince those agencies."

"You know, I just might be able to help. You'd be surprised," he said, trying to get his mouth around this outrageous lie, "you're better off than most. But I'll tell you what."

Leo took a card from his wallet. He had them printed when he rented the house, cards that said he was associated with the Top Girl Agency, a completely false claim, but if the play was ever going to work, Whitney was the type of girl he had in mind for it.

She swallowed a sip of wine from her fresh glass. "You're so nice. I wish I'd met you a couple weeks ago."

"That doesn't matter," Leo said. "The important thing is, we know each other now. I could be an important contact for you."

"Your hair is really cool," Whitney said. "Take off your sunglasses so I can see your eyes."

Leo drove her back to the house. She didn't have any clothes with her besides the cut-offs in her knapsack, but stripping off the bikini was Whitney's idea. Leo let her run with it. Hunting down a roll of Kodachrome, he realized Vicki could've passed him ten times while he was out there on the Drive charming the pants off of Whitney and he never would have known it, but Vicki was going to have to wait. He was having too much fun right now to worry about Vicki.

Whitney put on a CD that featured the Iggy Pop oldie, "Real Wild Child." She ignited a spastic dance around the living room, throwing a kick that knocked over a lamp and broke the lightbulb, Leo snapping away at the action. She kept right on moving, ending up in his face, giving him her tongue. He carried her to the couch, his fingers squeaking on the sweat-slicked small of her back, and fucked her wearing all of his clothes. She wanted to quit and videotape it, but Leo didn't own a Handicam. He promised her he'd buy one, and he promised himself the same thing. A camera and a tripod, too.

That Top Girl front he laid on her came back to haunt him. Even though Whitney checked out the competition and had to understand her brand of sexy was not what the agencies were looking for, she'd taken what he said to heart. Leo moved things around to let her know, not in so many words, that she wasn't going to be modeling fashion in this or any foreseeable lifetime. What client wanted those big rounds boobs blowing his product off the page? But if they required a face, for cosmetics or jewelry, maybe Whitney had a shot.

Her eyes came off violet, Elizabeth Taylor-eyes in the right kind of light, blue-grey in another, slate-grey from a third angle, slate-grey and sparkling. Leo didn't think she'd be that tough of a sell. It'd involve calling in favors and creating some he'd owe, but Leo had the juice to get it done.

First things first. That dirty picture book masquerading as a portfolio had to get kicked to the curb, and in a rush, if Whitney was going to get anywhere in the business. But she had to replace it with something. He called Stuart A. Homes-Leighton. A monied Brit who fancied himself a homeboy, Homes-Leighton had been kicking around the Beach for the last few winters, arriving at New Year's, breaking out after Easter for destinations north. He got a lot of shit for his receding hairline and his double chin, for his fire-engine red hair and the pasty English skin that turned a luminous lobster in the sunshine, but mostly, he got shit because he was from a rich family and the other scenesters were jealous of him.

He had a raft of shortcomings, weaknesses that played right into Leo's strengths. He would do anything to be around models. Professionally, he was vulnerable: He was a solid photographer, but the agencies all treated him like a troll. And he was a wicked blowhound. The mere suggestion of lines was enough to bring him running. There was no way he was going to refuse this job. He didn't, calling Leo back ten minutes after Leo left a message with his service.

Homes-Leighton rolled up in a 1974 Oldsmobile Delta 88, red with a white convertible top. The odometer had flipped at least once, but the engine ran smooth and her body was solid aside from a raggedy patch-up somebody slapped on her left rear quarter panel. He could afford any car he wanted, but he went out of his way to look like he was struggling. This was a Homes-Leighton thing Leo didn't get. The way Leo saw it, the more money, the better. Why hide it?

He had a delicate creature named Fraunces in tow, and when Leo said, "Hey, Francis, what's up," Fraunces cued him to the phonetics and spelled out the name for him. He was as tall as Leo and he might've weighed a hundred and thirty pounds with lug bolts in his pockets.

Leo went out to the Olds to help Homes-Leighton hump in his gear. He said, "Where'd you get this guy?"

"Fraunces is the mack-est of all make-up daddies."

"I'm not paying him," Leo said.

"No, I am. By the hour. So if your girl's good to go, let's set this shit off."

Leo introduced everybody, fumbling Fraunces's name again. He thought the living room would make a good set, and Homes-Leighton agreed, stalking the corners, rearranging the furniture, opening the windows and fluffing the shears. Homes-Leighton was wondering what kind of shots Leo had in mind.

"Concentrate on the face," Leo said. "Let's get some head shots, do a few, I don't know, three-quarters? You're the photographer, killer. What do you think?"

"I'm with that," Homes-Leighton said, though he didn't mention which part of it he was with.

"What we're trying to do is demonstrate that she photographs well. Am I right?"

"No diggity-doubt," said Homes-Leighton.

"Stuart? Nobody says that any more. The whole Eton-homeboy thing, it's over. Okay?"

Fraunces sat Whitney in a dining-room chair. She had what looked like a stainless steel poncho draped over her shoulders, and he was working on her with a brush, stroking powder under her cheekbones.

"Honey," he said, "your eyes are flawless." He had a clamp on her eyelashes, teasing them up and out. Applying mascara that made a sharp contrast with her blonde hair, he frowned. "Who did this to your hair?"

A hurt look hit Whitney's face. "My cousin," she said. "He's a licensed cosmetologist."

"If this is any indication of his work," Fraunces said,

"his license ought to be revoked." He flipped her hair forward and back, dissatisfied with both positions. "What do you expect me to do with this hair?" He pushed it away from her face and gathered it up in back.

"What's wrong with my hair?" Whitney said.

"Besides the color, the cut and the style, nothing at all."

Homes-Leighton was peering through the lens of his camera. "That's a phat look for her."

"Fat?" Whitney said.

"Cool," Leo said. "He means cool. That's a good look for you, with your hair up. Really shows off your features. Just pin it up," he said to Fraunces.

"I am a make-up artist," Fraunces said. "I am not Anne Sullivan." He let Whitney's hair fall.

Whitney said, "Who's Anne Sullivan?"

Fraunces turned back to Whitney. "A few more hours, I'd dye that hair. Blue-black, honey. Those eyes would shine like diamonds."

"I don't want black hair," Whitney said.

"What're we shooting here," Leo said, "the cover of *Vogue*? This is a test."

Homes-Leighton said, "Word."

"But I don't want black hair," Whitney whined.

Leo shut her up with a stare.

Fraunces went into his kit and came up with a mouthful of bobby pins. Covering her hair with a silk scarf, he knotted it at her forehead. It gave Whitney a Twenties kind of glamour. Perfect.

Homes-Leighton posed Whitney in front of a screen, chattering instructions. He snapped pictures, providing his own soundtracky babble, like he was starring in a TV commercial.

"Look left, that's it, chin up. Gorgeous. Okay, chin

down, eyes right. Beautiful, baby. That's the way."

Whitney got loose and started to have a good time, and while Homes-Leighton changed rolls, Fraunces attacked with a brush or a cloth, or his naked finger, a swipe, a stroke, a dip or a dab.

Homes-Leighton dove in. "Okay, give me a sexy look."

Whitney took a stab at a fuck-me stare.

"Sassy-sexy, pouty."

Whitney plumped her lips.

Leo thought, if he says, Make love to the camera, I'm gonna hit him with a chair. He lost track of how many rolls Homes-Leighton had shot, but they'd been at it for over an hour.

"This is fun," Whitney giggled.

Homes-Leighton said, "You're a natural." A line of sweat stained the band of his backwards Kangol cap.

"I think we've got what we need," Leo said.

Fraunces said, "I should hope so." He was looking at a wristwatch with a transparent casing and a transparent strap.

Leo pulled a full vial of coke out of his pocket. "Lunch time," he said. "Who wants to do a bump?"

"Two hundred," Homes-Leighton was saying, "what's up with that?"

"What's up with that is, your memory sucks, buddy. I told you two and that's what you're getting." Leo stuck two new hundreds into Homes-Leighton's hand.

"What about Fraunces? I gotta hit him off." He made a fist around the bills. "That's gotta come out of here?"

"Stuart, Stuart," Leo said, spreading his fingers into a stop sign. Arguing over money with a guy whose family could buy the town. "Let me ask you a question. You have a good time today?"

"That's not the point," Homes-Leighton sniffed, rubbing his nose.

"Then let me ask you another question, blue-blood. When was the last time anybody hired you to do a photo job at any rate?"

Homes-Leighton tilted his double-chinned face into profile.

"What you get out of this, besides the two hundred, which, by the way, is the going rate for tests, and also by the way, you could wipe your ass with and I know that, is some quality prints for your book. How do you know Whitney isn't going to be the next Christy Turlington?"

"A little short for that."

"Okay then, Kate Moss." Leo knew this was a stretch, but fuck it. "What I'm saying is, here I am, doing you a solid, and you gotta force me to make you feel bad."

Homes-Leighton caved. "Alright. But you gotta throw for the lab fee."

"Not a problem," Leo said. "Just like we talked about."

Leo looked out at Fraunces, who was in the front seat of the Olds with his arms folded. Leo'd broken out all the blow he was going to do with them, and he needed them to get lost so he could get high the way he wanted to get high.

"So listen," Leo said, "if you got everything you need, there's a few things I wanna take care of around here…"

Homes-Leighton got the message. He put Leo through the mechanics of a handshake that started with a hug and ended with Homes-Leighton snapping his fingers.

Leo was almost rid of him when Homes-Leighton turned around and said, "Oh, shit. Did you hear? Remember that grotty white trash guy?"

Leo said, "Which one?"

"You remember," Homes-Leighton said. "He was short and he had an ante-bellum name. He was tight with your Cuban homeboy. Beauregard, Beaumond. That's it, Beaumond. Remember him?"

Leo felt like he had a golf ball blocking his windpipe, saying, "Yeah?", but it came out a squeak. He cleared his throat. "What about him?"

"I heard they pulled his body out of the Glades. Somebody popped a cap in his ass and dumped him out there."

"How'd they know it was him?" Leo's limbs went cold.

"Dunno," said Homes-Leighton, suddenly sounding very English, "dental records? Why're you wearing that look? If you ask me, it couldn't happen to a nicer guy." He said a few more things Leo wouldn't remember, Leo just staring as he backed the Olds out of the driveway.

Chapter Ten

The bus hissed into Port Authority and circled up a number of ramps before coming to a stop with a jerk. Harry wanted to check out the overhauled Times Square that had been making all the network newscasts, but today wasn't the day for it, so he walked east a block to Seventh and jumped into a cab.

One of the last of the Single Room Occupancies, the Downtowner was home to assorted lowlifes and deadbeats, drifters and hustlers in pocket for a week or two. The building was still warehousing its share of welfare barnacles until the government installed them in plusher digs, but one lifer, subsisting on a shrunken trust fund, was the grandson of a shipping tycoon, and on any given week, the register featured a handful of nine-to-fivers, hanging on till they found apartments they could afford. For extra flavor, the Downtowner was a favorite landing strip of Midwestern rockers grinding out Econoline tours.

The glow from the sidewalk warned him, but now, standing in the lobby, Harry was blinded by a bank of lights aimed at three girls on a sofa, primped to pose. They were young, but they were not tender, huffing low-tar cigarettes and bitching about the cold, their clodhopper platforms and knobby knees sticking out from under their mini-skirts.

The front desk was formerly boxed off behind scratched plexiglass that had a cash slot and a two-way speaker. But the partition was gone, and so was the old desk. In its place stood a sleek modern model, fake mahogany buffed to a high gloss. The dingy wallpaper behind it had been stripped off and painted over. Harry's shoes sunk into new carpeting. It looked like the Downtowner had swallowed a stiff shot of its own cut-rate publicity.

Harry was relieved to see Davey Boy, not too much of a boy any more, but still front and center. He was looking horribly pleased with himself. He had his hair done in a South Beach bob, that all-one-length hairdo Leo wore, grown out from the bristle cut that had been trendy the last time Harry saw him. His eyes were riveted straight ahead, and he was fussing with that idiotic haircut like he was waiting to be called for his close-up.

If he planned on fronting like he didn't know Harry, he was going to need some straightening out, but on the other hand, Davey hadn't seen him in a while, and people did tend to forget you when you weren't around all the time.

Harry said, "Hey, Davey Boy, what's up?"

No change in his expression, Davey said, "What's up, Harry?"

Davey was mesmerized by the glare reflecting off the models' shins. Stepping out from behind the desk, one eye peeled on the girls, he walked Harry a few paces back toward the door.

"Listen," he said, "things have changed around here."

"Yeah, you got rid of that ugly wallpaper."

"I mean no more of the old stuff," Davey said. "No non-paying guests flopping in your room, no hookers, no drugs."

"No phone, no pool, no pets. You just stock the lobby with third-rung models, or you still rent rooms?"

Davey cut a nervous glance toward the photographer's assistant, who was trying to get the lights right. "You know what I'm talking about," he said. He pushed a lock of hair behind an ear, repeating the motion to make sure it was secure. Harry'd seen Leo do the exact same thing. "All I'm saying is, we can't have what we used to have."

As far as Davey was concerned, Harry was a degenerate drug dealer, and Harry couldn't blame him for thinking that. Through most of his last stay at the Downtowner, Harry was moving blow.

"What do you mean, we? You were dead on a jones, Davey Boy, and if you weren't copping from me, you would've been getting it somewhere else. Is that my fault?"

"Do me a favor," Davey said. "Lower your voice. Management has taken great pains to change the image of this place, and we don't need your kind of trouble here. Really."

Harry was close to slapping Davey Boy, but he held

back. He was exhausted and he needed to sleep. Plus the Downtowner's location was ideal, directly across the park from Julia's co-op. So instead of saying any of the things he could've said to Davey Boy, in the end he just said, "I need a room with a toilet and a shower."

"I got one," Davey said, all proud. "Top floor."

"How much is it gonna run me?"

"Five hundred for the week."

Harry peeled five Franklins off his knot. "Is that all?" he said. "Haven't you got something a bit more expensive?"

Davey handed him the key to room 801 and another key that would get him through the front door they locked after midnight. Harry headed toward the elevator, past the lights and the light stands and the photographer's assistant and the photographer and the girls.

"Hey, Harry," Davey Boy said when the elevator dinged, "don't be sore."

It was the sort of damp, grey morning New York was worth about six months of, drizzling off and on since before the sun came up. Bright green budlets shivered on skinny branches, as if they knew better than to come all the way out on this day that was sharp with the lingering doubt of winter.

The rain made everything stink.

Harry was across the street from the park, walking north on Avenue A and toward a clatch of punks huddled under the awning of a Syrian grocery. They wore clothes too dirty to use for rags, and they slept in condemned buildings for the realness of the experience, though most of them had warm, clean beds in some warm, clean suburb to go back to when the novelty wore off.

A voice burbled. "Spare a quarter so I can buy this fine gentleman a beer?" Trying to sound cute.

Harry locked eyes with a dusty bag of blood and bones who talked and presumably walked, though at the moment his ass was firmly planted on the concrete. For a guy who didn't have the price of a drink, he was way over budget on jewelry. Silver studs punctured both nostrils and both lips. A chain of hoops lacerated each ear. His partner, the fine gentleman, was out cold on his back, feet flat, knees up. A spiderweb tattoo in indigo spread up from his neck and over his jaw.

Eyes shut against its circumstances, a mangy pit bull lay on the sidewalk and sighed, though Harry could see the dog wasn't asleep. And they had a second mascot, a pale girl with creamy, teenaged skin. She'd had a bath during the last twenty-four hours, had slept indoors the night before, and was way too cute to be within a half-mile of these bums. She put the cadge on Harry, too, and he was about to let himself get touched, until he noticed her eyes were zipped a vacant, heroin blue.

"Sorry," he said. "I can't help you out."

"Sorry?" the perforated dirtball said. "You're not sorry."

Harry had pulled even with where the kid was sitting, and thought for a second of kicking him in the teeth, just to see what all that metal would do to his face. See if he'd rather have that for an answer. But he didn't do anything, and he didn't say anything, and as a matter of fact, the kid had it right. He wasn't sorry.

The apartment was up four flights of stairs, a two-bedroom Harry's mom and pop nailed down in 1955. Including the last rent increase, it cost $197.63 a month. The current landlord got skunked with Harry's old man and a few other tenants for life, but he maintained the property, anxious to keep the building attractive, and the turn-over on his one year-leases high.

Harry and his father hadn't seen each other in over a year, but the most affection the old man could muster was a pat on the shoulder. He moved away from the door to let Harry inside.

"Son," he said.

He looked good. He was wearing a pressed blue shirt and navy blue slacks that rode high on his waist and shimmered with a thousand dry cleanings. Harry wrapped his arms around him and pulled him close, the old man's bones going stiff as Harry planted a kiss on his cheek. He broke the clinch, taking both of Harry's biceps in his hands, and gently shoved him away. Giving him that same shoulder pat, he sat him at the table.

It was covered with a yellow oilcloth bright with blue gardenias, giving the room a hopeful, morning feel. A stack of placemats covered with the same pattern sat in the center of the table, under a plastic vase stuffed with plastic daisies, their plastic hearts a shade or two off the yellow of the cloth.

There wasn't a single dish in the sink, not even a glass on the drain board. Harry said, "What'd you do, Pop, hire a maid?"

"I was just gonna brew up some java. Could you go for a cup of bean?"

"If you're gonna make it, then I'll drink it. But don't go out of your way." Harry was looking for an ashtray. He got up and opened the cupboard where they used to keep them, but there weren't any there.

"If you're gonna smoke," his father said, "open that window and blow the smoke outside." He leaned against the sink and stared at the gurgling Mister Coffee, scratching his wrist in a way that didn't look like he had an itch.

"Forget it," Harry said. "I can't stay anyway."

"I put it down, you know. Fifty-something years of the goddamn things, I finally gave 'em up."

Harry said, "That's real good, Pop. They don't do a thing for you."

"But you don't realize how it's ruining you till you quit. When you see how good you feel, you think, what the hell was I doing to myself all those years?"

He must've broken down and bought new glasses, retro-style, wire frame-numbers. If the old man had worn glasses in the '50s, this would've been the pair. The lenses had a slight emerald tint. He brushed his hair straight back with a gel that knocked out the curl. There was plenty of white speckled into it, but it still hadn't gone all the way grey, and neither had his fussily clipped mustache. Harry took this as a positive sign for his own prospects.

The old man took a carton of milk out of the refrigerator, and the sugar bowl from a different shelf than it used to sit on when Harry lived here. The coffee was almost done brewing.

"So," Harry said after a minute of awkward quiet, "you still gigging or what?"

"I sit in with this meringue band, but their dates are always way out in Brooklyn. I don't know where I'm going when I get there, and then I gotta hang around till four in the morning to get paid. They work every weekend, but I don't go with 'em every time. Depends on how I'm feeling. And I jam with these neighborhood kids." He laughed. "Swing cats."

"Swing?" Harry said. "Who plays swing?"

"Kids, I'm saying, younger than you. Standards and

jump blues, like that Louie Jordan stuff. Very popular with a younger crowd. But it's strictly for love, that gig. I go home some nights, twenty, thirty bucks."

"You're too pro to play for that kind of money. Don't they know who you are, Pop?"

"You got that right. You know I gigged with Louie, dontcha?"

"Paramount Theatre, 1950."

"Did I tell you the story?"

"Once or twice," Harry said.

His father shrugged, disappointed, either because he couldn't steamroll Harry with the details for the hundredth time, or because his memory was slipping and he honestly didn't remember having told him.

He poured coffee into a pair of mugs. Then, from a cabinet under the sink, behind the cleanser and the Windex and the laundry soap, he pulled out a bottle of off-brand whiskey with the Irish flag on its label.

"Gotta be five o'clock somewhere in the world, right?" He spilled some booze into his mug, and was about to do the same to Harry's when Harry stopped him.

On second thought, he said, "I'll take half a shot, Pop. In a glass, neat."

His father said, "No water?"

"No water."

"Because you know what W.C. Fields said about water."

"Fish fuck in it," Harry said, but the stale punch line made him wince.

An extra serious voice on the radio made Harry aware it was on, describing a piece of music they were about to hear, and then tiny, muted horns came across, trumpets for sure, and other brass, softly.

"Since when do you like classical, Pop?"

He downed some whiskey-laced coffee. "Since forever. He's very subtle, Mozart, but he was tearing it up in his own way. Dig the way those strings come in behind the horns. Gradually. You gotta take the time to appreciate him, but it's worth it." The old man closed his eyes, his hands around his mug.

Harry drank the whiskey. They weren't talking about anything, the way they never talked about anything, but this newfound appreciation of Wolfgang Amadeus, which was not bad at all, was making Harry suspicious. His father had never owned a single recording of any kind of classical music, did not attend concerts or operas, and had never said a single word about it before today.

Something was up. But figuring out what it was wasn't why he was here. Truth was, he didn't really care. He could've gone another year without seeing the old man, no problem. What he wanted was to know how close the law was to him, and he wanted to find out without having to come right out and ask. If they were on his trail, and there was no reason to believe they wouldn't be by now, with Leo or Aggie or Bryce Peyton giving him up, this'd be one of their first stops.

"How's Arthur doing?" Harry asked.

"Good," the old man said. "Arthur's doing good. You don't need to worry about Arthur."

"I'm not worried about him, Pop. I just asked how he was."

"Well, if you're so concerned, why don't you give him a call?"

It seemed like every conversation with the old man ended in some kind of confrontation. Harry wanted to get out of there before that happened. He decided that if the cops had paid a visit, the old man would've said something about it by now.

"Anyway, listen," his father said, "I know this sounds terrible, but I'm gonna have to ask you to leave. Rosa's due home any second and I don't want you to get her upset."

Harry wasn't sure what the old man had told Rosa about him that would make his presence so upsetting, whoever Rosa was, but she explained a lot of things. The home economics kitchen, the secret bottle of hooch, the bright, summery tablecloth. He felt stupid for not figuring it out sooner.

Harry wanted to use the bathroom before he split, and in order to get there, he had to pass through the back bedroom, the room he'd shared with Ernie growing up. The flowery lingerings of an old-ladyish perfume thickened the air. An oversized bed hogged up most of the space, and the dresser and nightstand were dotted with cheaply framed poses of Rosa's grandchildren, an infant with a drooly, open-yawped grin, a pair of girls with ribbons in their hair. They could've been twins, sporting newly sprouted permanent teeth three gauges too large for their bright, thin faces.

Harry didn't know what the sleeping arrangements were, but he noticed the old man kept the front bedroom, where he used to sleep with Harry's mother, intact. He had a portrait gallery of his own, but every single one of the pictures was of him. The old man with Charlie Parker, signed by Bird and wishing him all the best. The old man with Mayor John Lindsey, with Max Gordon at what must've been the Vanguard. The old man fronting his Joe Healy Six, eyes squeezed tight in black and white, ripping off a righteous solo.

Solo. That was the old man. Kids or no kids, Mom or no Mom, Rosa or whoever, the old man was a solo act.

It didn't bother Harry. Why should it bother him?

Heading down the stairs and lighting a cigarette Rosa would never get a whiff of, he said out loud, "Who gives a fuck?", but he did. He did.

You were going to find Jimmy De Steffano in one of three places: pulling a job, on Rikers Island, or swilling two-for-one suds in this saloon long overrun by NYU students. If Harry hadn't been so distracted, he would have made it a point to avoid this route, but as it happened, here he was on the sidewalk with Jimmy, behind door number three.

"Just the man I wanted to see," De Steffano said. "I heard you were back in town."

It hadn't been two days. Harry said, "From who?"

"Bad news travels fast." De Steffano had reverted to his paroled physique. No jailhouse muscles puffed him up. "C'mon, I'll buy you a beer."

"I wouldn't get arrested in this shit hole. Why do you drink here?"

De Steffano cocked an eyebrow at a mouse-haired chunkette, the ordinary, easily flattered type. The kind they bred in the heartland, who was pudgy and astigmatic and got a genuine thrill out of hanging around a New York hood, smallish even by small-time standards, but a real live criminal all the same.

"We gotta stand here all night?" He was wearing a wife-beater under a leather car coat, rushing the season, catching a chill. "Let's go inside."

"I can't. I got something to do."

"You're hurting my feelings. You don't see me for a year, now you won't give me the time of day."

His black hair gleamed in the street light, the back and sides clipped as close as the shadow of goatee that darkened his chin. A crucifix and a crooked horn hung from a chain around his neck. Jimmy D, hitting all the strides.

Harry told him he had to be somewhere, which was about half true, and De Steffano, determined to talk, abandoned the NYU girls for some later hour.

They veered right at the metal cube that marked Astor Place. The skateboard army was out on maneuvers. Peacocking goofy, Easter egg-colored hair, their jeans were so baggy that two of their skinny asses would've fit into a single pair. Unlike the concrete jockeys blighting Avenue A, these kids didn't bum change, and some of them were real athletes, executing swirls and jumps on boards that never left the bottoms of their sneakers.

Three skaters circled a garbage can they had dragged into the street. One made a pass at it, measuring the distance it would take to vault it, swinging wide, powering himself up the block. He idled thirty yards from the target, sucked in one deep breath of concentration. Right leg churning, he started his run, blue-green hair blown back, his billowing sweatshirt flattened against his chest.

De Steffano said, "Ten bucks the kid don't make it."

"The kid makes it easy," Harry said.

"A sawbuck says no."

"You're on."

Harry was afraid his boy had jumped too soon. It looked at first like he'd crash mid-bucket, but as he neared the peak of his arc, he was soaring, arms stretched out for balance, the board at his feet throwing gravity a big fuck you. Landing soft on the asphalt, he had three feet to spare.

"Everybody's gotta be good at something," De Steffano said. He forked over the tenner. "What I was doing at his age, I was trying to get laid."

"So's he," Harry said, thinking not much had changed in Jimmy's life, except he was committing more serious felonies. And how much had changed in Harry's life? He was still picking up ten dollar bets from Jimmy De Steffano.

"How was Florida?" De Steffano said. "You didn't say nothing about Florida."

"Florida was a fucking disaster. The weather's nice, though."

"Not in the summer it ain't. In the summer there, you die. And then you get your hurricanes."

"Alright," Harry said. "So much for Florida."

"I got something going," De Steffano said, getting to the meat of their walk-and-talk, "that I think is right up your alley."

Harry said, "I don't wanna hear it."

"Thing is, it needs perfect timing. Two brothers, Hasids, working the diamond racket. They make the same deposit out of the same satchel at the same bank every Thursday at ten o'clock. We need four guys, one van, and one car. We grab the brothers and throw 'em in the van. We ride 'em around and dump 'em in Brooklyn, where our fourth guy is waiting with the car. We switch vehicles and we're gone."

"This sounds real familiar." Harry was thinking back. "Didn't somebody try this a few years ago? Bunch of guys got dead, and it was a set-up besides. Like the Feds were in on it? Remember?"

De Steffano didn't remember.

"Yeah, a Fed got it, a crook got it, and one of the Yids got it. They were brothers, too. Where'd you get this brainstorm? Out of a stack of old newspapers?"

"Cookie Levitas has been hot to pull it for months."

"Cookie Levitas. Another loser primed to take another fall. Pass."

Assuming they made it out alive, this asinine adventure was a straight ticket to Attica. Jimmy was airtight on a job, but he was no planner. And Harry was nowhere near up for this James Bond shit.

"Which alley of mine were you thinking about, Jim? Kidnapping? This is my life, it isn't a movie. If I decide to pull anything right now, anything at all, I gotta make sure it's fast, it's clean, and I get away. Tell me something. What've you got pending?"

"They got nothing on me," De Steffano said.

"Then they're waiting for you to make a move. And you're a fucking idiot. Go off half-cocked on this crazy caper. With your sheet? You'll get life. You've gotta start trying to think realistically. Like consider getting a job."

De Steffano's eyes went blank.

"I'm serious. It'd be a lot less work than coming up with these schemes. Something soft comes up, like that warehouse thing, you move on it. You keep a finger in, but you're basically legit. That's my advice to you."

"I'm asking you to grab a skinny, bearded freak and conk him on the head. That's the extent of your involvement, for twenty-five percent of the take. Advice," De Steffano hissed, "who the fuck are you to give anybody advice?"

They stopped walking. A bum shambled up, shaking a coffee cup, but De Steffano's black glare sent him packing. He looked left and right, as if he were searching for a witness to Harry's assault on his honor.

"Fine. I don't fucking need you. Go file your W-2 forms."

They were near the corner of Spring and Lafayette, by the entrance to the 6 train. A group of women with swollen ankles chattered in Spanish. A guy holding his briefcase between his knees was trying to get a cigarette going in the wind.

"I'm heading this way," Harry said, meaning this was

where Jimmy got off. "Good luck with everything."

"Luck," De Steffano said, "you need luck. I got skills." He backpedaled north up Lafayette, and had just turned to retrace his steps when Harry made a right on Spring.

De Steffano was dead wrong. Whatever way you wanted to think about it, luck was something nobody could do without. Wasn't that why he wore the crooked horn? To ward off the evil eye and bring good fortune? No, you needed luck, no question about it. And you needed the desire to not let things keep happening to you, to not just get done in by life.

At a lot of queasy junctions in Harry's past, De Steffano's ravings would've made perfect sense. Minus any real idea of what he was doing, he'd let himself get sucked into the whirlpool of bad planning and bad luck and wind up in the same place De Steffano was heading, the joint. The difference between then and now was this: Harry was all done letting things happen to him.

Chapter Eleven

The sun hung on the western horizon, a blood-orange ball in Martinson's rear view mirror. He was grateful the sinus attack or migraine that might've been coming on in Ft. Lauderdale had reversed itself, and he was almost feeling good as he drove east over the Causeway and back to the Beach. There wasn't enough time to stop for flowers and make the last part of visiting hours, but it'd be okay to skip them this once, go sit with Josephine for fifteen minutes before heading back to the station house.

Riding the elevator up, he intruded on some family

crisis, a mother, a daughter, and two brothers, all in tears. They had the same blue eyes and the same brown hair, except the youngest, a boy, who was blond. They stopped talking when Martinson got on behind them. He looked at his shoes until he got to his floor.

Right away, he knew something was wrong. He felt that cold tingle in his fingertips, walking down the hall. The machines Josephine Simmons was hooked up to had been wheeled out of the room. Last week's flowers were holding up pretty good, and her get-well wishes were still lined up on the nightstand, but her bed was empty and the linens had been stripped off of it. Arnie was hoping they'd transferred Josephine out of Intensive Care and into another unit, but he knew that wasn't what had happened.

He went looking for the young doctor with the curly hair. At the nurse's station, a heavyset woman in hospital whites was talking on the phone. Martinson rested both of his thick hands on the upper level of the desk, wanting her to hurry it up. The caller was phoning about a patient, but didn't know the patient's last name. This nurse was saying they weren't going anywhere without that.

A doctor about Martinson's age, with square shoulders and a golf-course tan, walked up to the desk. He had the same lean, in-shape look Kramer sported. Martinson was surprised to see a pack of Salems bulging out of his smock pocket.

Martinson said, "I was wondering if you could help me."

The doctor didn't say anything, cocking his head to one side, waiting.

"I noticed that Josephine Simmons wasn't in her room."

The doctor's name was Gustavo. It said so on his nametag. He took a breath and blew out a tired sigh. His head came perpendicular again and he said, "Are you a family member?"

He asked the question out of reflex. There were no black Martinsons, at least not that Arnie was aware of.

"She doesn't have any family members. I'm Detective Martinson, Miami Beach Police."

It was freezing cold in this unit. And it wasn't him. It definitely wasn't him. That tingling in his fingers had quit. With the sun down and the humidity almost nonexistent, there was no reason for the air-conditioning to be set so high. It couldn't be good for these sick people.

"Miss Simmons passed about an hour ago," Dr. Gustavo said. "She was just too frail to recover from that kind of beating. It was a miracle she held on as long as she did. I'm sorry."

Although Arnie knew this was what the doctor was going to tell him, he said, "I'm sorry, too." He didn't know what else to say.

Doctor Gustavo shook his head. "Outside of her age, she was perfectly healthy. There was no reason she couldn't have gone on another ten years. Who knows? Maybe more." He shook his head again. "It's a hell of a thing, to get that far in life, and then have it end like this."

Martinson had been thinking the same thing the last time he was here, but he was all done thinking about that. He was concentrating on Anton Cantor, wondering how old Anton would feel now, with a murder beef hanging over his head. As soon as Martinson had the time, he was going to re-check Anton's alibi. Maybe there was something he missed the first time around.

But if it wasn't Cantor, it was somebody else, and that

somebody else was going to have to pay. No matter how fucked up it seemed most of the time, this world would not tolerate the murder of a spindly old lady walking home with four dollars worth of groceries. It couldn't. Justice existed, as an independent, true objective. It made no difference how twisted the path toward it was, or how long it took, there was such a thing as justice. It was real, Martinson thought, heading back to the parking garage. Justice was real, and this wasn't it.

Acevedo was talking long distance with New York City Detective Don Kellogg. Kellogg spoke like they were living in some previous era of telecommunication, shouting into the receiver as if they had a staticky connection, which they did not.

After the FBI faxed her Harry Healy's criminal records, she'd sent them along to Detective Don Kellogg, who'd been Police Officer Don Kellogg when he busted Healy for assault in August, 1994, his last fuck-up before the one that landed him in the Dade County Stockade.

He said, "I see our boy is moving up. This memo says you want him in a murder investigation."

"We found one of his fingerprints at the scene," Lili said.

Kellogg whistled, and Lili heard him shuffling papers on his end. "Healy's a hard-ball. A hothead. Like it says, he was working as a bouncer in this joint when he gave the complainant, William T. Dryden, a beating that put him in the hospital. What Dryden did I don't remember, but Healy's mouthpiece managed to get the charges dropped, as you can see."

Kellogg's New York accent was so thick, Lili would've thought it sounded phony if some actor tried it out in a movie. He took a sip of something that sounded like it was hot.

"As it happens," he said, "and you're going to think this is weird, but that's the way the world works, I'm following a tip right now on a hood named Jimmy De Steffano. The reason you'd care is that De Steffano and Healy are the oldest of running partners. Check out Healy's first arrest."

May 23, 1978. Grand theft, auto. James Albert De Steffano was driving the car. Healy was seventeen. He drew a year's probation.

"My snitch says Jimmy's planning a diamond heist, and my feeling is, he's stupid enough to try it. I'm gonna put some heat on Jimmy D, do a little preventive policing. If Healy's in the city, he won't be too far from De Steffano, I guarantee you that. Want me to call if he turns up?"

"I'm in after eight," Lili said.

If she'd had anything better to do, Lili would've gone home and changed, but when she dialed into her answering machine to check the messages, the only person who'd called was her mother, twice.

Martinson walked in around 7:45 with his tie untied. The waistband of his pants was losing its grip on his rumpled shirt. "How'd it go?" he said.

Lili showed him Healy's record. Martinson glanced at it and unfastened the most recent mug shots.

"The French girl did a pretty fair job describing him, don't you think?" He held the composite next to the photographs. "He does sort of look like Robotaille."

Lili said, "Robotaille's better looking," and immediately wanted to take it back. "There is a slight resemblance though, yes."

He was balancing his one-armed reading glasses on

the end of his nose. "Never got him with a gun," he said. It looked like he needed to have his prescription changed, the way he was holding the folder out and away from his face. "This assault charge looks like it came from a bar fight. Murder's kind of a big jump."

"Meaning what?" Acevedo said.

"Meaning I'm not sure I'm crazy about him for the shooter."

Lili wasn't sure she was crazy about this shift in Martinson's thinking. "How'd you make out in Lauderdale?" she said.

He scratched the shadow of whiskers under his chin. "I did a lot of sitting in traffic." Stretching his neck forward, he rolled his head from left to right. "Healy was working in the club, like that deputy said, and I talked to the owner of the place. He gave me a woman Healy was seeing while he was there. She said he took off last week, she didn't know where."

"You believe her?"

"I don't believe she doesn't know where he went, no. My money's on New York. But I didn't need her to tell me that."

"Kramer said he thought you had a contact in New York."

"I grabbed a perp for New York a few years ago. But what am I gonna ask that cop to do, scour all five boroughs for one of our suspects? Anyway, I hate to use up a favor before it's absolutely necessary."

"What about the FBI?"

"Slow down a minute, Lil."

She couldn't understand why Arnie was dragging his feet. Why didn't they just go and collar-up on this Healy?

"I contacted the arresting officer on Healy's last go-round before he came here," she said. "Turns out he's working a tip on an old associate of Healy's, a guy by the name of"—she checked her notebook—"Jimmy De Steffano. Healy takes his first fall at age seventeen in a stolen car? Who's at the wheel?"

"Jimmy De Steffano?"

"You got it. And this cop says if Healy's in New York, it won't be long before he tries to contact De Steffano."

"That's a hell of a coincidence," Martinson said. He set the file on his desk, folded the one arm of his glasses, and stuck them into the pocket of his short-sleeved shirt.

He was not in good shape. Lili knew that he did almost no exercise, and that his diet was straight off the Mesozoic menu. But still, he looked strong. Close to fifty or whatever he was, exhausted, distracted, Arnie Martinson didn't look like anybody some punk would want to screw with.

Lili took a call from the desk sergeant. "This is Schimmel," Schimmel said. "I got a woman here who wants to speak to somebody upstairs."

"About what?" She listed for a few moments to what the desk cop was saying, and hung up the phone.

"Somebody else wants to weigh in on Pfiser," Lili said. "There's a girl downstairs with a dog in her purse."

The dog was a long-haired teacup Chihuahua. Arnie knew this because he asked, trying to establish some rapport with this girl. It was called Mimi.

The name the girl gave them was Victoria Leonard, and she had a kind of ruined beauty. An orange halter that tied at the neck and across the back exposed the dead-end of a peeling sunburn, and a bad tit job some strip-mall plastic man had tossed off. Though Arnie wasn't convinced there was such a thing as a good tit job.

Mimi's snout peeped over the thatched bag she was

riding in, and she had a head cold. She was coughing, little yips in the back of her throat, and at one point launched into a seven- or eight-sneeze jag that left her muzzle wet with doggie snot. Victoria found a tissue in the bag and wiped Mimi's nose.

Martinson could feel himself giving up on this day, after the terrible news about Josephine Simmons, and realized he hadn't said anything to Lili about her death. Maybe after they were through with Victoria Leonard, he'd bring Lili up to speed. Or it could wait till tomorrow. Arnie was the only one who knew about his visits to the hospital, and he wanted to keep it that way.

He bought a bag of chips and a Kit Kat bar from the vending machine. The three of them, not counting the dog, went to sit in an interview room.

"Just let her say what she came here to say," Martinson told Lili before they walked in. "Go soft. We can question her later."

Victoria spent a lot of time blowing on coffee that wasn't hot to begin with, a Styrofoam cup she loaded with sugar and powdered creamer. She was born in Idaho and moved to L.A. when she was eighteen. She wanted to be an actress.

She said, "What a surprise, right?"

Mentioning this was five years ago, if she was telling the truth, it meant she was only twenty-three, a shock considering how rugged she looked. Arnie would've guessed ten years older. Ten hard years.

Acevedo had her notebook out, but she wasn't writing. She was regarding Victoria Leonard with her eyes narrowed, like she was coiled to pounce on her the second she got the chance.

Arnie swallowed some of the coffee in his cup. Maybe the reason it tasted so bad was because they needed a new machine. He was going to ask Kramer about getting them one. They had to be able to do better than this.

Victoria smiled a smile that showed her jarring white teeth. Twenty-three years old, Martinson thought, capped teeth and breast implants. The kid was a mess.

There was a television producer, a very successful television producer, Victoria said, that loved her. He put her in many episodes of a show that ran for three years in syndication. Maybe they had seen it. It was a cop show called *Do or Die*.

Martinson didn't know that one. Acevedo went, "Mmmmmm."

After those three years, the show had run its course. The producer couldn't sell it to anybody, and it ended. Victoria drifted into projects she was far too talented for, things she never imagined she'd have to do, especially not when she was shooting *Do or Die* and watching herself on TV, twice a day sometimes.

Arnie assumed she meant porno, and maybe Acevedo did, too, but Victoria said, "Not what you think."

They were a series of cut-and-run features that cost nothing to make, relatively speaking, movies that went straight to video or cable. She played the girl in the bikini, the hapless co-ed in five beach-blanket slasher movies. She'd have half a dozen lines before she got killed, and she got killed in every picture. They shot the principal photography in a week, and a project could go from script to screen in a month.

In the meantime, she was getting older.

Acevedo pushed herself away from the table. Victoria picked up on her body language.

"I know I'm not old," she said. "And I was even younger then. I mean my face was getting old, because everybody had seen it. And you wouldn't believe how fierce it is, the competition. These producers, they can find a hundred girls right behind me to do exactly what I did, all cute, and all younger than me."

Suddenly, nobody would hire her. She didn't work for almost a year. They both knew how fast money went when you didn't have any coming in. And it wasn't like she'd been thrifty while she was making it.

Victoria had gotten close with an actor from one of her movies, a guy named Lawrence Lendesma, who lived here. Actually, Lawrence was a model, but he was trying to make it in acting. It was what they all did. Lawrence was why she decided to come to South Beach.

Victoria and Mimi landed in Miami on December 27th. But once Lawrence had to deal with her face-to-face instead of coast-to-coast, things between them changed. Acevedo rolled her eyes.

"It was Lawrence who introduced me to Leo. We met at a New Year's Eve party Leo was throwing at his house."

"Who's Leo?" Acevedo said, and Martinson shot her a glance that was supposed to remind her to save the questions for later.

But when Victoria looked at him, he said, "Go ahead."

Victoria hit it off with Leo, and he invited her to stay at the house. He had this big house he was living in all by himself.

It was a good thing, too, because she was very low on money, and a girl who was low on money could get herself into a lot of trouble down here on the Beach. Or anywhere, for that matter.

Leo was nice to her, the way they're all nice at first, she said, but life around that house got extremely freaky after Leo moved in two of his friends. One of the boys, Alex, she never did get his last name, he was nice. Alex was cute. Victoria liked Alex. But she did not like JP

Beaumond. That was the other one. There was something wrong with JP Beaumond, besides the fact that he was short, dirty and mean, and he was always trying to rub his scratchy whiskers against her face. They were together a few times, but he was gross, and one night after she told him no, JP came into her room and raped her.

Victoria Leonard said, "I think I'm pregnant." She started to cry.

She dug through her dog bag, trying to come up with a clean tissue. Martinson handed her a box and topped off her cup with some more lousy coffee. Mimi, who had recovered from her sneezing attack, licked Victoria's wrist. They waited. The dog seemed to be waiting, too, for Victoria to regain her composure. It didn't take long.

"Leo was always talking about his Dutch Uncle."

Okay, enter the Dutchman.

He had arrived in South Beach right around the time Victoria did, though Leo knew him from before. Some kind of European wheeler-dealer. Throw a rock on Ocean Drive and you were liable to hit a few of them.

"Why did he call him that?" Arnie said.

"Because he was older and he had lots of money and because he was... Dutch?"

Arnie said, "Yeah, but... never mind. Keep going. I'm sorry."

Anyway, he was looking to make a big cocaine score. According to Leo, Leo put the deal together, but Leo was always talking like he was such a big shot.

It was a night like any other night at Leo's house. The four of them awake into the morning, snorting cocaine and drinking. Leo brought it up as a joke. Manfred, Leo said, would be the perfect sucker to rip off. He laughed. The boys laughed. Victoria laughed because everybody else was laughing, but she wouldn't have known Manfred from a bag of apples.

But JP brought it up again. JP had taken the idea seriously. Like very seriously.

Victoria broke small bits off the Kit Kat bar and fed them to Mimi. The dog's ears pricked straight up for Victoria's babbling baby talk, and she smacked her tiny chops for those crumbs of chocolate.

It was easy for her to get next to Manfred. She approached him one afternoon on the beach and poured out this sob story, how she was a little lost lamb with a little fuzzy dog, thousands of miles away from anybody who cared about her. She might've cried. She was, after all, an actress.

Manfred said Victoria reminded him of his daughter. He had a daughter about her age.

"He was a wreck. He drank too much and he snorted too much, but he had a good heart. He was just a sweet guy, and he was easy to get over on. The whole time, he thought my name was Jennifer, because that's what I told him."

He had a very definite agenda of his own for Victoria/Jennifer. This was what people did to you in this life, she said. They used you.

"They will if you let them," Acevedo said.

It was funny. The boys used her to get at Manfred, and Manfred used her to get at other boys. And he sure knew how to pick them. One of these college kids turned out to be such a complete homo that once she lured him back to the room, he spent the rest of his vacation in Manfred's bed.

Acevedo said, "I don't understand. He needed you to help him pick up guys? On South Beach?"

"Manfred said anybody could have the queers here. The ones he went after were supposedly straight. They were straight, all right. Straight to the next man."

Anyway, Manfred was delighted with the way things were working out. He let her stay in his room. He gave her money and he gave her drugs. He bought clothes for her. Leo's plan was working like a charm.

According to Leo's information, the big cocaine deal was supposed to be made in Manfred's hotel room. As soon as it happened, she was to alert Leo. She was kind of bleary on the details, but one day she saw Manfred shaving pieces off a brick of cocaine wrapped in butcher paper. He had it stashed in a suitcase at the top of the closet. She made the call.

She lied and told Manfred she'd decided to go back to L.A. She packed up her things and went back to the house on Pine Tree. But then she heard that Manfred was dead. She'd been hiding in Key Biscayne ever since.

"I'm not particularly bright, okay? I know that. But I'm sure Manfred's death had something to do with that cocaine deal, and I think I know who killed him."

Chapter Twelve

After a few extra lies and a few extra bucks and calling in a favor he wouldn't return, Leo airmailed Whitney off to Lawrence in Daytona. Whitney had been fun while she lasted, but she cost too much money, and Leo was sick of her. Somewhere along the line, Whitney had gotten hold of the silly notion that she was in love with Leo, which Leo couldn't blame her for, but worse, she had decided that Leo was in love with her. He might've let it slip a time or two in the heat of the moment, but it most definitely was not true. He vowed to be very, very cautious, from now on, what he said to these girls.

Now that Whitney was out of the picture, though, that left a crucial slot that needed to be filled. Leo, who was not a young man who sat on his hands where women were concerned, made a date with his dream girl of the season. She was a tall stack of everything good about Italy, and her name was Valentina.

Valentina seemed to belong to another century. Not the Renaissance, which was what people always said because they didn't know what they were talking about, but she had a style, a classic old-world beauty that put miles of ground between her and every other person on the Beach. No tattoos, not a single one, anywhere. No metal stuck out of her nose or eyebrows. Her black hair wasn't dyed. Her heart-shaped face had the saddest cast, as if she had witnessed sorrows beyond description, which Leo was pretty sure she hadn't, but whatever it was, it was killing him. Leo was far from the only smooth-skinned lifestyler attempting to coax the panties off Miss Valentina, so he had his work cut out for him, but that was all right. Nothing like a bit of unfriendly competition to get the blood flowing.

He did a bump out of the jar he had stashed in the freezer, his third of the evening or maybe his fourth, but who was counting? Leo measured a two-finger shot of tequila, cut a wedge of lemon, and shook out some salt on his wrist. A lick, a swallow, a suck of citrus, he was just about ready to go. A reminder: buy a fifth of Cuervo. Make that two fifths.

It'd be absolutely wrong to have tequila on his breath behind the wheel of the Jag. These cowboy cops pulled you over for everything as it was, but they were particularly hard-assed about young guys in expensive cars. Exhaling Jose Cuervo Gold into the face of some gung-ho redneck, very bad mechanics.

While he was scrubbing his teeth, Leo decided his shirt wasn't working at all, and neither was his pasty, nightclub pallor. Too many late nights taking divots out of his afternoons at the beach. Which is why the white shirt failed him. He looked like an undertaker's apprentice. The Kid needed some sun.

But now that he'd changed into a mint-green mock-turtle that played nicely off his eyes, how could he stick with these black cap-toe lace-ups? Black shoes were like anti-Miami, and what he was shooting for with Valentina was a splash of traditional Beach glamour.

White loafers. White loafers were the key. White loafers and a white cotton windbreaker. Except when he gave himself a final exam, he noticed a chocolate stain near the zipper. Back upstairs one last time for the linen sports coat that originally belonged to his grandfather, a guy who knew a thing or two about looking sharp.

There was authentic H_2O running through the plumbing of this fountain, trickling streams that would've made a soothing sound if this warhorse of a mariachi band weren't camped out in front of it. They must've completed their Ocean Drive circuit then migrated up here to Lincoln Road to haul out the exasperated strains of "Guantanamera" for one final flogging before calling it a gig.

The guitarist's bowling-ball gut had propelled a button off his shirt, and a bunch of the dingleberries that should've been should've been hanging from the brim of his sombrero were missing in action. It seemed to Leo that some of the profits needed to be re-invested in that costume.

He practically tripped over Valentina's table. Four people were seated behind four place settings, and Leo found himself shambling up like somebody's poor cousin. A minion from Valentina's agency sat to her right. Announcing a photo opportunity, he blinded Leo with a flash from his disposable camera. A frumpy, frizz-haired girl sat across from him, but Leo forgot her name the instant it left Valentina's lips.

Valentina's brother was there, too. His name was Paulo, he was preposterously handsome, and to Leo's horror, he was wearing the exact same linen sports coat as Leo, except his was offset by a deep tan. Al Pacino-looking motherfucker in a white dinner jacket, making Leo disappear.

Paulo was in complete control. He got the waiter's attention with a smile, and the waiter had a chair under Leo in two shakes, sticking him on the end between Paulo and Valentina. He half-filled a wine glass with Montepulciano and poised to recite the specials.

"I'm actually not hungry," Leo said. "I just stopped by to say hello."

"The food is fabulous," said the agency minion, whose name was Gregory, a butterball queen with a too-round face and a Fred Flintstone nose.

Paulo said, "It *is* good," in an accent it was hard to detect.

The menu the waiter handed Leo was in Italian, and it didn't give up any clues to what the dishes might be in English. He didn't want to eat, but thought it'd be polite to have a plate in front of him. He took a sip of wine, but he didn't want that, either.

When the waiter came back, Leo asked for a mozzarella, tomato and basil salad, the tomatoes would go down easy, and a Cuervo Gold margarita, straight up with salt. That'd go down easier. Except he needed to prime it with a shot. He nodded to Valentina, then to Paulo, and went inside to the bar.

All the action was outside. The dining room was deserted and the bartender was manning an empty bar, a short guy in a maroon vest. Leo barked back a tequila and headed toward the bathroom.

He took the opportunity to check his hair. Nothing wrong there. He slid into a stall and sat on the bowl. Twisting his Bullet-gram into the open position, he huffed a bump up his left nostril, and a bump up his right. He washed his hands and tilted back his head, letting some florescence up his nose. All clear. All clear and feeling good about life.

His margarita was on the table waiting for him. Leo sat down and crossed his legs. They felt safe in that position. He was glad to see everybody smoking. Lighting up a cig of his own, he tried to pick up the conversation.

The frumpy chick was a childhood friend of Paulo and Valentina. This was her first trip to the U.S. and she was flying to New York to accompany Valentina on some big modeling job. All this came through Paulo. The frump spoke no English.

Paulo disliked the New York assignment. "Valentina should be concentrating on her studies," he said. "What does this prove? That she's a beautiful girl? Anybody can see that. This fashion business, if you ask me, is shit. No offense, guys."

He was a bit of a spoilsport, this brother.

"She's going to be major," Gregory said. "Major." Looked like old Greg was getting himself a nice buzz on, that goblet sloshing wine at the end of his pudgy fingers.

He snuffed one extra-light cigarette and lit another.

Leo was trying to think of something to say. He licked salt off the rim of his glass and took a swallow, then drew a breath as if to speak, but nothing came out. Oh, well. Fuck it.

Frumpy's name was Chi-Chi. That was it, Chi-Chi. Paulo was pleading some case in Italian, but Chi-Chi refused to get involved, swabbing a hunk of onion foccaccia around a saucer covered with an olive oil film, her cigarette still burning in her left hand.

One waiter came to clear plates and another followed, shouldering a tray he set on a stand that a third guy opened on the flagstones.

"It's the life of a gypsy," Paulo said, "a vagabond. And it's dishonest. Those magazines that make her look like a tramp, they give people the idea it's a glamorous, sexy world they'll be excluded from if they don't buy the junk advertised inside. What bullshit." He was trying to get Leo on his team. "Do you know how many girls are being sent home right now?"

Or, like Whitney, to Daytona. The brother was dead right on that one. This was a very stressful time for the girls, the end of the season. But Leo couldn't feel too sorry for them. The ones going back to Eugene, or Akron, or Wichita, they'd be back for another crack next year, or they wouldn't. Whose problem was that? Anyway, his question didn't apply to Valentina. There were big things ahead for her.

Chi-Chi said something to Paulo, but he wasn't about to let the subject change.

"Will you please?" Valentina said. "You're embarrassing me."

Paulo took a poke at his sister in Italian, and she fired right back, prompting a comment from Chi-Chi, and then nobody was listening and everybody was jabbering at once.

"Hello?" Gregory said. "Family Feud? This is not why we came here."

"Paulo can't get over the fact I'm determined to live my own life," Valentina said, getting in the last word.

Chi-Chi did her best to re-set the tone, getting quiet and tucking into her pasta. "Eat," she said to Gregory in English, "eat," like somebody's grandma.

If there was one thing Leo couldn't deal with while he was getting his groove on, it was conflict. Gregory and Valentina stared at their plates, and Paulo, his chin jutting, beamed his glare across the table. High tension. Leo didn't dig it.

Sometimes he wished he could play the *Mister Wizard* game he used to play when he was a kid. *Mister Wizard* was a cartoon named after some wise old creature of the forest that had the power to grant wishes. His steadiest customer was a turtle, whose name Leo forgot, an ambitious turtle with big dreams that Mister Wizard would fulfill on a weekly basis.

One time the turtle wanted to be a baseball player, a pitcher just like Leo. So Mister Wizard transported him to some cartoon league where he was facing a team called the Giants, who turn out to be real giants, smacking overmatched turtle ass all over the diamond. It was like Giants 72, Turtle nothing, before the turtle decided he had enough.

At the end of the story, the turtle would go, "Help, Mister Wizard, I don't wanna be a baseball player"—or astronaut, or private eye or whatever he'd wanted to be that week—"anymore." And Mister Wizard would rescue him with the incantation, "Drizzle drazzle, drozzle, drome/ Time for this one to come home," and bring him back to the forest.

What Leo used to do, he was his own Mister Wizard. He would just say to himself, Help, Mister Wizard, I don't wanna be in the principal's office—or church, or at Aunt Helen's—and then, working his own magic, bang, he wasn't there anymore. He would travel so deep into himself that everything around him became non-existent. He did this right up till the time he was eleven or twelve and told Duane Measler about his game and Duane Measler said Leo was weird. He quit it after that.

A real-deal Mister Wizard situation, this. He was an afterthought, a fifth wheel at the table of the breathtaking Valentina, whose jealous brother was on the verge of undoing a season's worth of hard work. With a frizz-haired frump who couldn't hold up her end of the conversation, if there even was a conversation to hold up. And Gregory. Gregory wasn't even that bad, as far as these guys went. But Leo kept anticipating he'd come up with something witty or even stupid to say to break up the glacier creeping over this scene, and Gregory stayed mute, twirling linguine on his fork.

"I must have a bladder the size of a peanut," Leo announced. "When you spot that waiter, could you order me another margarita? I'll be right back."

He went straight into that stall and snorted two big blasts up both nostrils. There.

Stopping for another quick pop at the bar was a strong temptation, only Paulo was at the bar waiting for him. He said, "Having a good time?"

Leo said, "Uh, yeah?" He wasn't sure which way he was supposed to answer.

"I'm sorry you had to sit through that. My sister is very

beautiful, but she is not very mature. I didn't mean to make you feel uncomfortable. I was out of line, and I apologize."

"That's nothing," Leo said. "Let's go back and sit down."

"All the same, I wouldn't want you to get any ideas about her."

Leo said, "Ideas?"

"Come on, Leo. We're men. We both know why you're here. You weren't expecting Chi-Chi and you weren't expecting me. You might've been braced for the queer, but you're not interested in him. You're a lot of cheap things, but you aren't homosexual."

"Hey, wait a minute." Leo's nose dripped cocaine runoff. He sucked it in and wiped what escaped on the back of his hand. Wow, did he need a drink. What happened to that bartender, the short one in the little red vest?

"Valentina is a rare jewel. If you think my parents raised her to be trifled with by a third-rate, cocaine-sniffing hoodlum, you're dead wrong, my friend. I suspect you realize she's out of your class, but I'm here to reinforce your fears."

Did this guinea have any idea who Leo was? That he'd straight-up wasted a psycho killer? He started to say, "You don't know me at all."

"You're wrong there, too." Paulo turned up the wattage on a bright, sinister smile Leo didn't care for the looks of, not one bit. "You don't think I know you, but I know you. And I'm warning you. I'm threatening you. Stay away from my sister."

Paulo turned and walked back to the table, slow, cocky, chest out, just about daring Leo to follow him.

Leo wasn't biting. After he found the bartender, he hammered down a double, and, feeling more together, took his time with the return trip outside. He left a twenty under the plate he didn't touch, and said goodnight, giving them three lies where one would've been plenty. In the future, a point of form: Never tell three consecutive lies.

Valentina shot her brother a dead eyed-look. Standing to shake Leo's hand, Paulo pumped that smile for all the malevolence it was worth.

Leo walked the length of Lincoln Road. Turning left on Lennox, then right on 15th to Alton, he covered the last couple blocks to Kilkenny's, where he should've gone in the first place. Leo was grateful, though not at all surprised, to find Jo Ann wearing a pleated mini-skirt and red suede boxing shoes, carrying three Bud Longnecks high on a tray.

Leo had one eye open on a vicious hangover that started at his temples and wrapped around his head like a turban. His lungs ached up through his chest. His nostrils were crusted shut. Opening his other eye, he felt twice as bad. The few clothes Jo Ann had been wearing were in a heap on the floor, and it hurt to look at her red suede boots.

Right. Jo Ann. Jo Ann was snoring directly into his ear, and no matter how long he planned on playing dead, whoever was ringing the doorbell was not going to stop. The sunlight honking in through the staircase window seemed to have a sound to it, all mixed up with blasts on the bell, and now, some extra-rude knocks.

Leo opened the door on a pretty, athletic brunette wearing a beige suit and shades. There were braces on her teeth and she was holding a badge. It took him a few seconds to register this, shirtless, shoeless, the top button on his Levi's unfastened. This cute brunette, who was on the young side, but way too old for trips to the orthodontist, was a fucking cop, and she was at his house. The cops were at his house.

They must have identified JP Beaumond's body. Though Leo had his JP story all together, and though he'd been waiting for this since the afternoon Stuart A. Homes-Leighton mentioned they'd carted Beaumond's corpse out of the Glades, a knot of acid churned in his gut.

He said, "Good morning."

"Good afternoon. Leo Hannah?"

"That's me."

"I'm Detective Acevedo from the Miami Beach Police." She put the wallet with the detective shield in her pocket and took off her sunglasses. Her eyes were the same green as Leo's, and she was very fair-skinned for a Cuban chick. Maybe her mother was white.

Leo snuck a peek at the coffee table in front of the television, at the plate with the remnants of last night's blow-fest. He stepped outside and closed the door. "What can I do for you, Detective?"

"On the night of March fifth, a Dutch tourist was murdered in his hotel room on Ocean Drive. You probably heard about it."

Okay, curveball. She wanted to talk about Manfred instead of JP, and she had to know that Leo knew him, or she wouldn't be standing here.

"Awful," Leo said. "Terrible. You know, I knew that guy."

"Manfred Pfiser. How did you know him?"

"Let's see, how did I know him? That's a good question. I just sort of knew him from around, a familiar face from the Beach. You know, bars, restaurants, that sort of thing. Hey, how're you guys making out with your investigation?"

"It's coming along. Would you be able to recall the last time you saw him before he died?"

"I'm sorry," he said, "I just woke up and I'm a little hazy. What did you wanna know?"

"I was wondering about the last time you saw him. Alive."

That was a low blow. It was supposed to imply that Leo had seen Manfred dead, which he had not. "I think it was a couple days before he died. But I'm not sure, that was what, two months ago, and my memory isn't the best, you know what I'm saying?"

Posing in the brightness without a shirt, all waxed up like he was about to shoot a print ad, Leo felt he could use a pair of shades out here, the new Armanis.

But the cop was pin-spotting the Jag, and now she had her notebook out. "Where do you work, Mr. Hannah?"

"I don't. I mean I'm not right now. I've been doing some modeling jobs. That is, I've been testing a lot, but I don't have adequate representation at the moment. What you need in my line of work is a good agent."

"Do you own this house?"

"I rented it for the season. Which reminds me. The lease is about to expire. I'm gonna be looking for a new place to live."

"Are you married?"

"Nope. Single all the way, baby." Shit, error on Leo. She might be cute as hell, but she was still a cop.

"Kind of a big place for one person, isn't it?"

"Let me tell you something. For a long time I lived in two rooms on Meridian Avenue. I promised myself that when I moved, it was gonna be into a house. But now look at me. I've gotta move again. Ain't that a bitch?"

"I don't understand what you mean."

Bullshit. How could she not understand what he

meant? What was he speaking, Swahili? She was pulling his chain, but that was okay, because he could pull right back.

"Making plans," Leo said. "You make plans, they jump up and bite you on the ass. Like in your mind, you expect things to go one way so you chart your course accordingly, but reality turns out to be something totally different."

He wasn't having such a bad time talking to the cop. But if she was going to be much longer, he needed to get himself squared away with some cigarettes and a pair of shades. Coffee'd be great, too.

"Would you excuse me a moment? I'd like to go put on a shirt."

He didn't ask her in, and she didn't ask to come in, which was good. If only there was a way to get this chick to tip her hand, let him find out what she knew. Although it'd look bad for him, asking questions. Cops didn't answer questions, anyway. Finally, he thought, fuck it, let her fire away. What could she do to him?

He took a piss in the upstairs toilet and let go of the fart that had been looming out on the steps. The flushing toilet stirred Jo Ann just enough for her to roll over and ask him what time it was. From the way the sun was blaring, Leo figured it had to be around noon, but Jo Ann went back to sleep before he could give her an answer.

The Armanis weren't on the dresser where he swore he'd seen them last, and he wasn't crazy about the way the Black Flys looked with this haircut. Not to mention they were the same frames everybody on South Beach was rocking the last couple seasons. But they beat staring into the glare of a South Florida afternoon.

His Marlboros were on the coffee table next to the

plate. There was a nice-sized rock left. He shoved the plate into the refrigerator for safekeeping.

The cop was nosing around the Jag and scribbling something into her notebook, the license and serial numbers, probably, but that wasn't much of a worry, because the ride was totally legal. Except now the law had a line on it. He'd have to go talk to that dealer, see what he could do about bailing out of his lease.

Leo sat down on the steps, as relaxed as he could be with a throbbing headache roaring back at him. The first few Marlboro drags triggered a coughing fit that brought tears to his eyes. Better think about giving up the smokes one of these days. Make a note.

The cop headed back up the gravel and turned an ankle, but she hardly broke her stride. Her lap-lines were eye-level, and he was staring right at her pussy. Underneath the linen and whatever kind of underwear she had on, Leo bet that pussy was sweet. He never fucked a cop, but he was young still. He wouldn't mind starting right here.

"What year is that car?" the cop wanted to know.

Dumb bitch. She could've got it off the serial number. He got to his feet. "That's a '97," Leo said. "You know what the factory calls that color? British Racing Green. Don't you love that? British Racing Green."

"Now that's a rental, am I right? What'd you do, get that for the season, too?"

"They won't let you do that," he said. "I got a two-year lease on it."

She peered over his left shoulder, like she was considering what to ask next. Leo thought she might be trying to look into the living room, but the curtains were drawn like they always were, and there was nothing to see anyway, not with the plate in the fridge. "I understand you're very fond of entertaining, Mr. Hannah. People come and go all hours of the night, loud music, naked women in the back yard. You're a regular party boy, aren't you, a real good-time Charlie, with your house and your Jaguar and your hot tub."

Now who the fuck told her that? Was this the cop getting tough with him?

"At the beginning of the season, when I was excited about having the place, I wanted to share my good fortune with my friends. We did have a few late nights, but I felt they were abusing my hospitality. You invite people over, open your home to them, and what do they do?"

"They suck up your booze and snort up your coke, and then you can't get rid of them. Was Manfred Pfiser ever a guest at one of your parties?"

"We weren't exactly what you'd call friends."

"More like business associates."

No mistaking it now. The cop was turning up the heat. "What business would I have had with Manfred?"

The cop said, "You tell me."

"We were acquaintances, you know, I knew the guy a little bit. Hi and goodbye, that's all. We didn't exactly swim in the same pond."

"What if I told you we have a witness who puts you with Manfred Pfiser on the day he was killed?"

"I'd say that witness had the wrong date, off the top of my head, but like I said, that was months ago. I could be wrong."

"It was six weeks ago, and burnt-out brain cells or not, I'd say if I knew somebody who was murdered, I'd recollect pretty much to the second the last time I saw him. But that's me. Can you remember where this meeting took place, on that vague last date two or three days before he was killed, that you saw him?"

This was turning into a complete buzz-kill. "One of those places on Ocean Drive. We sat down and had a drink."

"You and your faulty memory, I don't suppose you could tell me which place?"

Leo racked his brain for the name of one café, just one, any one, so he could give her an answer, but she wasn't waiting for it.

"Now what if I told you we have another witness who not only puts you in the company of Manfred Pfiser on the afternoon of the day he was killed, this witness places you at his hotel. Right in the same room with him. On the day he was murdered. What would you say to that, Mr. Hannah?"

How? He'd be there, what, all of ten minutes? Fifteen? But that didn't matter now.

"I know what it was. Now I remember. Manfred said he had a jacket for me, a sports coat my size. He wanted me to come up to his room and try it on. Manfred was queer, I don't know if you knew that, and I figured he was gonna try and make a pass at me, but I went with him anyway, to humor him. That was the day he was killed?"

"Here's what you're telling me. You knew that he was gay, and you were expecting an advance of some kind you claim you weren't interested in, but you accompanied him to his room."

Leo said, "Yeah, well."

"He was merely an acquaintance, right? That's what you said? But he wanted to give you an article from his wardrobe."

"One thing I will say for him, he was very generous."

"And at five feet eight, and a hundred eighty pounds, he owned a jacket that would've fit you. I think you can do a little better than that, don't you, Leo?"

The cop closed her notebook and put her shades back on, pair of cheap shit Persol knock-offs she probably bought in some drugstore. "What can you tell me about a man named Harry Healy?"

"Never heard of the guy," Leo said, and instantly realized what a stupid lie he just told.

"You spent forty-eight hours with him in the same cell at Dade back in February."

Of course she knew he knew Harry. What an idiot.

"I figured you two would've gotten the chance to chat."

She drew a breath like she was going to say something else, but pulled up short, and left Leo standing on the steps, wobbly from the beating she'd dealt out. She turned around and Leo reflexively checked her out. Lotta junk in the trunk. This chick was like the Beach Police Department's very own Trojan Horse. And they came for him while he slept, just like the fucking Greeks.

"By the way," she said, turning around again, "remember how you said your plans had a way of backfiring? If you had any to leave town, consider that this is them jumping up and biting you on the ass. We're gonna need to talk to you again."

She smiled a smile that under any other circumstances Leo would've made for flirty, a smile that showed her braces, but was sexy as hell. She had gorgeous hair, too, and a booming ass, but she was trying to cut off his balls, right here at his very own seasonal rental. Help, Mister Wizard. Jesus Christ, Mister Wizard, help.

Chapter Thirteen

The bar on Grand Street was so slam-packed with cheap-suited finance grunts, Harry figured it must be the eve of one of those shifting, unknowable holidays, giving the place all the charm of Fraternity Row on Career Night. For a few years there, it felt like these guys had gone away, but there was no denying it anymore: They ruled once again.

The suits barked out orders like they were trading shares, hanging bills over the shoulders of the guys in front of them. Irish Mike snatched the money out of the air and stuffed it in the till.

On his bad nights, and Mike had plenty of those, he was bitter about tending bar. But it was the perfect job for him. He had that thing that made you want to give him money. He could be funny, he was polite most of the time, and he recorded the pet subjects of his regulars in a mental file.

Mike needed bigger pants. The pounds he'd added around the breadbasket doubled his waistband down. He was sporting a five o'clock-shadow beard, but it didn't make him look hip or masculine, it made him look like a bum.

Harry decided he'd go kill an hour or so somewhere else when Mike caught his eye and pulled down a bottle of Dewar's. He capped the pourer with a tumbler, tipped the bottle upside down, and let the whiskey run into the glass. Pouring a drink for himself, Mike shelved the scotch, and threw down the measure in a gulp.

By the time Harry was ready for his third Dewar's, Mike had found a Louis Armstrong cassette, and it was playing over the bar's sound system. Harry couldn't possibly hear Satchmo and not think of his father. The old man was a huge Armstrong fan. What jazzbo wasn't? Give him a kiss to build a dream on.

Mike pointed at Harry, touched his own thieving heart, then pointed back at Harry. He guessed it meant Mike wanted a word. The crowd was leaving, and there was room at the bar.

The way Mike drank, Harry wondered why he bothered with a glass. Another dog-choking shot, down the hatch. He had to be drunk. Maybe this wasn't the best time to talk to him. Then again, what were the odds of catching Mike sober?

He wanted to know what happened in Florida. "I can tell by that tan, you must just be getting back."

"Couple of days ago," Harry said.

"Jesus, I'm glad to see you," Mike said. "Haven't been this tired in a long time."

"You work hard," Harry told him, and on nights like this, he did.

"I could use a little something to pick me up."

Harry had wondered when he was going to get around to it. Mike didn't give a shit what had happened in Florida, or anywhere else in Harry's life.

Mike was an on-again-off-again blowhound, with a dry-out, two detoxes, and a rehab on his resume. Mike had been doing it for years. Whenever they let him out, he'd lip-serve their one-day-at-a-time jive, which coincidentally was the precise span of Irish Mike's typical rehabilitation. One day.

"So what've you got for your old buddy?"

Harry laid a twenty on the bar, to coin up for his

drinks. "I gave up on that shit," he said. "All it ever brought me was grief."

"I hear you woofing, big dog." Mike forced a phony smile that deepened the lines at his temples and made his face look like it was going to crack. "But that's no reason to quit. Cut down, sure. I could see wanting to cut down."

Harry said, "Remember that girl, Julia? I was hanging out with her about a year ago?"

"What about Julia? I told you stay clear of her, didn't I?"

Mike popped a beer for an ossified suit. The guy counted out some singles and held one back, to make sure Mike knew he was setting aside the whole, entire dollar for a tip. The guy got his beer, a light. He stood there cuddling it.

"Is there somebody you can call," Mike said, "that can straighten me out? I could really go for something right about now."

Pretending to think a minute, Harry walked over to the phone, dropped in a quarter, and punched out the Downtowner's numbers. Phil the night guy snapped it up after half a ring. Maybe Phil was expecting something of his own.

Harry said, "Phil, this is Harry in 801."

Phil said, "What can I do for you?"

"Have I got any messages?" He could feel Mike's stare boring holes in the back of his head. He turned and winked and turned around again.

Phil said, "Who knows you're staying here?"

Harry angled his profile to let Mike lip-read him saying, "Hey, I'm just asking."

"No messages for you. Can I be of any further assistance?"

"That'll do it, Phil. Thanks."

"The guy's all done for the night," Harry told Mike when he got back to the bar. "Can't do anything right now."

"Done for the night? Fuck. What kind of coke dealer is he? It ain't even four yet." Mike zeroed in on that suit, frozen in the same spot where he bought his beer. "Hey, buddy," he said, "We're closed."

The guy's jaw slackened, and he trained his blurry vision toward the source of this noise. "Closed?"

"That's right, closed." Mike slipped the bottle out of his hand, and the suit pawed the air.

Mike was way too creaky to be vaulting any bar, but he did hustle around it to grab the guy's arm. He pushed him toward the exit. When Mike shut the door and bolted it, the guy cocked his head like a terrier faked out in a game of fetch.

This was the six hundred pound gorilla, a mighty monkey indeed, ventilating a hapless, beer-gutted soak too looped to stick up for himself. Not that Harry felt sorry for the guy, but Mike was nasty with him, and for what? For nothing. Because Mike needed to get beamed up and Harry wasn't holding.

He asked for another scotch.

Mike said, "I'm gonna need some money for this, you know. You can't just drink here for free."

Harry slid the twenty at him. Mike snapped it up and spitefully rang an eighteen dollar sale into the vintage NCR. The drawer flew open and Mike banged it shut without making change. He reopened it and started counting the night's take.

"I'm trying to find out about Julia," Harry said. He peeled another twenty off his roll, to replace the one Mike had stuck in the register. "I'm assuming she's still in town."

Mike said, "Uh-huh." He wound a rubber band

around a stack of singles. "Julia, right? Sharp-looking chick, tall brunette?"

"That's the one, Mike. So do I get my drink, or what?"

"Sorry," Mike said, "sorry," reaching for the Dewar's. "I'm a bit rattled tonight." He poured until Harry said whoa. "This one's on me. Happy days. What went on with you two, anyway?"

"What went on was, we took a trip to Florida, but then I got into some shit and I had to stay."

"Told you that bitch was trouble. You gotta listen to old Mike."

"Okay, you were dead-nuts on that one, but what I'm trying to do is get the rap on her now. Did she move some guy in? Is he banging my girl? Is he drying his ass with my towels?"

Mike was counting again, the fives this time, counting and nodding, maybe listening, maybe not. "You know what I was thinking, Harry? I was thinking you could ask somebody else."

"The problem is, everybody I know that knows her is a friend of hers. They're not gonna give her up. She's got 'em all convinced I'm a monster. You follow me?"

"He's not the only blow dealer in New York, is what I'm saying. You gotta know somebody else."

Jeez. He was still fixated on getting his coke. "No, Mike, *you* gotta know somebody else. Cause I'm out of it. Like I said. Only you must not have heard me, because if you did, you wouldn't keep fucking asking. I don't know anybody, and I don't wanna know anybody, that's gonna make a fifty dollar drop at four o'clock in the morning."

"I'd go a hundred," Mike said, putting the singles with the fives.

"Try the car service on Avenue D. Go talk to Hector."

Hector was most likely in Rikers, but Harry was hoping Mike would run into some desperate crackhead and get robbed. "Otherwise, First Avenue, 8th Street, 9th Street. Those guys are always open."

"Scrubbing powder," Mike said. "Pure, unadulterated street garbage. I don't put that trash in my body."

Ah, yes. It was the cheap stuff that hurt you. "You remember the last time you saw her?"

Mike said, "Who?" He was halfway through a stack of tens, and had to start over. His totals were bound to be miles off. "Oh, yeah. That tall girl with the dark hair. What's her name?"

"Julia, Mike. Her name is Julia."

"Right, Julia. You gotta be careful of girls like her."

"Seen her lately?"

"She was in, I don't know, one night last week. Why? What've you got going with her?"

"Was she alone?"

"She came in alone and got guys to buy her drinks until her boyfriend showed up. You know the guy."

"I know what guy?"

"The boyfriend. Kind of a big nose, real Italian-looking. You used to be friends with him."

Harry said, "Who?"

"Jimmy," Mike said, "Jimmy De Steffano."

Harry was right. Hector was still on the good-boy bench, and the car service was shuttered, but Hector's cousin Junior had moved the operation, and he was running it out of a bodega on 2nd Street. Junior carved him a gram of rock from his private stash. For old time's sake, he said.

Harry bindled the gram into a fifty, and that more than got him past Felix, the four-till-midnight doorman at

Julia's co-op. After Harry assured him he'd keep his name out of it, Felix slipped him in with keys he should've been fired for using.

The apartment was basically one big room with an arched, wall-length window that faced east and let in lots of light but didn't offer much of a view. In another part of town, the pad would've passed for a loft, the rambling space split into rooms by furniture, about twenty-five percent of it plasterboarded into a bedroom, and through there, the bathroom.

Julia's estimated time of arrival, one half-hour. To get showered and changed and telephone vicious, half-true gossip to friends about other friends who were either in or out of their dinner plans. He hoped she showed up alone. He didn't want to deal with De Steffano, not right now. Jimmy no doubt did backflips to convince Julia how tough he was, and if he felt any pressure to put his money where his mouth was, Harry'd have to kick his ass for him, and he didn't want to do that.

Irish Mike's tidbit stung Harry. He was wounded, but not because De Steffano had scooped up Julia. All anybody ever did was act according to his character, and Jimmy was always the kind of guy who'd get your girl in bed the second your back was turned. No point expecting him to change now.

But De Steffano'd had a golden opportunity to come clean. Instead, he'd let Harry find out through somebody else. That's what got him. Julia wasn't his girl anymore, and what he had to keep in mind, the one thing he did not want out of this life or any other, was Julia Stencyk hanging around his neck like a stone. But De Steffano could at least have told him.

Every bill was due. Phone, three months worth of

cable TV, Con Edison. A charge account had been turned over to a collection agency, one of Julia's financial managers having fallen down on the job.

Harry sorted through Julia's jewelry box for a pair of diamond-stud earrings he'd bought her during a flush period. He found them easy enough, slipped them into his pocket, and started opening dresser drawers. There was a copy of his birth certificate in here somewhere, and he wanted it.

He should've avoided the drawer where she kept her photographs, but he didn't. There were recent photos of Julia with Jimmy, among the same faces and in the same places that she used to hang out in with Harry. He dug through stacks of snapshots and landed in the Harry era, Harry and Julia with some castmates from her sitcom, all grown up and doing pretty badly. Harry and Julia flanking the old man after a gig. Harry looked pretty drunk in that one.

What do you know, Miami Beach. Harry and Julia entwined on the sand, the ocean rolling behind them. That must have been their first day there. Wait a minute. Behind them, featured in a series of three photographs of Harry and Julia kissing—he recognized this girl, the deep suntan, those shoulders. It came to him slowly. She was the girl from Manfred's room. Jennifer.

He heard the locks clicking and walked out to the front room to meet Julia, who let out a little yelp and dropped the shopping bags on the floor.

"How did you get in here?" she said.

He held up the picture of Jennifer and said, "How do you know this girl?"

"What are you doing here? You want your stuff? Take it. I've been saving it for you."

"Answer my question," Harry said. "How do you know her?"

"How dare you go through my things? I should have you arrested right now."

She picked up the phone and started pushing buttons. Harry grabbed the receiver out of her hand and smashed it against an end table, a contained explosion that sounded like a shot.

"This girl," he said, "was in Manfred Pfiser's hotel room on the day he got shot. I made a delivery for him, and when I got back to his hotel, this girl was gone and Manfred was dead on the floor. Who is she and what did she have to do with it?"

Julia said, "I don't know what you're talking about."

She got a cigarette situated between her lips, and sent out the search party for a match. But she didn't have one. She never did.

"For an actress, you're a terrible liar." Harry got up close to her, and dug his fingers into the fleshy part of her arm.

"You're hurting me."

He squeezed, and it buckled her knees. "Julia, honey," Harry said, without raising his voice, "I'm gonna do a lot more than that if you don't start giving me some answers." He applied more pressure, then let her go.

"I met her in Los Angeles on a job, and she was in Miami when we were there. Her name is Vicki. She's an actress."

The white marks from Harry's fingers had turned to red.

"What do you know about a guy named Leo?"

"Leo Hannah? They're friends. He and Vicki and Lawrence Lendesma. They're Miami people."

"So you were in on it, too."

"In on what? Have you lost your mind?"

Harry took a step toward her and Julia put up her hands. "She called me in March. She wanted to know when you were getting out of jail."

"And you fucking told her?"

The cigarette quivered in Julia's mouth. She walked over to the stove, held back her brand-new Cleopatra hairdo, and hunched over a burner. Straightening up, she took a deep drag.

"She said Leo wanted to make contact with you, that you two met in jail, and he was looking forward to seeing you when you got out."

"How did she find out about Leo and me?"

"I don't know."

"Julia—"

"I swear to God, Harry, I don't know."

Harry brushed past her. All the things he'd wanted to say to her, everything he'd wanted to get back, none of it meant a thing.

Downstairs, Felix was worrying a powder-fed facial tic, his upper lip pulling back to reveal new, managed-care teeth, his jaw pulsing to a beat only he could feel. He was holding the door for a toddling relic in mink.

A thick chill dampened the twilight, the top third of the Empire State Building glowing pale through the settling fog. People swarmed on the sidewalks, umbrellas up, but the mist in the air was hardly like rain.

Harry felt sick, and leaned against the wall of a building for support. What was going on? Leo and Julia... Vicki, who he'd only met once, and Jimmy De Steffano, who he'd known all his life... was there anyone who wasn't going out of their way to make him suffer? His own father couldn't get rid of him fast enough, for god's sake.

An image came to him then, Aggie at the bus station,

just before she slapped him, asking "All I want to know is, where do I fit in?" And then the answer he'd given her.

The tears were bitter. He let them go.

Chapter Fourteen

Nobody took the trouble to give the boy a name, just two initials that didn't stand for anything. It wasn't the first time Martinson encountered this phenomenon, or even the second, and it wasn't all that much of a phenomenon around Campville, JP Beaumond's birthplace, a roach turd on the map a short shot east of Gainesville.

Five feet, four inches, one-hundred and fifty-nine pounds, his mean, dull eyes struck a near-perfect match with his mouse-brown hair. These mugs were snapped before Beaumond went to jail the last time. His record indicated he had a tattoo of a rebel flag on his left shoulder, and a chunk of meat gouged out of his left thigh, most likely an old stab wound.

His first run-in with the law came at age nine, when for no reason that was mentioned, JP slit the throats of six of his neighbor's chickens, and the neighbor pressed charges, along with the county chapter of the ASPCA. Beaumond's family was ordered to make restitution for the birds.

A few years later, the underage JP snuck out of a package store with a pair of Colt 45s, the bottled variety, then broke one of them over the head of the clerk attempting to apprehend him. This led to a brief hospitalization for the clerk, and a juvie bid for the ambitious JP, now moving up in the world, at a detention home outside of Middleburg. He earned two county bounces for a B&E and an assault, respectively, and did his first state jolt at the not-so-tender age of eighteen, after the deceitful JP borrowed his brother-in-law's car, then neglected to bring it back. Two years on the inside, six weeks out, the unlucky JP had a return engagement at the Big House for selling three-and-a-half grams of cocaine to an undercover policeman in St. Augustine.

Which brought them pretty much up to the present, although in JP Beaumond's case, everything was past for him now, and there wasn't going to be any future. Somebody made certain of that when they shot him twice with a .25 caliber pistol and rudely pitched his body into a canal in the Everglades.

Hardly a week went by that some law enforcement agency wasn't pulling a stiff out of that grassy river, a body some tour guide or fisherman found floating. Arnie thought by now even the dimmest bulb realized this feed-the-guy-to-the-alligators crap never panned out. An alligator would not eat a man unless he was starving, and being absolute boss of his neighborhood food chain, the alligator was never starving. Lazy, yes. Cowardly, yes. Hungry, no. All the same, somebody out there must've been feeling a bit peckish: Beaumond had a big bite taken out of his side.

It was a thoroughly unprofessional dump job. The victim's wallet was in the hip pocket of his pants, and it contained twenty-seven dollars cash, a suspended Florida driver's license, and another one from Georgia, assigned to Clement Snipe. It had JP Beaumond's picture on it. Also, Visa, Master, American Express, and Automobile Association of America cards, all in the name of Theodore Kistler.

It was too bad Beaumond was dead. Martinson wasn't

sorry the world was minus one Campville native of JP's standing, but he would've liked to talk to him. He must have finally pissed off the wrong guy. Leo Hannah, for instance. Or this Alex character Victoria Leonard was covering up for. Plenty of other people, too. But Arnie Martinson was in no way obligated to investigate the murder of this piece of shit, a Dade County headache all the way down the line.

Lili was rarely in this part of town after dark, and she was getting a good dose of why. The sidewalks were clogged with noisy Italians, Germans with seven-figure Swiss bank accounts, and blonde bunnies who seemed like they'd been raised in Midwestern towns but were too frail to be farm girls. Hip-hugging corduroys showcased their narrow figures, exhibiting brown bellies and pierced navels. Every fifty feet or so, one would uncork a mind-bending whinny, and throw her arms around another girl who looked just like her and happened to be approaching from the opposite direction.

The sneakers that encased each and every one of their feet made Lili's pumps feel like mukluks. She looked like somebody's maiden aunt with her wavy hair, mannish and out of it in this blue blazer over the white button-down shirt. But she wasn't competing with these girls, she was at least ten years older than most of them, and she wasn't doing a night on the town, she was working.

Though it was before eleven, there was a line outside the Calabash. A velvet rope divided patrons from a doorman holding a clipboard. He was wearing a pin-striped suit and a pair of black and white wingtips, a grey hat with a snap brim that dove down over his left eye. His hair needed to be cut. The gel that held it together was failing. He took shallow puffs from a gold-filtered cigarette, chatting with a grim, steroid-bloated bouncer. Lili felt the nervous energy radiating out of him like a stink.

She tugged the collar of her white, button-down shirt, then walked right up and badged him.

He said, "How you doing tonight?" His skin reflected the violet neon of the club's sign.

"I'm looking for somebody named Alejandro or Alex. Tall, thin, mid-twenties. Probably Cuban."

"I know two guys named Alex," the doorman said. "One's a French guy who owns a restaurant on Alton Road, and the other one is married to my sister. They have two kids and they live in Sarasota."

He reached over and unclipped the rope to let four people pass, then re-attached it. When the bouncer pulled the door open, Lili looked in and saw the club was deserted. The line was getting longer. Why were they making these people wait?

"He hangs around with a guy named JP Beaumond," Lili said, and saw the doorman's eyes flash on the name. He took two quick steps toward the stanchion, where he raised the rope again, letting in six more bodies.

"Beaumond, huh? Don't know him." He walked to the curb, his heels clicking, and flicked his gold-tipped cigarette into the street. He patted his pockets for the pack. He was lying.

"I'm going to go in and see if any of the staff can help me."

"No problem," he said, glad to be rid of her. "Be my guest."

He signaled the bouncer, who opened the door, and Lili stepped into a cloud of music and swirling, cobalt light. The name Calabash must've been picked from a hat. There was no discernable theme in here, and the overpowering air-conditioning, coupled with the absence of a single stick of furniture, made the club feel as cold as it looked.

It was an enormous square, like a low-ceilinged aircraft hangar. The few souls inside threaded the emptiness like they were waiting to meet a guide. If they were scouting out a place to blend in, there wasn't one. And nobody to blend in with, except maybe the hardball security crew deployed in strategic spots around the floor.

The bar was built of concrete and corrugated steel, a forbidding hulk that hummed with an industrial wasteland vibe. Three bartenders stood behind it, doing nothing but folding their arms against the chill.

Lili keyed in on the balding one wearing black jeans and a black t-shirt that said Calabash, South Beach in tiny letters where a pocket would've gone. Six feet, one forty, light build. He ran his hand over his scalp, smoothing his wispy hair back-to-front.

"What can I get for you?" He rested his elbows on the bar. His skinny arms matched the rest of his body. Lili showed him her badge and asked about a tall, Cuban kid named Alex.

"Not by that name," the bartender said. He leaned in, his head close to Lili's, to holler over the blare. "I try not to bother too much with their names. It gets like that when you've been at this as long as I have."

He straightened and blew out a sigh. Lili smelled vodka on his breath.

"What about a guy named JP Beaumond?" Lili showed the bartender his mug shots.

"Oh, yeah," he said. "Him, I know. We threw him out not too long ago, caught him selling coke in the bathroom. Little piece of swamp trash about four feet tall. Extremely bad news. He's well known to the bouncers on the Beach, I mean, enough so they'd keep him out of a joint."

"Then how come your doorman didn't know him?"

"Did you show him the pictures?"

Lili didn't answer. The doorman had hinked on the name. Maybe he had something working with Beaumond.

"Because Ralston knows everybody. But if I was looking for this creep, I'd try the Switching Station. They don't do much with models or trendies, but they draw a late-night crowd of local skanks. Might be a bit early but it's worth a shot. And if you strike out there, go to Loby's Ron-Da-Voo."

The dealers who were holding scattered away from the unmarked, city-owned vehicle that was as much of an advertisement for Beach law enforcement as any patrol unit. Lean, brown-skinned teenagers, their long, slow legs took them in various directions as Martinson rolled up to the curb.

Anton Canter stood his ground. He was leaning, arms crossed, against a Dodge with missing hubcaps. Wearing tear-away sweatpants in U of M green and orange, he posed one ankle over the other, one sneaker toeing the asphalt. A gold-plated rope with a Mercedes-Benz hood ornament was fastened around his neck.

Martinson climbed out of the car. Canter stared him down until Arnie got right up next to him, eliminating his personal space. He picked up his chin and looked off to his right.

Arnie said, "Hello, Anton. How are you today?" He could feel the heat coming off the kid's body, his temperature no doubt going up, bracing for this roust.

Canter said, "What you want?"

"I was just wondering how you were doing. Funny I'd think to find you here, all this nefarious activity going on all around you."

"I live up the block," Canter said, still looking away. "You know that. Where you want me to hang out?"

"Look better for you if you were hanging out at your job," Martinson said.

"Less you count Mickey D's for the minimum, there ain't no jobs."

"And why would you wanna do that, when there's all this money to be made out here? What's your P.O.'s name?" Martinson scanned the empty parking spaces, sighting the usual curbside flotsam, cigarette butts, broken glass, spent butane lighters, looking for Anton's stash. "Never mind. I can look it up."

Canter was too experienced to have the stuff on him, but Martinson knew it wasn't far away. "Still doing your outpatient, Anton? I could check that, too, but I figured I'd save myself the time and just ask you. Give us the chance to catch up."

Canter mumbled something into the breeze.

"I'm sorry," Martinson said, "I didn't hear you. You've got to learn to enunciate, Anton. I mean, I'm standing right here, for Christ's sake."

"Every Tuesday, I said."

"Down to once a week, huh? Is that enough? Because I thought that drug program taught you something about people, places and things. Like what you'd want to avoid if you wanted to stay clean. Now look at you. Associating with a known criminal element, in a very dubious location, doing something I consider to be questionable at best. Judging from your present circumstances, I'd say you were all set to go and get yourself dirty."

He was standing so close to Canter the upper part of

his chest was touching Canter's shoulder. Anton took a step to the right.

There was a screwed-up paper bag under the Dodge's rear wheel on the driver's side. Martinson picked it up and reached into the bottom of it. He pulled out a handful of crack vials.

"Ho, shit," he said. "What's this? You dirty little piglet."

"That got nothin' to do with me," Canter said. "That mess was in the street."

Martinson was going to stuff the vials into Canter's pocket, but the sweatpants didn't have any pockets. "Yeah, but what if I said I found these on you? Who they gonna believe Anton, me or you?" He put the vials back in the bag and folded it.

"That's entrapment," Canter howled. "That shit's against the law."

"Against the law?" Martinson laughed. "Take a look around, Anton. The only two out here is me and you."

He unsnapped the strap on his holster. Anton Canter was all done posturing. Martinson had his undivided attention.

"I can do whatever the fuck I want." He smacked his open palm into Canter's chest, knocking him off balance. "You understand me?"

This felt good.

"You remember Josephine Simmons, don't you? The old lady you beat half to death?"

Canter said, "I didn't do it."

"She died."

"I didn't do it and you know I didn't do it."

"I know you got an alibi," Martinson said, "and I know it checked out. The first time. That's all I know. But the State of Florida takes murder very seriously. So there's going to be a whole new investigation now because it's a whole new crime. Isn't the criminal justice system wonderful?"

"I swear to God," Canter said, "I never laid a finger on that woman."

"Then you better start thinking about somebody who might have, you little cocksucker, and the next time I talk to you, which is gonna be real fucking soon, you better think about giving me that name."

Martinson tugged on the gold rope with the Mercedes logo, and Canter's head came forward. He pulled it again, harder, but it stayed around his neck. Tightening the slack, the third time he used both hands, and snapping the clasp, he pitched the necklace into the gutter.

The Switching Station was an overgrown dive with delusions of glamour, and though it might've been plush once, that was a long time ago. Track lights illuminated the dregs of a shag carpet, and three high-backed booths lined one wall. A hanging lamp threw a dim puddle of light on a pool table. Somebody had taped an OUT OF ORDER sign on an unplugged pinball machine.

The bartender at the Calabash was right. The Switching Station had the dead-eyed makings of a tough, freaky crowd. Walking in, Lili counted six patrons and that number was instantly thinned by two. A pair of rugged Cubanos slipped out the second they made her for a cop.

Somebody's grandmother was bitching about her landlord in a drunken, foul-mouthed Spanish, but Lili didn't recognize the accent as Cuban. Salvadoran, Costa Rican. Something. A sideburned Romeo listened to her woes, nodding compulsively.

The bartender was dressed as a woman, but it

wouldn't be right to say he was in drag. He was making no effort to fool anybody. He had beefed-up arms, broad shoulders, and a thick, muscular neck. Sporting a pigtailed wig, he also had a dense mustache in addition to a solid five day-growth of beard. He was shirtless under a gingham jumper, a tragic Dorothy taken a twisted trail west of the Yellow Brick Road.

Lili badged him and showed him JP Beaumond's mug shots.

"Yeah, I know him. Pulled a knife in here once." He had a rumbling voice, not a queenie lilt. Lili had never seen it done quite like this before. The wig, the clothes, the beard. The guy must've been on the cutting edge of some new gay style.

"Is he a regular here?"

"He's been in a few times. I wouldn't say regular. What'd he do now?"

A pockmarked poppo called him away. There was one other customer at the bar, a white male, maybe twenty-five. He was wearing a Ricardo Montalban suit, and had his heels hooked over the rung of his bar stool. He tapped his feet in the air, eyes darting, waiting for the action to start.

When the bartender came back, Lili said, "Actually, I'm looking for his buddy. Young kid, tall, probably Cuban. You ever see him come in here with anybody matching that description?"

"You gotta mean Alex. This other guy, the short one, he's fairly new to the scene. Alex's been around for years."

"So you know him?"

"Like I said, he's been around for years. Miami native, if I'm not mistaken. Last name Hernandez, Fernandez, something real common. Did you try the Ron-Da-Voo?"

"Not yet. Have you seen him lately?"

"Not since the night the short guy pulled the knife. They came in together. Alex's fucked up, like everybody else who hangs out here, but he wouldn't hurt a fly. What kind of trouble is he in?"

"I just wanna talk to him."

"I'm sorry to hear that," the bartender said. "He really is a gentle, sweet-hearted kid. But that other one is a chemical spill. Completely toxic. He'll never get in here again, I can tell you that. Just do me a favor," he said, tossing a pigtail over his shoulder. "Don't give me up, okay? It'd be bad for business."

"Not a problem," Lili said. "I appreciate your help."

"And I appreciate yours."

This was years before the hype washed over this town like a tidal wave, when all of South Miami Beach was sick with a poverty and an off-the-graph crime rate no European land baron or transplanted nightclub impresario, no Hollywood schlockenstein wanted to touch:

The punk's name was John Colangelo, a Times Square hustler whose bloom was so long off his rose he'd been niggled into running a short con with his boyfriend, Rudy Burkalter. They took out some classified ads and a PO Box, and had suckers mail in checks and money orders made out to their bogus company. It was a rock-bottom bunco scheme, but they weren't after any prizes for originality. And it wasn't like they were making millions or even thousands, though they did have a few hundred bucks coming in every week, enough to cover the rent on their flop, enough to keep them in jumbos and T-Bird.

The fight was most likely over money. Colangelo grabbed the first thing handy, a cast iron frying pan, and whacked Burkalter with it. Then he hit him again. And again. Twenty-six times all together, until Burkalter's head was a squishy nub on top of his neck. Colangelo emptied their post office box one last time, cashed the checks, and hit the road.

Who knows what he was thinking? Maybe he just wanted to go where the weather was warm.

But Miami Beach was not then and not now an ideal location to go on the lam. First of all, it was an island, and east of the city, you were in the Atlantic Ocean. West, you'd run into the Everglades. South, there was one lonesome road in and out of the Keys. And north was the direction Colangelo had run from. He was at the end of the line.

Before long, somebody made him for John Colangelo, who was wanted for the murder of Rudy Burkalter. That same somebody, his greedy heart set on some imagined reward, phoned the NYPD and informed them that John Colangelo was occupying quarters in an Ocean Drive fleabag, where he was registered as Jerry Collins.

Homicide detective Pat Judice called Beach police and gave them the rundown on John Colangelo. He also gave them the name of the hotel where Colangelo was holed up, a building that had since been torn down to make way for the inevitable forces of progress, a hotel whose name, at the moment, escaped Arnie Martinson.

Colangelo was not there when Martinson and Frank Matzalanis arrived to collect the debt he owed New York State, not to mention the memory of Rudy Burkalter. So they waited. They waited six hours. And during that six hours, Colangelo, with an overwhelming longing to return to his salad days, or perhaps just in need of some company or some cash, made a date with a Philadelphia businessman. The businessman's wife, it turned out, was in another hotel room way up Collins Avenue.

Martinson was stretched out on the lumpy mattress, and Matzalanis sat on a rickety chair, with the lights off. By then, it was dark. When they heard voices in the hallway, they stood up and positioned themselves on either side of the door. They drew their weapons. The door opened, and as Colangelo reached for the wall switch, Martinson stuck the barrel of his .38 caliber service revolver into John Colangelo's right ear. The key still clammy between a thumb and a forefinger, Colangelo raised his hands. His trick let out a bark before he broke down in sobs.

Pat Judice arrived the next day with a partner, and they flew back to New York with John Colangelo. Colangelo confessed. He copped a manslaughter plea and was sentenced to not less than fifteen years. He would be just about eligible for his second shot at parole now.

Judice was a ginger-haired man with a dozen years in on the hotshot Homicide Division. Arnie was wondering how he was getting along.

"Pretty good," Judice said, over the long distance line. "I feel pretty good for a man my age."

"I don't know what kind of time you've got," Martinson said, then used up some of it breaking down the Manfred Pfiser case. How they were getting close to a guy named Harry Healy.

"A precinct detective up there's working something on a known associate of Healy's, a loser by the name of Jimmy De Steffano. They took a fall together way back when, and this precinct guy, he figures they're never too far out of each other's sight."

Pat Judice said, "What's the cop's name?"

"Cop is named Don Kellog and he works out of the, let's see, Ninth Precinct. The Ninth."

"Right. Don Kellog, Ninth Precinct."

"Collared our man not long ago, as it turns out," Martinson said, "before he made detective."

"Nice," Judice said.

"Anyway, I need this Healy soon as I can get him. I'm not squeezing you, but we could really use a hand with this."

"I'm not making any promises, Arnie, but I'll help you out if I can."

"That's all I'm asking," Martinson said.

Judice said, "I've gotta go rid the streets of crime."

"Whatever you can do to make this happen," Martinson was about to say, but by that time he was talking into a disconnected line. Just then, he remembered the name of the hotel where he arrested John Colangelo. It was called the Sao Paulo.

The computer hit thirteen times on the name Alejandro Hernandez. Six of them were incarcerated, and of the two out of seven who were still in their twenties and free for the time being, one was five feet, two inches tall, and the other one was black.

A similar search on the name Alejandro Fernandez spit up eleven names, nine of whom were currently guests of the state, so Lili requested the records of the two on the outside. They were the same height and the same age, but the one who had a criminal record stretching back to his sixteenth birthday had also managed to lose an eye somewhere along the way.

That left one Fernandez, Alejandro, also known as Alex. Born: 7/3/68. Height: 6'2". Weight: 140. In this photo, he was a doe-eyed kid with close-cropped hair, taken when he got busted for possession of a controlled substance, a quarter-gram of cocaine. The judge suspended his sentence. Lili got into her car and drove to

15th Street in Hialeah, the address listed on his record.

The Medical Examiner's report stated that if Pfiser was shot while he was standing, then he had been killed by a person shorter than himself. This eliminated everybody but Beaumond. Only they couldn't ascertain whether Pfiser was standing. In that case, why not Healy for Pfiser? Why not Leo Hannah? And why not Fernandez, Martinson had said, and Lili thought sure, why not?

The house was finished with stucco, like most of the other homes on the block. There was a grapefruit tree in the front yard, and the dug-out circle around the base of its trunk had been filled in with white stones. A line of shrubs banked the front of the place, six squat bushes trimmed to identical height. Two taller ones, shaped to resemble Christmas trees, grew on either end of the row.

The driveway was paved and sealed with tar, giving it a smooth, blue-black sheen. The front stoop was shallow, six feet wide by four feet deep, but evidently, somebody enjoyed watching the world from this perch: A lawn chair leaned against the stucco.

The screen door looked in on a sofa covered with a knitted blanket. A painting of a bullfight's final stages hung behind it.

Lili pushed the doorbell and got startled by a buzzing twice as loud as it needed to be. The laughtrack of a sitcom was rising and falling somewhere in the house. She was going to hit the buzzer again when Alex Fernandez came into view, tall and lanky, his Soul Train afro intact.

She said, "Alex Fernandez?" She had her badge in her right hand.

The kid tilted his head like he was about to say Yeah, pivoted off his left foot, and disappeared. Lili ran toward the driveway side of the house. Another screen door banged shut. She rounded the corner to see the long-legged Fernandez scrambling over a chain link fence, his feet moving as he hit the sod in his neighbor's back yard. Lili took off after him.

She hopped the same set of fences, her gun flapping against her hip in its holster. She yelled for him to stop, that she was the police. That was stupid. He knew exactly who she was.

He continued in a southerly direction, loping through a second set of yards. Lili felt confident on the hard pavement of the street, the asphalt and concrete, where the footing was certain and it was easier to run. Fernandez had veered east on 13th Street, and Lili caught a flash of one sneakered foot before it vanished around a corner. She followed it.

He cleared another fence and landed in a yard guarded by a snarling German Shepherd. Drool flew from its snapping jowls. Fernandez raced the animal to the back fence and won, the dog leaving all four of its feet in a last lunge the kid beat by some miracle.

Lili ran alongside the fence. She was closing the gap. Her breathing was deep and steady. If Fernandez wanted to run all day, that's what she would do. She yelled, Stop, Police a couple more times in a couple more places, and as he hit 11th Street, he showed signs of weakening. His arms pumped crazily. His head lolled.

He came to another fence. Spooked by his confrontation with the dog, he dashed past the fronts of a few houses. Lili gained ground. "Your time's up," she yelled. "Where're you running to?"

He headed down an alley. Lili was right behind him.

Coming to 9th Street, he pulled up short and shot a look back. He took two steps to his right, kicked it into gear, and broke east again, toward Palm Avenue. The light was against him. Two lanes, both directions, heavy traffic.

He dashed into the intersection, clearing the northbound vehicles. Lili got hung up on the curb. She yelled one last time for Alex Fernandez to stop. Looking over his shoulder, he sprinted off the safety island and directly into the path of a late-model Buick. They collided with a crunch of steel and bone. Fernandez got knocked ten feet into the air, and flipped a reverse somersault, his ankles bent back over his head, forming an inverted U. She was close enough to see the shock on his face. Thinking about it later, Lili would've sworn they made eye contact while he was still in the air.

He hit the street with a smack. The driver of the truck that ran over his legs and snagged him and dragged him had less than a second to hit the brakes, which he did, with an air-piercing screech. It sounded like a lullaby next to the scream he let go of when he jumped out of his truck and saw what he had done.

Chapter Fifteen

Sweet.

Oh yeah, this was sweet.

Just as sweet as sweet could be, live from Hialeah, Chopper Lens pointing straight down on the corner where Alex Fernandez had been hit by two cars and killed. Cut to a ground shot, and a picture of Alex's mother, her wide mouth wailing one unbroken, dry-eyed sob. The frame went shaky after a few seconds, one of

Fernandez's uncles, Leo thought, taking a swing at the cameraman.

Leo felt sorry for Alex. He felt sorry for Alex's mom, for his sister, and for the uncle. On the other hand, the hand that counted, he didn't have to worry any more about Alex blabbing to the cops. He'd done the right thing, waiting him out. Fernandez was dead and Leo didn't have a thing, not one thing, to do with it.

But here was the true genius: Fernandez got run over jetting from the same sexy cop who was here busting Leo's balls just a day or two ago, Detective Lili Acevedo. Well, according to the television, Detective Lili Acevedo was in deep shit. The Fernandez family had hired a lawyer, and he was suing the City of Miami Beach for $163 million, due to the reckless and irresponsible behavior of Detective Lili Acevedo. A young man had been cut down in his prime, an act of criminally negligent homicide, if not outright murder.

There was footage of Acevedo wearing her cheap-ass sunglasses, surrounded by cops and lawyers of her own. The head of her union, his mustached cop's face hogging the screen, was convinced a subsequent inquiry would reveal Detective Acevedo acted in full compliance with Department guidelines regarding the pursuit of a suspect. She had not fired a single shot. At no time did she draw her weapon. He was one hundred percent confident she would be cleared of any wrongdoing.

In the old days, the days before sexy Cuban detectives, before Beaumond and Fernandez or even Manfred, when he had fresh leases on a six-room house and a fine British automobile, Leo might've taken a margarita into the back yard and gotten into the Jacuzzi to feel the warm sun on his face, dreaming his dreams of endless possibility. What happened? It wasn't that long ago.

He didn't feel so much possibility now. For one thing, somehow or other he had managed to spend nineteen thousand dollars in three months. All he was doing was spending money, so he couldn't claim it as a total shock, but where could almost twenty grand have gone? This was after the house and the Jag, twenty thousand of his grandfather's hard-earned dollars roaring up and down the Beach.

And then he thought of something else: Vicki, who must have been the one who'd ratted him out.

There was a moment back there, when Leo was on his roll, that he was looking for Vicki, and he was going to take care of her, too. He was sitting at that Ocean Drive café. His eyes mine-swept the crowd for her, because he knew if he just sat there long enough, Vicki would pass by. But then he forgot her. Didn't give her another thought after that evil afternoon until a minute ago, when it was too late to do anything about her. This was why you had to watch. The one kink out there against you, if you didn't eliminate it, was the one that would take you down.

His path was so hard and bright, and he let Whitney get in his way. Whitney, a pain in the ass who caught his eye and cost him money and made him forget Vicki, who by all rights should be alligator shit right now. Okay, the alligator part didn't work out, but still.

Another thing pissed him off. What had the cops done with Harry Healy besides crash Leo's door one sunshiny morning and throw the guy back in his face? Leo figured he'd found the perfect patsy once he worked out that Vicki knew Harry's girlfriend. And though the girlfriend told Vicki she was done with Harry forever, she knew pretty much to the second when he was getting out. When it turned out Manfred knew Harry, too, come on, who could blame Leo for setting this up?

But then instead of calling when Harry got back to the hotel, Vicki got scared and ran, leaving it to Leo, and that meant to Beaumond and Fernandez, to take care of business.

That's where it had gone wrong. Leo'd just meant for Healy to absorb the heat from the robbery. He fully expected to see Manfred, if not the next day, then the day after. He didn't think that pig-ignorant, white trash piece of shit Beaumond was going to shoot him.

Leo was so glad Beaumond was dead. He was so happy he'd killed him. But where did that leave Leo now?

More bad news: Between Whitney and Jo Ann, Leo was down to an eightball. Not counting the quarter ounce he had stashed in the freezer, tucked between two slices of a loaf of Wonder Bread, where nobody would ever think to look for it.

The sun burned yellow outside, but every curtain and blind was shut tight against the day. Leo spilled some coke onto his plate, carved up a juicy fat line, and mowed it down. The sounds coming from the carport turned out to be the central air kicking on, but the upstairs part of the house was making noises, too. He checked the closets and looked under the beds. He searched the carport again, then took a quick peek into the back yard, before he was satisfied that everything was chill.

The phone rang and he picked it up without thinking. What a mistake.

"Hey, baby," Whitney said, "What's going on over there?"

"Nothing," he said. "I'm not feeling too good today." He downed a shot of Cuervo and tried to get his lie over with a few fake coughs.

"You don't sound too good."

"No," Leo said. "Matter of fact, I just took a bunch of stuff and I'm gonna go lay down. Try and sleep this thing off, whatever it is."

"Have you got a fever?"

Leo touched the back of his wrist to his forehead. "A fever," he said, "yeah, I think I do."

"You better be careful it doesn't turn into something else," she said. She wanted to know if he'd talked to Homes-Leighton.

Homes-Leighton had left a bunch of messages, when was it, the day before yesterday, but Leo hadn't called him back. "I haven't heard from the guy," he said.

She started to thank him for hooking her up with Lawrence. He had gotten her some unpaid extra work on this movie he was shooting. Whitney was hurting his ears.

"I feel like I'm gonna pass out," he said. "I'll call you when I'm feeling better." He was never going to feel well enough to call Whitney, but whatever.

He hung up and unplugged the phone. He wasn't taking any calls today, he wasn't making any calls, and nobody better show up at his door, that's all he had to say.

He had divided another pile into four bumps when it hit him: The dining room was a very dangerous location. The edges of the curtains were framed with light, and if somebody had been looking in, they would've seen him with his plate and his straw and his finely chopped powder. The only place that was safe was the upstairs bathroom. Leo climbed the stairs, went in, and locked the door. Stepping into the tub, he pulled the shower door closed. He sucked up two quick lines, then two more. He took his toothbrush and scrubbed that tequila taste out of his mouth until the foam he spit into the sink was speckled with blood. Soon as he could find his car keys, he'd drive to the liquor store, stock up, and get himself set so there'd be no reason, no reason at all, for him to leave the house.

His mission succeeded, yielding a half-gallon of Cuervo and a carton of Marlboros. But the ride home just about made his heart stop. A white-haired police lady followed him for a two-mile stretch. She was driving an '89 Grand Marquis, robin's egg blue, the seat pushed forward as far as it would go, her head just peering over the dashboard and her wrinkled fingers gripping the wheel at the ten o'clock and two o'clock positions, just like they taught in Driver's Ed, a deep-cover cop they were using to trick him.

Instead, Leo tricked her. He deliberately drove past his house, making a series of quick turns that got her confused. Losing the old bitch speeding through the back streets, he made a sharp turn into the driveway, and pulled the Jag all the way into the carport.

He supposed the coast was clear enough to prepare a cocktail, but what Leo could really go for right now was a nice hit off the pipe.

If he could figure out what he did with his pipe. He remembered hiding it from Whitney. It was under something. The kitchen sink. Behind the Ajax and the Drano and the Formula 409, wrapped in a remnant of a blanket he used to polish the Jag.

The house was getting dark, but Leo left the lights off. He secured himself in the closet of the spare bedroom. He had all the light he needed, right here in his palm.

He sparked a dime-sized boulder that almost didn't fit in the bowl, sucking till the chunk glowed orange and the chamber was trapping a fearsome grey cloud. Smoke boomed into his lungs, right to the top of his throat. His ears crackled with a buzzing, like crickets on a crazy-hot afternoon. He held the hit, and when the buzzing died down, he let it go. Lights blinked. Lights winked and lights flashed at the edge of his peripheral vision.

The racket that echoed from every corner of the house forced him to investigate. Flashes followed him down the hall—that's how he knew the lights were strobing inside his head, and not outside of it. Reconnoitering the living room, his back flush with a wall, he raked his shin against an end table. When he got to the kitchen, it went quiet, waiting till he got back upstairs before it started up again.

He sifted the bag for a tasty rock, but it was getting powdery in there. Selecting three pebbles, he cooked them and held the smoke, listening for that cricket buzz, but this blast was weak, just a hum, and it faded after a few seconds.

Now there was trouble outside. Big trouble in the form of a cop parked at the curb. The car was the same model as a police cruiser, without the gumballs and the splashy paint job. No tricks this time. The guy looked a lot more like a cop than any white-haired granny or sexy Cuban chick, that was for sure.

Leo could make out the cop's profile in the streetlamp glow. High forehead, short cop's haircut, squared-off jaw a few years from going jowly. He was holding a spray inhaler to his nose, took a blast in one nostril, then the other, just sitting there. Probably waiting for Leo to do something stupid, like flip on the lights, give the cop some kind of sign he was home. He retreated to the spare bedroom and slipped into his closet. He'd wait right here. He dared the cop to try to come in and find him. He dared him.

He was sure an hour had passed, but it might've been more, when he combat-crawled back to the master bedroom. He peeked over the windowsill. Leo had won. The cop was gone. The cop was gone and it was safe to go downstairs.

A good thing, too, because as Leo headed down the stairs to go switch this powdery bag for the chunky fat one in the freezer, he heard glass breaking. He traced it right away to the sliding door. A tiny crash, then the clink-clink of shards raining down on the linoleum. The definite click of the latch being turned. The heavy door slid a few feet on its track.

It couldn't be the cop. This had to be a burglar, somebody thinking he wasn't home because the house was so dark. Then, rounding the corner from the dining room to the kitchen, it wasn't dark at all.

The lights popped on and Leo saw it wasn't the cops and it wasn't a burglar, it was that fat little fucker Negrito with some greaseball sidekick. He was taller than Negrito, like that was saying anything, and he was wearing a suit that was tight under the arms. His horrid tie featured diamonds, swirls, and stripes, red, blue and beige against a silver background. He had a gun in his hand and so did Negrito.

It dawned on Leo that he had made two very serious miscalculations. One, he should have run away from the sound of the breaking glass and not toward it. Two, he should've kept the gun he used to shoot Beaumond. He wasn't looking all that bright right now, up against Negrito and this other spic with the shocking taste in neckwear, no weapon to protect him.

Leo said, "What the fuck're you doing?"

The muzzle flash surprised him. He didn't think you'd be able to see it in the light.

Negrito's shot hit him in the shoulder. It spun him around and it took his legs and he cracked his head against the kitchen table. That hurt. He put his hand to his forehead, feeling for blood, thinking this had turned a lot more serious than it had originally seemed. The second shot went in below his fourth rib, and he wouldn't swear to it, but he thought he heard a third. Leo Hannah left this world wondering why people always made such a big deal over dying. It was the easiest thing he had ever done.

Chapter Sixteen

Harry wanted to meet his brother somewhere far from his office, where the restaurants weren't jammed with the cheap suits from Grand Street, guys who had two settings, overdrive and dead. Arthur had been one of those cheap suits in the '80s, but he'd emerged from the decade a wealthy Healy, his heart still beating and his record unblemished. His wingtips had licked a crazy Fred Astaire on the outskirts of some headline-grabbing scandals, and he'd hustled with guys who did Fed time, but he'd steered clear himself, and the end result was he still had a desk at Salomon while his buddies had to content themselves with lecturing at universities.

Harry didn't know exactly what his brother did, and he got further confused when Arthur tried to break it down for him. The bottom line was, if Wall Street was rocking in one direction or the other, Arthur got quoted in newspaper stories, and because he was good at describing the action in terms anybody but Harry could understand, he frequently popped up on cable TV shows like the one Aggie saw him on, holding forth on what it all meant. Arthur in suspenders and one of his monogrammed shirts, amused and giving the impression the subject was serious, but not too serious.

The restaurant he picked out was known for its sushi. Harry hoped they served something else. He wasn't too big on raw fish.

Arthur was blowing out a cloud of cigarette smoke, sitting at the bar and chatting with the bartender. His suit was grey and his shirt was grey, and a burgundy pocket square peeked out of his pocket and matched his tie. He hugged Harry and kissed him on the cheek.

Harry followed him to a podium, where a guy with coal-black hair was waiting. He nodded at Harry and shook Arthur's hand, then penciling a line thorough Arthur's reservation, he said, "Right this way." Their table was in a corner.

"Perfect," Arthur said. He shook the guy's hand again, this time with a folded bill in his palm.

Harry said, "I thought you had juice here."

"I've got juice everywhere."

"Then why'd you tighten up the maitre d'? The joint's deserted."

"Yeah, tonight. What about tomorrow," Arthur said, "or Friday? I get an oil guy in from Texas. His wife reads about Soho in *Newsweek*, and they mention this restaurant. We show up at eight-thirty, no reservation, we're looking at a two-hour wait. I explain the situation to my man, and as soon as something's free, we're dining. I look like a big man in front of my client and his wife. If it costs me an extra twenty or thirty when I'm here, so what?"

Harry lit a Marlboro, and he was looking for someplace to put the match. "Why did he seat us in non-smoking? Don't you wanna smoke?"

"I always want to smoke," Arthur said. "Unfortunately, I can't do it in the dining room. You're going to have to turn that off."

"You're kidding," Harry said.

"He's not kidding," their waitress said. In spite of the tattoo that marred the milky skin on her shoulder, she looked wholesome, with muscular thighs and a high, round ass. She pulled an ashtray out of her apron, and set it on the table. "Sorry."

"Not your fault," Arthur said. "You didn't vote for that ordinance, did you?"

"As a matter of fact, they didn't consult me."

Harry huffed a last drag and squelched his smoke.

"There's all these, like, draconian social laws," the waitress said. "Don't smoke, don't eat, don't drink, don't, don't, don't."

Arthur said, "Draconian?"

"That's right. I said draconian and I meant draconian. I've been to college. What are you guys drinking?"

Arthur asked for a vodka and soda and Harry ordered a beer. He studied his brother. His haircut was flawless. His clothes, immaculate. Personal demeanor, enviable. How could you lose if you were Arthur Healy?

"This is how you know you're getting old," Arthur said. "I'm probably her father's age, but I'd love to bang her. Take a look at that walk."

Harry watched the waitress switch her hips back to the bar.

"Just like a woman," Arthur said.

"Speaking of women, how's your wife?"

The waitress brought their drinks. Arthur ordered sushi and a salad. Harry looked through the menu, ordered the Szechuan sirloin. Szechuan. What kind of restaurant was this?

"The old man told me you ambushed him the other day. He seem okay to you?"

What was there to say? The old man was the old man. Harry said, "Fine," and then to change the subject, "How're the kids doing?"

"Teenagers," Arthur said. "They're a constant worry. Last week, Odette went on her first date where it was just her and the boy. I thought I was going to start crying."

"What is she, sixteen? That's old enough. What was the kid like?"

"Very tall. Captain of the basketball team."

"He doesn't sound too threatening."

"He wasn't. But when I pulled him aside to slip him a few bucks, I told him, with this big smile on my face, he doesn't have my little girl back under my roof by midnight, I was gonna set his car on fire."

"What time did he get her home?"

"You think I was watching the clock?" Arthur stopped chewing, arugula and a bit of onion impaled on his fork. "It was eleven twenty-four."

Arthur handled his chopsticks like he'd never used a knife or fork, dislodging a fish chunk from its marble pedestal, dipping it into a shallow bowl of soy sauce clotted with atomic green mustard. Harry wondered where he picked up these Asian table manners. Certainly not at home. Arthur was pure self-invention, and this invented self was very pleasing to the world. Harry was more or less self-invented too, except it won him friends like Jimmy De Steffano.

"How's that steak?"

"Very tasty," Harry said. Which it was. Very tasty. It just didn't taste very good.

"How about you?" Arthur said. "How're you doing?"

Harry said, "To tell you the truth, Art, I'm in a lot of fucking trouble."

The dining room had filled up around them. The waitress hustled to stay on top of her section, people asking for more water and more soy sauce and more cocktails, but when Arthur smiled at her, she stopped in her tracks.

He ordered a lichee mousse that came in a martini glass, a mint leaf sticking out of the top of it. Harry asked for a double Dewar's, neat. Maybe he'd get drunk. Then maybe he'd go find Jimmy De Steffano, that shouldn't be too hard, and give him a beating, just for fun.

"You understand now," Arthur was saying, "your first mistake." A smear of mousse had the nerve to settle on his top lip. He wiped it away, eyes narrowing at the stain on the napkin.

"Which mistake are you referring to?"

"The one you made by not calling me."

"I thought about it," Harry said. "I did."

"Then why didn't you do it?"

"Because I was ashamed." And he was. Ashamed then, and even more ashamed now.

Arthur's hand cut the air. "We retain legal counsel immediately," he said, more to himself than to Harry. "First thing in the morning, you call me at the office. I get to work early."

And that put the matter to rest. No questions regarding guilt or innocence. Arthur had all the details he needed. Decide. Act. Be in charge. Nothing could go wrong as long as he was pulling the strings. He straightened his tie and set his jaw, like asking for the check was the first step of this new challenge and there was no way Arthur Healy was going to fail.

If Arthur was going to hire an attorney, Connor Merrill was exactly the kind of brand-name mouthpiece he'd come up with. He made his bones in the '80s, like Arthur, when he demolished a set of RICO beefs the Feds were hanging on two mob bosses. Crooked bureaucrats were fitted for halos under his counsel, and there was a judge still sitting on a bench somewhere in Texas thanks to Connor Merrill.

Whenever Merrill showed up on TV or in the papers, it was to issue a tight-lipped no comment. After a case was decided, Merrill would read from a single page, a paragraph or two that took thirty seconds, and he didn't hang around to answer anybody's questions. Connor Merrill was old school.

His corner office had views that looked north and east for miles. The 59th Street Bridge looked close enough for Harry to touch, Queens spreading out on the polluted horizon, the hills of Harlem visible up Lexington Avenue.

Harry was sitting on his leather couch. Merrill was sitting on the chair that made it a set, relaxed and confident in the way that people who have money are relaxed and confident.

"Do me a favor," the attorney was saying, "lose the charming low-life routine."

He was wearing a navy blue suit, serious and precise. A taut, trim man, Merrill's eyes were slate grey, and his thin nose was perfectly aligned on his narrow face. His hair was going silver at the temples, but only there, and Harry wondered if the rest of his follicles weren't receiving some sort of cosmetic assistance.

"Let's get back to Leo," Merrill said.

"It was like he was waiting for me."

"Are you trying to tell me you were framed?"

"Framed seems too advanced for Leo. But yeah, he set me up."

Merrill leaned in, his suit sleeves riding above his ruby

cufflinks. "You understand I can't help you if you're lying."

Harry was stung. "I'm doing the best I can."

Merrill got up and walked to his desk. It was uncluttered with snapshots or books. He didn't use an in-and-out box. The only items taking up space on it were an ink blotter and a telephone. He slid a yellow legal pad out of a drawer.

"Is there anybody who can corroborate your story?"

"There's this chick Vicki, the one who was in Manfred's room when I went to go pick up the package. She knows he was alive when I left. But she wasn't there when I got back."

"The good news, Mr. Healy, is that the burden of proof is on the state. We don't have to prove you didn't do it. They have to prove that you did."

Harry got off the leather couch and went to stand by the windows. Merrill seemed far away. "You don't believe me, do you?"

"If I'm going to represent you, I have no choice but to assume you're telling the truth."

Somehow Merrill was managing to make Harry feel guilty, even though every word he'd spoken was true.

"What we're going to do is negotiate your surrender, and let them worry about building a case against you for this murder you didn't commit."

"What about all the other charges?"

"We'll get to them. Let's take care of your biggest problem first. You're going to go spend an extremely quiet evening at home, wherever home is, and you're going to be back here at nine o'clock tomorrow morning. Do you understand?"

Harry said, "That's it?"

"No, that's not it," Merrill said. "But that's all you need

to worry about for now." He stood up, and Harry was dismissed, like a bad boy who was finished serving his detention.

He rode the elevator for thirty floors. It was raining again, like it had every day since he got to New York, and it was icy cold. Walking down Third Avenue, trying to get his teeth to stop chattering, it felt more like November than April. He pushed his hands deep into the pockets of his jeans and lowered his chin.

One of the thoughts Harry tried to keep on the run, with the help of a lot of scotch, was that he'd played an important part in bringing himself to this point. It wasn't as if things had just been done to him. Bad thinking led to bad decisions, and bad decisions led to stupid actions. It made him feel dizzy, this whole interconnectedness of things. Every event in life was knotted around the thing that happened before it, and led straight into the thing that came after it.

If he hadn't been involved with Julia, what were the odds of him meeting Leo? A billion to one? And if he'd ever bothered to make something of himself, he wouldn't have been delivering cocaine to parties that had guests like Julia. He wouldn't have worked for Frankie Yin, and he never would've met Manfred. Poor old Manfred. His poor Dutch Uncle. Was it Manfred who set off this chain reaction of bad juju? Or was it Harry? Or just destiny?

Another thought was chasing him, and he let it catch him in the foyer of a Chinese take-out joint. Harry bought a Coke with a ten-dollar bill. He asked for his change in coins. This drew a fractured complaint from the counterman, but he gave it up anyway.

A Bud Light clock on the wall said it was five after three. Harry pictured Aggie staring at her computer screen, typing in a line, maybe reading it out loud, a half-eaten cup of yogurt sitting on her desk.

She picked up on the first ring. She said hello twice.

Harry said, "Hi."

She didn't recognize his voice.

"It's Harry," he said.

Now that she knew who it was, she wasn't talking.

"I called to see how you were doing."

"I'm fine," she said. There was a sinking pause, like she wasn't going to say anything more, but when Harry let the line stay silent she said, "How're you?"

"I'm coming back."

"Detective Arnie Martinson will be thrilled."

"My brother hired me a lawyer. I'm giving myself up."

"So I should look for you on the six o'clock news. What'd you do, call to warn me?"

"No, I called to say I've been thinking about you. And that I missed you. Depending on the way things shake out, I was thinking maybe we could get together."

The street door banged open and a deliveryman pushed past. He was wearing a yellow rain slicker and a pair of yellow boots that buckled up the front, like a kid's.

"I think we've got a chance," Harry said. "I really do."

It sounded like Aggie was smoking. She said, "A chance at what?" Then she said something else Harry didn't hear because a recorded voice was talking over her, telling him to put in more money or his call was going to get cut off. He dropped in four more quarters.

When the beeps stopped, Harry said, "A chance at being together."

"How could you even be thinking about that? For all you know, you could be going to jail for the rest of your life."

"All I'm saying is, I really care about you, Aggie."

"Harry," she said, "I've gotta go. I wish you all the luck in the world."

"Can I call you?"

"I didn't hang up, did I? Although I probably should have. Goodbye, Harry."

Davey Boy was talking on the phone with his feet on the desk. Harry nodded on his way to the elevator, but Davey had been blowing hot and cold since Harry rented the room, friendly or not according to his mood. Today, not.

He wished he'd thrown the extra twenty-five a week for a TV. At least it'd take his mind off of things, and he could have drowned out the game show blaring next door, cartoony bleeps and buzzes knifing through the plaster.

Glancing through the sports section of the *Post*, he saw the Mets had dropped their home opener, the Yankees got snowed out in Cleveland, and the Knicks were scuffling toward the playoffs. A column by the guy who covered the team predicted they wouldn't make it past the first round.

A vampire cult in Florida made page one. Some sixteen-year-old had lured a classmate into the woods, dragged a machete across the kid's windpipe, and drank his blood. The cops said it was the initiation into a secret society, and a bunch of teenage bloodsuckers who flipped had lined up to testify against the lead vampire. This was outside Orlando. An entire state of freaks, Florida. And Harry was going back.

Voices filtered through the door. Whispering voices, vibing wrong, a threat in the tenor of their hissing. Harry was about to get up and check it out when the door blew open and somebody screamed police. Two guys pinned him to the bed and turned him on his stomach, the flash of a third guy pointing a gun. They tore back his arms. Harry heard a pop, his shoulder dislocating again, and a spiking pain engulfed the joint. If he ended up in the Florida State Pen after all, he was going to get the surgery done on that shoulder, for sure.

The cops pulled him to his feet.

"You guys," Harry winced through his gritted teeth, "have got this all wrong."

Chapter Seventeen

The lawyers for the union assured Lili the Review Board inquiry would amount to nothing, and Kramer called her reassignment a public relations move, but Acevedo wouldn't be back in the field until the heat from the Fernandez thing burned out, and that was going to take some time.

Which was a shame. By all rights, it should've been Lili who went to the airport and met the U.S. Marshalls who had Healy in custody. Instead, Kramer sent Robotaille and Martinson. He wanted to make sure there was a Beach detective on each of Healy's handcuffed arms, and he instructed them to bring the suspect through the front door.

Martinson wanted to book him as quietly as possible. They didn't have enough evidence to charge him with Manfred Pfiser's murder, they were just busting him on a parole violation. But Kramer alerted his friends in the media and every TV station dispatched a crew to Rocky Pomerance Plaza. It was a slow trudge from the street to the entrance, a classic perp walk.

Healy kept his mouth shut and his chin up. No flashbulb flinching, no shackled peek-a-boo, no burying his face under a hooded sweatshirt. He stared straight ahead, and let Robotaille and Martinson lead him through the front door, where three uniformed cops intercepted the jostling bodies.

Due to some screw-up between New York and the Marshalls' office, Healy arrived without his lawyer, but rather than turning to stone, he wanted to talk. He had a lot to say. Unfortunately, he wasn't able to tell them anything.

"Just so you know I know," he told Martinson at one point, "I don't have to answer a single one of these questions until my attorney gets here. But to tell you the truth, I'd rather be talking to you than sweating my ass off in some jail cell."

Lili was standing with Kramer outside the interview room, watching and listening through the two-way glass. Martinson made Healy run through his story another time. Healy wasn't disrespectful, but his breezy tone was bugging her. He seemed relaxed, almost relieved, like a man with a weight off his shoulders.

Martinson told him they lifted a fingerprint that belonged to him off the stereo in Pfiser's room. Healy didn't deny being there.

"I shut it off," he said. "It was blaring some Patsy Cline thing. I wiped down the scotch bottles and the glasses, but I forgot about the stop button on the stereo."

He had drained his second can of Coke, and now he was wondering about coffee. Martinson shifted his gaze toward the mirror, nodding his head yes, and Lili had to go fetch him a cup.

"Light and sweet," Healy said.

Martinson was waiting outside when she got back.

Kramer was chewing the inside of his lip, and everybody stayed mute as Arnie took the coffee and went back in. He set the cup on the table.

Healy led Martinson, for the third time, to the point where he ditched Pfiser's rented Mustang in Hollywood.

Arnie went soft. Acevedo was waiting for the chance to burn Healy down, hopefully before his lawyer got there.

"Tell me about your relationship with Leo Hannah."

"There was no relationship. I saw the guy exactly twice, once in jail, once on Ocean Drive. That's how much I know him."

"Were you aware of a conspiracy to rip off Pfiser?"

"I told you who's gonna help you is that chick, Vicki, who was in his room. She told Manfred her name was Jennifer. What does that tell you?"

"Why did you agree to meet with Pfiser when Hannah suggested you go see him? Didn't that make you the least bit suspicious? You just said there was no relationship."

"What can I say? I needed the two hundred."

Martinson said, "Who got the package, Harry?"

"What difference does that make?"

"I thought you said you wanted to talk. Help me out with this."

"Two queers in a motel room. This is the worst cup of coffee I've ever had in my life."

"What do you want for free? Tell me about JP Beaumond."

"I told you I don't know the guy," Healy said, and Martinson pushed Beaumond's mug shots at him again.

"JP Beaumond," Martinson said. "I'm just trying to get this clear in my mind."

"I don't need to look at him any more. I don't know him."

"What about him?" Martinson gave him a picture of Alex Fernandez.

"Ditto."

"In or out of the company of Leo Hannah."

"Look, you guys want me to help you make your case, I'll help you make a case, but I can't tell you what I don't know. You seem like a decent guy, but I think we're about done here. Where's that fucking lawyer? He's costing my brother a fortune."

Kramer was worrying a button on his sleeve, and he hadn't stopped chewing his lip. He was looking at Lili but she refused to meet his eyes. She was getting the awful, empty-gutted feeling that Healy was telling the truth, that while he might have been guilty of a lot of things, the murder of Manfred Pfiser wasn't one of them.

Healy was lawyered-up tight with a hot rod from New York named Connor Merrill, and Merrill hired a Palm Beach bulldog, Otto Wagner, to help him navigate Florida statutes. Kramer gave Acevedo her crack at Healy, but she didn't have any more luck with him than Arnie did. For his final interview, it was Kramer, Martinson, Acevedo, and both attorneys, with Assistant DA Whitaker Graves observing through the glass. Healy gave them a written statement. It didn't sway one letter from what he had been saying all along.

Graves was a serious young man with a pinkish complexion and scowl lines creasing his forehead. Kramer's lantern jaw was pulsing.

"What do you make of this guy, Arnie?" Kramer said.

Martinson said, "He didn't do it."

"What have we got left?"

"We've got Victoria Leonard," Lili said. "We figured she was lying to protect Fernandez. I wonder if she'll stick to her story now that he's dead."

"Would we have any shot at all with a grand jury?" Kramer asked Graves.

"John, your own detectives think somebody else did it."

"The Medical Examiner's opinion eliminates Healy," Martinson said. "Any grand jury would have to hear from him."

Graves said, "Forget this guy, John."

Kramer took a deep breath, let it out slowly. He was thinking about the bank of cameras set up in front of the building. He'd need to throw them something. He said, "What's happening with that thing on Pine Tree?"

Dade investigators recovered gravel from the cuffs of JP Beaumond's camouflage pants, and its composition matched the mix lining the driveway of Leo Hannah's house on Pine Tree Drive.

They also found fibers, manufactured by a company that sold carpets to General Motors in the late '80s, stubbornly clinging to those same fatigues. Martinson figured Hannah shot Beaumond on Pine Tree, dragged him out of the house, and loaded him into the trunk of an '89 Cadillac. Then he drove to the Glades and dumped the body. The car, what was left of it, had been found in Liberty City. It was registered to a Theodore Kistler of Biloxi, Mississippi, who identified Beaumond as the man who carjacked him in St. Cloud.

Martinson picked up the ringing phone. A voice talking through a handkerchief asked for him.

"This is Martinson," he said.

The muffled voice said, "People are saying Junior Fabricant for Josephine Simmons."

"Uh-huh," Martinson said. "Who's this?" He knew

who he was talking to, he just wanted to string him out.

"Don't worry who's this. Junior Fabricant for the old lady."

"Junior Fabricant." Martinson wrote the name on a slip of paper.

"That's right."

"Good work. You get an A in citizenship," Martinson said. "A for Anton."

There was a short lapse of dead air, and Anton Canter clicked off.

Lili was standing at the window, the late sun throwing an aura around her body. She stepped out of the fading light and headed over to where he was sitting. "It just seems like a lot of work for nothing."

He wanted to tell her that disappointment and frustration were a big part of this job. If that's all she learned from this case, she could take it with her through the rest of her career, which would continue decades after Martinson was comfortably retired, a notion he was giving more and more thought.

He asked her, "Did you ever try to keep a garden?"

Lili said, "I live in an apartment."

"Nothing but work," Martinson said. "Weeding and planting and watering, and then the animals get after your tomatoes or whatever, and you wonder why the hell you bother."

"I didn't know you had a green thumb."

Arnie said, "I don't. I'm drawing a comparison. The same way you have to trust that one season it's all going to come together and you're going to harvest that bumper crop, in this job you've got to trust that your work is worthwhile, even when the results suggest otherwise. Does that make sense? As you get older, you roll with the punches a little better. That's all I'm saying."

She walked away, and Arnie called her back.

"Hey, Lil," he said, "have you ever taken that drive to Key West?"

"Not since I was a kid."

"The weather's supposed to be beautiful Sunday. I was thinking of going for a ride. An old friend of mine owns a restaurant there, and if you're not doing anything…"

Lili laughed. "Are you asking me out?"

"That's what it sounds like to me."

"Would that be appropriate? In light of current sexual harassment guidelines, I mean."

"I'm not sure," Arnie said, "I'd have to refer back to my sensitivity training manual."

Arnie didn't think he was her type, and he didn't think Lili was his, either, but maybe it was time he found out.

She said she could be ready by around eleven. "By the way, we're supposed to be in the lieutenant's office for a pow-wow on this Hannah thing. Robotaille's working a lead, and Kramer wants to fill us in on the details."

"Alright," Martinson said, "let's get on it."

Chapter Eighteen

Four months after Harry moved in, Aggie started throwing up in the morning, and it was obviously more than a virus or some fluke stomach bug. She went to the drug store and brought home a test, and when that came back positive, she made an appointment to go see her doctor. He said she was eight weeks pregnant.

Harry did not think this was bad news. Just the opposite. He was thrilled.

Although Aggie had been wanting to have a baby, she didn't know if she was ready for it. She didn't know if this was the right time.

Fair enough. Who was ready to be a parent? But if everybody thought that way, they might as well give the world back to the monkeys.

His attitude was good, but his attitude alone didn't do enough to reassure Aggie.

"Think of it as having nothing to do with me," she said.

"That's stupid," Harry said. "It has everything to do with you."

"Then think of it as an independent event. Think about being a father. Think about me being dead, and you having sole responsibility for this child. How's that look?"

Harry despised hypothetical problems. They were a waste of time. He'd rather deal with the reality of a situation, and the reality of this one was, there was going to be a third tiny existence in the apartment that was going to need to be fed and burped and have shoes bought for it.

"Statistically," he said, "I'll be around for another thirty-five years, minus a few on the back end if I don't quit smoking soon. What're you now, twenty-nine?"

"Twenty-nine," she said.

"Odds are you make it to seventy-eight. Not a bad run, all things considered. That's almost fifty years. You're going to be tied to me for thirty-five of those fifty years."

There. Right back at her. "Which is like what, seventy percent of the rest of your life? Think about it."

"I have thought about it, only you make it sound like you're selling insurance."

"Gambling is what I had in mind," Harry said, "but insurance is good. It's like taking a stake in the future. I'm not saying I have any confidence in the future, but it's going to get here regardless. I say we have the kid."

Lying in bed a couple nights later, imagining a son, Harry thought about playing catch with his boy. It was the fear most often mouthed by guys who were scared they were too old for children. The fear of catch. As if this were the single, defining experience of fatherhood. But how taxing was tossing a baseball? And when did his old man ever play catch with him?

They were both awake. Aggie said, "Do you really think you're going to be tied to me for the rest of your life?"

Harry said, "Mmmmmm," since there was no point in pretending he was asleep.

"After we have the baby?"

Harry said, "Does this mean it's been decided?" All the guys living in mortal fear of being too old for catch, it wasn't like they'd been out there throwing baseballs at their fathers, either.

"Answer me," she said.

"If we're going to be any kind of parents, the answer is yes."

"Doesn't that scare you?"

"Nothing scares me," Harry said, though that wasn't true. The prospect of being mangled in a car wreck, now that he was driving all the time, on point against motorists in their seventies and eighties, that scared the shit right out of him.

"Your life is going to change," Aggie said, and she rolled onto her side, facing away from him. "In a hurry."

It already had. Not long ago, he was hustling blow and holding his breath until Jimmy De Steffano wired up their next heist, doing bouncer gigs for Frankie Yin. Now he liked to be asleep by midnight, so he could be up at seven for his maintenance man job.

She was right. Life changed in a hurry. Like if you were sailing through an intersection without a care in the world, and some half-blind octogenarian came ripping into your ass, your life could change in a second.

Connor Merrill turned out to be worth every penny Arthur paid him. Harry had to serve out the rest of his minimum, ninety days, but after that he was back on his parole deal. Florida broke his balls on the terms: Three years, with five more of probation thrown on top. Any fuck-ups during that time, he was going back in, two years, no questions, no nothing. It was as harsh as they could make it. But the bottom line was, for now he was out, and he had Merrill to thank for that.

Aggie hooked him up with the job. She knew somebody in the company that managed the apartment complex, and they were looking for a guy. Harry was responsible for cleaning the pool, a cinch if you did it regularly, for cutting the grass, and for vacuuming the carpets in the hallways. He had to fix little shit that broke, a door, a window, but if there was a major problem with plumbing or electricity, Harry called in the plumber or the electrician. Maintenance man was not a spectacular career, but it beat the hell out of being in jail.

For his latest challenge, management had decided it was time to paint, so Harry was in charge of hiring and supervising the painting crew. Painting was easy. You had to make sure the new color covered the old color, and you had to be neat, or else you wound up with paint all over the fucking place, and that was about it.

But he couldn't keep any painters. Seven dollars an hour was not a lot of money, and Harry understood that, but the guys who answered his classified would work a day, demand their pay, and that'd be the end of them.

One clown came back when he was short of wine money, to cadge a five-dollar "advance."

For a while it looked like Harry's permanent crew would consist of himself, Cedric Baker, and a Seminole Indian named Pat Mule Deer, but Pat went and got blasted on schnaaps, busted up a bar, and took on the Sheriffs when they arrived, in an eerily familiar scenario. He left Harry a message on the office answering machine, asking Harry to bail him out, and that was the last Harry heard of Pat Mule Deer.

Cedric Baker appeared on a Tuesday, with a metal lunch pail and work boots spattered mostly white. He was from some podunk in South Carolina that was so small it got absorbed by a neighboring town. Compared to picking strawberries, as far as Cedric was concerned, painting was genteel employment. And he painted with pride. He had a delicate touch with a two-inch brush, deftly cutting trim, no running, no dripping, before Harry went in after him and whacked the walls with his roller, or when they could get away with it, the Power Painter.

Cedric had to take two buses to get there, but he was on time every morning with the lunch bucket and a thermos of what Cedric said was iced tea. Harry knew it was spiked, and Cedric knew that Harry knew, but whatever it was, it didn't slow Cedric down.

Harry bumped him up to eight bucks an hour, then started paying him for his half-hour lunches and two fifteen-minute breaks. They finally settled on three-fifty for the week. Harry pulled his ad from Aggie's newspaper, hoping to go the rest of the way, just Cedric and him.

Cedric had caramel-colored skin and hair that was turning silver. His Adam's apple jutted from his throat, and his shoulders were stooped from a lifetime of bad posture, but he was quite a hit with the ladies. He lived with a woman he called the missus, though they weren't married. Cedric had yet to divorce his third wife, the last in a series of joyous unions that yielded six children, flung all over the East Coast. One of the exes operated a beauty parlor in Queens. Cedric spent five years with her, five of the most miserable years, he reckoned, of his whole up-and-down life.

"We stayed in an apartment over the shop," Cedric recollected, "out there by the ballpark. Between the trains and the traffic and the airplanes screaming over your head, you never heard so much noise. And that's just outside the house. The woman never shut up. Run her mouth all day with them hens, come up the house, start running in on me. I got so I couldn't take no more of her, and one day I up and left. Headed back for Carolina."

Left her on her own with two of his kids. Didn't Cedric think that was kind of shitty?

"She weren't depending on me for nothing. She was making herself a good living." Cedric swabbed his brush in a puddle of eggshell white, and straightening, cut in a right angle over a window, back and forth, back and forth. "Had herself another man, too."

Ah-ha.

"Long before I was out of the picture."

This was later on in the day, when his thermos was empty, that Cedric did all this talking. He spoke slowly, and when he talked for any length of time, like now, his voice lost power.

He graduated from the can't-live-with-'em-can't-live without-'em school, and Harry thought, after his third time, no charm, Cedric ought to know what he was talking about. Harry had his own dim views on marriage, but he kept them to himself. After a while, he just stopped listening.

Aggie was washing the dishes before she put them into the dishwasher, and Harry watched her, her belly bulging against the denim of her Levi's. Her boobs were swelling, too. Complaining that they hurt, she wore a specially designed bra, even when she was at home.

Her doctor told her she could tend bar into her third trimester, or until she got too uncomfortable being on her feet. Aggie hadn't breathed a word of her pregnancy to Bryce or anybody else at Sailor Randy's, but she liked the idea of pulling in sympathy tips once she started to show.

Harry hated it. Bartending was a rotten job for a pregnant woman, and she could've quit without a problem. They'd have been all right for money. The newspaper was covering her obstetrical bills.

But it didn't have to do with money. The job represented independence. They'd had two or three arguments about Sailor Randy's before Harry figured this out, but when he did, he dropped the opposition. Let her work there if she wanted to. Pretty soon, she wouldn't want to.

He said, "The Catholics are going to give you a hard time about baptizing this kid, if you're not married."

She measured a scoop of powdered soap. "Spending a lot of late nights with your Catechism?"

"I'm just saying, you know."

"Let me ask you a question, Saint Ignatius, when was the last time you were even in a church?"

"Not counting weddings and funerals?"

"No, throw them in, too."

"I can't remember. Two years ago?"

"Why are you so hot on making this kid a Catholic," Aggie said, "when you don't pay attention to it yourself?"

"I think we've got two separate issues here."

"And they are?"

"One, us getting married," Harry said, "and two, bringing up the baby in the Church."

"Who said anything about us getting married?"

"I think I just did."

It took her a while, but she said, "I don't know how I feel about that."

"I don't know how I feel about it either, but I'm leaning toward considering it might not be a bad idea."

"In an ideal world," she said, "a child would be brought up by a mother and a father who were married, providing a stable home environment." She was drying her hands on a dishtowel. "But we're light years away from an ideal world."

Aggie was good at re-routing a discussion out of the specific and into the general, in order to make some larger, philosophical point. In a minute she was going to be citing some obscure sociological statistic she read in the newspaper of hers, not talking about whether it was a good idea for them to get married. She'd get back around to that when she was ready, those impulses surfacing at the worst times, like when he was getting ready for work. They wouldn't have time to finish what they were talking about, and he'd have this conflict with Aggie hanging over his head. Or she'd get all wordy when he was trying to sleep. Harry sensed a middle-of-the-night conversation looming.

Harry extended Cedric's work for a week, retouching spotty patches, pitching in with the final clean-up, but by that Friday, there was nothing left to do. They finished at noon and killed time, Cedric squeezing hot drags from the generic cigarettes he bought on the Reservation. He could afford the real kind, but stuck to the raspy, no-name ones. That was brand loyalty for you.

They started drinking in the bar Pat Mule Deer made famous, a storefront joint that poured beer in plastic cups. Pick-ups and panel trucks crowded the parking lot. Drinkers, sunburnt and pale in shirts with name patches over their pockets, refigured dreams of late-life laziness as a few after-work belts in some strip-mall dive.

The barmaid had a big, girdled ass she stuffed into black stretch pants, and wore a blouse that allowed peeks into her bra every time she bent to get something. Her hair, blown into a bouffant, was bleached a starchy white. Late-forties, she wasn't lacking a certain molting charm.

Cedric ordered a Genny Cream Ale. Harry was surprised the stuff still existed, but it was popular with the old men, at seventy-five cents a glass. It went down better than Harry remembered, frosty cold, thick, sweet aftertaste.

When it was time for their third round, Harry switched to Dewar's White Label, served in a one-and-a-half ounce jigger. For his next one, he asked for a double, and the barmaid tipped two brimming measures into a plastic tumbler.

Cedric had started talking by then, his face pointing forward, glancing out of the corners of his eyes. He was theorizing about money, his second-favorite subject, where it came from, where it went. Money, he said, was like electricity. It was generated at a source and conducted until it found a ground, say the stock market or the auto repair shop.

"You might not have it anymore, but it has not disappeared."

Coming from Cedric, this kind of thinking bore the weight of an advanced mathematical equation. High-concept. Abstract, even.

"This bar right here, now this is a good example of what I'm talking about. You see all these men?"

He wasn't trying to trip Harry up. This was a sincere question, and Cedric was waiting for an answer. Harry said, "Yeah?"

"These men been working all week, making money. Some of it got to go to the house rent, the groceries, make the car note, you follow me?"

Harry was going to say something, but Cedric said, "Hold off. That money had to come from somewhere first. This man here," he said, making an arbitrary gesture at nobody in particular, "is a plumber. He unstopped somebody's sink today. Earned himself two hundred dollars for the job."

"Fucking plumbers are expensive," Harry said.

"That two hundred gonna stay in the plumber's pocket?"

"He's got his own bills," Harry said, speeding up the story, trying to get the barmaid's attention.

"As we know. But some of that income, you see what I'm saying, is what you call disposable. That mean he's gonna feed it down the sink, get it all ground up?"

"No, he's gonna blow a chunk of it over the bar," Harry said. "Get some new overalls he doesn't really need because he's sick of the ones he's wearing."

Cedric held up his hand. "Okay. That money he used to pay for the drinks, what is it, ten dollars, twenty dollars?"

"At these prices, he'd be hammered."

"We're not concerned with the condition of the man's head, Harold. What we're doing is following the money. Tell me what happens to it after that."

"Doris here sticks it in the till," Harry said. He had no idea what the woman's name was. The men called her sugar or darling, but she looked like a Doris if Harry ever saw one.

"Zackly." Cedric sounded pleased with Harry's conclusion. He was on the verge of making a profound point. "And then?"

"It gets counted up and deposited in some bank."

"You got it, son, you got it. Then what?"

"I don't know," Harry said. "The bank uses it to give somebody a loan, and they invest their profit someplace else. It's really not that complicated, Cedric. I mean, no offense, here."

"None taken," Cedric said. "The idea is, it all got to go somewhere. Now what would you say if that same plumber, what he did with his disposable income, he kept it in a shoebox at the bottom of his closet? He weren't saving it for nothing, he was just stacking it up so he could look at it, count it once in a while when he was alone. Defying the natural law of money. Interrupting the flow, what you think about that?"

"I don't think anything," Harry said. "I used to hide my money in a sock in my laundry bag, eight, nine hundred bucks, whatever I had laying around the house."

He thought about where his money was now, in the first checking account he'd ever had. It cost him twelve dollars a month if the balance dipped below a grand, which in Harry's case, it never climbed above. Twelve bucks a month. A hundred and forty-four a year. His money was costing him money. The dirty sock didn't seem like such a stupid idea.

"But that was so you could spend it later," Cedric said. "You wasn't hoarding it just to have it, like some fucking King Midas."

"Everything he touched turned to gold," Harry said.

"It ain't money that's the root of all evil," Cedric said. "That shit is neutral. It's the love of money. Seven thousand dollars, in a shoe box at the bottom of your closet, is about the most unnatural love I ever heard of."

Though he was trying to keep the volume down, Cedric's voice pitched way up high, his words coming out in a shrieked whisper. This was a ton of passion for a parable, which of course, it wasn't.

"I happen to know where that bundle is ripe for the plucking. Let's say me and you, we go get it." This was delivered in a low, tight hiss, barely audible above the Garth Brooks tune honking out of the jukebox.

"That would be the money interrupting the flow," Harry said. "The seven thousand in a sock."

"Shoe box," Cedric said.

"At the bottom of a closet."

"That's what I'm talking about."

"This closet," Harry said, "would most likely be in somebody's house, now wouldn't it? And we would most likely have to gain entrance to this house through some means of stealth. That would make it a burglary, which I believe is in direct violation of a very specific Florida statute."

Cedric blew air through his teeth, as if he knew what kind of guy Harry was all along. "And this would be the first statute you violated," he said, "in all your lily-white thirty-five years."

"I'm thirty-six," Harry said.

"And you done a lot worse than burglary, and don't you tell me no different."

Harry said, "We used to pull burglaries when we were kids and didn't know any better. You got a very low risk-reward ratio on your hands."

Cedric was laughing. "You'd think it was funny, too, if you knew how easy this job was."

"Then what do you need me for? The less guys involved, the less your chances of getting caught."

"We ain't gonna get caught."

"No, we're not," Harry said, "cause I'm not going."

"What I need," Cedric said, turning his cup between his palms, "is a set of wheels. If I go in and grab the cash, the man's gonna suspect it was me. But if there's a bunch of other stuff missing, I'm covered. Now how'm I gonna get that stuff out of there? Load it onto a bus?"

Harry said, "That's your problem, Cedric."

"Plus, it never hurts to have a lookout. Pretty easy work for thirty-five hundred, cash money."

Harry had to piss and he had to use the phone. It was back by the men's room, a single stall minus a door and a trough spotted with pink urinal cakes. It smelled like a paddock.

He dialed his house and got the answering machine, Aggie leaving instructions for what to do in case you wanted to send a fax.

"Hey, it's me," he said. "You there? Aggie? It's about eight o'clock." He was taking a guess at the time by the color of the dying day through the chicken-wired bathroom window. "I'm having a beer with the painting guy. Have a good night at work, sweetheart. I love you. Bye."

Cedric's cup was empty when Harry got back to the bar. "How you like to go look at some titties?"

"Sure," Harry said. "I don't wanna drive too far, though."

"It's just up the road," Cedric said. He was about to leave a seventy-five cent tip for Doris.

Harry told him to pick up his change. He counted his money and left a ten-dollar bill on the bar..

Cedric said, "What you doing, boy?"

"I'm leaving a tip."

"Ten dollars? You leaving a ten dollar tip?" Cedric was aghast. "That's too much. That's way too much."

"No such thing," Harry said, feeling like a big shot, "as too much tip."

Cedric wasn't exaggerating about how close they were to the go-go joint. Tucked between a triple-X bookstore and a tire discounter pushing steel-belted radials, it was maybe a mile from the last place. Cedric led the way past the bouncer, a house of a man attempting to fold his arms across his chest. He settled for the fingertips of each hand in its opposite armpit.

It was a cut-rate operation, huffing and puffing behind the trend to glamorize titty bars. They took chairs in front of the stage, a plywood square ringed by Christmas lights and backed by mirrors smoked with golden swirls. A waitress got on them right away. Another peroxide blonde, she was sporting a Dale Evans costume, hat included. Her breasts sagged under a fringed vest. Cedric went for a beer, and Harry ordered a scotch, not bothering to call the brand.

The dancer was nearing the end of her act, down to a g-string and a pair of high-heeled sandals too small for her feet. The last toe on each foot hung outside its shoe. Doing a loose march to "Disco Inferno," she stopped center stage, and shook her tits. Harry could make out the stretch marks on her jiggling stomach. She beamed a smile at the audience, her tiny teeth overwhelmed by a set of gums that went on forever. Cedric slid a dollar into her g-string and she left the stage to zero applause.

That message Harry left on the answering machine: He sounded drunk, even in his own ears, over the din of everybody's lies and the bloodless Nashville pop that passed for country music. He sounded drunk because he was drunk, drunk on scotch and beer.

He hoped Aggie wouldn't get the message. He hoped she was gone for the night. He was going to dive on the answering machine the second he walked in the door, erase that shit flickering with his boozed-up voice.

The waitress came back, Cedric lifting his beer off the tray, and told them some amount Harry didn't hear. He handed her a twenty and told her to keep five dollars for herself. She stepped away quick, like she wanted to escape this juicehead blunder before Harry caught on.

A bony Indian girl was doing a quarter-hearted grind to a ballad Harry remembered from way back. He was trying to think of the band that had a hit with it, an overworked cover of an even older tune, pure FM-rock, like at Sailor Randy's. The original version was in the old man's record collection. Done by the Everly Brothers, he thought. Don and Phil.

The stripper had a broad, flat face, deadpanning an expression of drunken boredom.

"Cowboys and Indians," Harry said.

"Hey, cool it," Cedric said, looking around.

"Why? That's what it is," Harry said, louder this time, "fucking Cowboys and Indians."

"This motherfucker is full of guys from the Rez. You wanna find out how mean they are, keep it up."

Cedric returned his attention to the stage, where the woman took off her red rhinestone top to expose small tits arranged high on her chest, big, brown baloney nipples.

"Cedric, man, these chicks are nasty."

Cedric said, "Nasty, right?" He was wearing a huge grin, his eyes glued to the gawky Indian girl.

"I mean like un-fine. This bitch is stone-cold ugly. She

wants to take her clothes off while I'm watching, she ought to pay me."

Glazed and lifeless, she timed the dramatic movements in her limbs to the singer's tortured treatment of the lyrics, like whatever emotion she was feeling was in her fingers.

"Nazareth," Harry said.

Cedric said, "What?"

"The name of the band. Nazareth. Had a big hit with this tune when I was a kid." Cedric was giving him a skeptical look. "I couldn't remember at first. Then it came to me."

The corners of Cedric's mouth crept up. "What're you thinking about, son?"

Harry said, "Nothing."

"No, I'll tell you what you're thinking about," Cedric said. "You're thinking about a shoe box that's got seven thousand dollars in it."

Whatever property taxes were being spent on around here, it wasn't streetlights. The four-room cottage was silhouetted against a moonless horizon, not even a porchlamp burning to scare them away. Most of his fear was dulled by booze, but the adrenaline that flowed on any job was pulsing, a flutter in his gut that if you didn't feel, you were probably dead. Harry, at this moment, was feeling very much alive, but it wasn't the thrill of the job that was moving him. It was something else.

The steady drone of air conditioners whirred up and down the quiet street. Television shadows bounced through windows. All of a sudden, there looked like lots of chances to get caught. Dozens of potential witnesses with nothing to do but take a gander outside and see a man with his arms full, waddling toward a '91 Grand Am, its lights off and its motor running, Florida license plate number 3TG-7751.

Child on the way, thirty-five hundred dollars could come in handy. And you didn't change a man overnight. That just wasn't how it worked. But looking at the cottage they were about to go into, all Harry could think about was the look he'd see on Aggie's face if it went wrong.

"Ced, I'm not gonna do this one."

"What the fuck," Cedric said. "We're here now."

"I'm still on parole."

"So?" Cedric said. "Who ain't?"

"Sorry, man. I'll drive you home."

"Fuck that shit," Cedric said. He got out of the car and slammed the door. He started walking toward the busy street that brought them here.

Harry put the car in gear and rolled down the passenger window, Cedric staring straight ahead, his brilliant plans shot down in flames.

"Get in the car, Cedric. The cops are gonna pick you up just for walking around this neighborhood."

Cedric kept walking. "I can take the bus. Don't need no pussy-ass white boy."

"That's shitty, Cedric. I didn't say anything about you being black."

They had reached the corner and Cedric's last chance to reconsider. Harry said, "Do you want a ride, or not?" and when Cedric didn't answer, Harry rolled up the window and hit the gas and drove back home to Sunrise.

After the fifteenth ring, somebody picked up the phone at Sailor Randy's, the voice on the other end hollering over the noise. It wasn't Bryce Peyton. Harry had to say Aggie's name three times. Two long minutes later, Aggie came on with a suspicious hello, loud music and loud voices behind her. Somebody emptied a bucket of ice into a bin.

"Hey, how you doing?" Harry yelled into the half-dark.

"I'm doing fine," she said. "How're you?"

"Good," Harry said.

"I can't talk to you right now. I'm really slammed."

"You still wanna get married?"

"Did I want to in the first place?"

"I just wanna be with you."

"We'll talk about it when I get home."

"I'll be asleep."

"Tomorrow, then."

Harry said, "I was drinking."

"No shit, Harry. Listen, I'm all backed up here. I gotta go."

The room was doing a see-saw. He closed one eye on it, got it to level off, and flopped on the couch. This was him, just about ready to be redeemed. Married or not, on or off probation, father-to-be, the future was bound to arrive, anyway. Harry was going to sit right here and wait for it.